I0562254

SPECTRUM DUOLOGY
VOLUME ONE

CURSE

PART ONE
WHITE CURSE

Also by D.N. LEO
http://www.narrativeland.com

There is only one happiness in life -- to love and to
be loved.
George Sand (1804-1876)

CHAPTER 1

She lay on the cold floor of a dungeon flooded with water. A bunch of tangled weeds tied her hands, and a pair of bony hands grabbed at her legs, pinning them to the dungeon floor. She thrashed her legs, pulled her arms, and tried to roll her body around—nothing seemed to work.

She couldn't scream, and she couldn't cry for help—she wasn't really the crying type anyway. "How long can I hold my breath?" she wondered. She was twenty-nine now. She was full of life and had been on the path to a better future. At least, that was what she'd thought.

The water was everywhere.

Ten minutes earlier, Orla had held tightly to a rusty steel pipe running across the ceiling of a dark and cold dungeon. Although she was flexible and as agile as a leopard, hanging in the same position with her feet braced against a small ledge halfway through a wall for an hour had pushed her muscle strength to the limit. The Thames River was not as patient as she, and the tides raised by the minute, flooding the drains and leaking water into the dungeon. She couldn't see the floor anymore.

She wagered that she would quickly have to get out and find another way to break into the building. She hadn't planned for a plan B. Her planning was so impeccable that the use of alternative plans was a rarity.

Orla had done a countless number of jobs of this nature. She was a high-profile, experienced antique transporter. She disagreed with those who referred to her profession as thievery. She wasn't a thief. She didn't steal and resell for profit. Instead, she provided a service to her clients who wanted to claim ownership of antique items. She removed items of interest from the current owners and transferred them to her clients. She didn't care about the person who had original ownership or what the new owner would do with the item. Most of the merchandise had ambiguous origins to begin with and had been dealt with by underground collectors—she doubted anyone could prove genuine ownership anyway.

Orla looked at the barred lid of a small door leading to the compartment above, the dim light coming from it shedding a bit of blue down to the dungeon. "What's taking you so long, Lorcan?" she mumbled to herself. All she needed was a signal from Lorcan that he had jammed all the securities in the above compartment, and then she could climb up to that barred door, on which she had loosened all the screws.

She heard the painful shriek of a cat from the above compartment, a thud, footsteps, and another shriek. A tiny kitten dropped through the bars of the door lid. It clawed at the bars, trying to hang on. Orla heard the sound of door closing from the above compartment. The kitten was losing its grasp of the bar. It meowed and shrieked at the same time.

She heard a bang from the far end of the dungeon. "Damn it," she cursed. She knew the floodgate had been broken. The water from the river gushed into the dungeon. In minutes, it would be completely under water. She had to leave right now.

Orla jumped down to the floor of the dungeon. She was five foot seven, and the water had risen to her waist in only a few minutes. She treaded ahead toward the exit.

From the door above, the cat clung to the bar with its claws. It cried out a meow. Orla looked up. Soon the cat would let go and drop into the rising water. The door was at the far end of the room, and she was already at the exit, but Orla shrugged and came back inside. She stood right underneath the door and reached her hands out. "Come on, let go of the bar. I'll catch you."

The cat clawed and scratched and few more times, then it let go and jumped into Orla's hands. As soon as it landed on her hand, it climbed up her arm and sat on her shoulder. Orla giggled. "You're as quick as a full-grown cat, aren't you? Now you're comfortable, safe and sound, and we have to get out of here quickly . . ."

Her legs were pulled from under the water. Orla was thrown off balance and fell on the floor. She gasped for air and tried to see in the dark. In the water, a rotten body with bony hands clawed at her legs and held them underneath the water. Its eye sockets sparkled in blue, and where the teeth and mouth were supposed to be, Orla saw something resembling a grin.

She shook her head to ensure that she was conscious. Still under the water, she reached toward her legs to free them from the bony hands. A pile of tangled weeds grabbed at her both arms, preventing her from freeing her legs. Orla gasped, kicked her legs, and wiggled her body as much as she could, but she didn't make any progress. She was running out of air.

She looked down again at the blue eye sockets and found the mouth of death still grinning at her—the sign she had not seen for a long time, and didn't wish to see again in her life—the sign of the black curse.

She heard Lorcan's voice calling out for her. He was entering the dungeon. He would save her. He had a knack for coming for her at the just right time. Her life was full of uncertainties, but Lorcan was her constant, the one thing that would never change. She'd never told him how she felt about him for various reasons—and most importantly, for his own sake.

The dungeon was a long way underground. She wasn't sure he would get to her in time. Maybe this time, he'd be too late. She struggled more, but the weeds and the dead arms wouldn't release her.

She felt a tug at the weeds. Orla looked up to see the kitten clawing at them. It clawed and bit at the weeds until Orla's right arm was loosened. She yanked her right arm free, untied her left arm, and sitting up, she reached to the bony arms and broke them both at once. The bony arms felt soft like jelly and mud now. They were not as hard as when they grabbed at her legs. She saw a flash of the dead body dissolving into the dark water. She had beaten the curse this time—or at least the cat had.

She surged up to the surface and drew in air. She stood up and saw the tiny kitten trying to paddle with its miniature paws, its bright green cat eyes frantic and pleading with her. She scooped the cat up and stared into its eyes. "You saved my life. You're no ordinary cat, are you?" The cat responded with a meow. Orla rolled her eyes and mumbled, "Naturally." She swished through the water, heading toward the exit.

Lorcan bolted at Orla when she was halfway up the stairs. "You didn't respond! Jesus Christ, Orla, the floodgate broke! You could have just let me know you were okay!"

Orla pulled out her phone and looked at it. It was dead in the water now, but it had never signaled her. She waved the phone at Lorcan. "I dropped it in the water. It's dead."

Lorcan looked at her up and down. "Why are you soaking wet? What's with the cat?"

Orla sneezed, and Lorcan wrapped his coat over her shoulders. "Let's get back to the van," he said.

Inside the van, Orla pulled out at set of spare clothes and got changed. Lorcan chuckled. "We can literary live in this van." Orla glared at him.

"What took you so long?"

"My device was jammed."

Orla stared at him for a second and then she rolled over laughing. "Your jammer was jammed!"

Lorcan threw this arms up. "It's not that funny. It jammed, and then it started working again without me even fixing it. Damn it. And why are you wet from top to bottom?"

Orla dried her long black hair with a towel. "It flash-flooded in the dungeon, and I slipped."

Lorcan cocked an eyebrow. "You slipped?"

"Yeah. You think I went for a swim in the Thames?"

Lorcan said nothing, his striking blue eyes leveled at hers for brief moment. He ruffled his thick black hair, making its ends spike up, then he pulled out his pack of cigarettes.

"We're not done with the job yet, Lorcan."

"You're not going back in there."

"The hell I'm not." Orla pulled up the zipper of her jacket and tied up her hair. Then she snatched his cigarette before he had a chance to light it. "This will kill you."

Lorcan shrugged. "If you want to go back in there, I want my cigarette."

She shoved the cigarette back into his hand. "This is the last one of the month."

Lorcan smiled. "That's negotiable." He lit his cigarette and took a drag. He glanced back at Orla and saw that she stood next to the van, holding the kitten.

Through the screen of smoke he exhaled, she was beautiful—tall, lean, milky skin, big dark eyes, full of secrets. "You're not taking the cat back in there, are you?"

"Of course. He needs his mother," Orla deadpanned and left with the cat in one hand and a carry bag in the other. Lorcan shook his head. He squashed his cigarette on the ground and followed her.

A moment later, Lorcan was helping Orla climb in from a window at the back door of the building. He had managed to cut off the security system at that end of the building.

"Are you sure? It can't be that easy to enter this building," Orla whispered.

"Well, the guy isn't exactly a high-profile drug lord. I think he's just an ordinary rich guy."

"Ordinary rich guys don't collect multi-million dollar antique collections without putting decent security systems in place to protect them."

"Maybe my skills make all security systems look ordinary then."

"I like that explanation better."

They entered a wider hall way that led to the collection room. The kitten trailed right behind Orla. It paused and hissed. In front of them was the collection room, trashed. Blood was everywhere. The body of an old man was on the floor in a pool of his own blood. A few feet away was the body of the mother cat.

The kitten kept hissing. Orla picked it up. "Shhh, it's okay darling. We'll take care of you." She slid the cat inside her carry bag, where it stayed still and stopped hissing.

Lorcan checked the man. "He's dead. We have to get out of here, Orla. Don't leave anything that might incriminate us."

"We're here already. He's dead. He doesn't need that vase anymore. We might as well take the merchandise for the client."

"Jesus Christ, Orla."

"It won't take long." Orla darted to the secured cabinet. She put her gloves on and worked on the lock. In a few minutes, she had the cabinet opened. Inside the cabinet was a large vase, prominently placed in the middle. It was too large to fit in the bag, plus she had the cat in there. She grabbed the vase and held it in her arm. As she walked toward Lorcan, the bony arm that grabbed at her in the dungeon poked up from the floor, grabbing and pulling at her foot. The cat hissed inside the bag. Orla stumbled and fell. The vase dropped to the floor, shattering into pieces.

Lorcan charged toward Orla. He helped her up. "Are you okay?"

"Did you see it?" Orla asked.

"See what?"

"Nothing. Don't worry. The vase . . . it's broken."

"That I can see. Leave it. We have to get out of here before the cops come."

"I have to get another one. Something else in replacement for this. It won't take long. We can't go back to the client empty-handed."

"No! I said no, Orla." Lorcan half-dragged, half-carried Orla out of the house.

A short moment later, their little van was zooming rapidly along the highway, heading back toward London. Orla sat on the passenger seat with the cat on her lap. "We can't exactly take care of a kitten, can we?" she asked.

"Why not? It'll just be like a kid." Lorcan smiled at her.

Orla narrowed her eyes. "It's a cat. Not a kid." Orla silently cursed herself. She couldn't offer him a better explanation. A kid between them would make a family. That was no-go territory for her.

"Right. A cat it is. Certainly." Lorcan glanced at the cat. "Don't worry. We won't call you Edward or anything like that."

Orla laughed. "Of course not. Losing his mother was tragic enough for him! What do you want to do about the murder?"

"Nothing. By the way, the police just received an anonymous tip regarding that murder. The tip must have come from Mr. Edward here." Lorcan grinned.

"He's *not* Edward."

"Right. No Edward then . . . Listen, do you want me to go talk to the client with you regarding the vase?"

"Why? You think I can't do it myself?"

"Of course you can. I'm just saying," Lorcan smiled, but the smile faded quickly. He kept on driving, while Orla absently scratched the cat's neck, sending it into ecstasy. The smile on her face had long since faded.

CHAPTER 2

Orla sauntered into the long hall of the most luxurious restaurant in London. She was tall, slim, and exotic with a river of dark long hair that wrapped around her shoulders. Her siren red gown flattered her flawless body and dazzled people so that they wouldn't notice her oversized handbag, in which she carried the merchandise.

Orla clenched her teeth when she saw Lorcan standing at the end of the hall, grinning at her.

"You said you'd let me handle this myself," she growled.

Lorcan smiled. "Don't pout. It really detracts from that stunning gown. I didn't see you all day yesterday—I miss you. I'll let you work with your client, thought. I'll be sitting over there, keeping my mouth shut." Lorcan pointed to a table.

"I'm not pouting. And if you keep interfering with my work, I'll leave you."

"You need me too much to leave me." Lorcan smiled and leaned in for a kiss.

A wave of strong jasmine suddenly engulfed Orla. A faint gray mist swirled through the air, forming a funnel and thickening around Orla and Lorcan. She pushed at Lorcan's chest to stop the kiss, puzzled. She didn't like what she saw and smelt. It had been a long time since she'd experienced these sensations, and she didn't care for them at all.

"Are you okay?" Lorcan asked, looking into her eyes.

"Yes, sure. I'm settling a job here. No messing around in public." She scowled.

Lorcan grinned again. "We'll mess around tonight in private then." He nodded toward the entrance. "A minion of your client is here. Don't take on any new jobs before we talk." Lorcan walked toward his table.

Orla wanted to punch Lorcan in the face. But it wouldn't be a good idea to do so in front of her client. She composed herself and turned around to see a tall man approaching her. He nodded at her. She cast a warning look at Lorcan, directing him to stay where he was, and walked toward the man.

"Mr. Turk?"

"Call me William, Orla."

"I have a table reserved." She smiled.

"Thank you." William nodded.

Orla caught a slight accent in his voice, but she couldn't quite make out its origin. It didn't matter where they came from—as long as they paid her, she was happy. After they had settled at the table, Orla put the bag on the floor and pushed it toward the man. William placed an envelope on the table and pushed it toward her.

She opened the envelope, pulled out the cheque, glanced at it, and put it back into the envelope. She slid the envelope into her purse and smiled at William.

"Please send my regards to your employer, and tell him I appreciate his business. I suppose if he isn't happy with the merchandise, I can't cash the cheque."

William smirked. "That's the reason he keeps using you. You're a smart cookie."

"Technically, he's using my services, not me. Prostitution is not my line of business."

The man nodded. "Getting a prostitute is a lot cheaper than your services, Orla. Trust me, he values your services highly. As a matter of fact, he has a new assignment. If you pull this one off, you won't need to work again for the rest of your life."

Orla felt the urge to sneer at the statement, but thought better of it, so she maintained a neutral expression. She could try for a poker face, but she would never be able to pull it off. Acting was not her strong suit, and she knew it. "You have no idea how much money I'd need to settle for the rest of my life. Don't speculate. Anyway, what's the job?"

"It's a prepaid ransom."

Orla arched an eyebrow. "Too good to be true."

William shook his head and chuckled. "You should hear me out first."

Orla nodded and absently gestured the man to continue.

"A computer game designer was kidnapped from her New York apartment. The kidnapper used her to blackmail her best friend, a reputable journalist, for some information. The journalist will be in London tomorrow. Your job is to rescue the computer game designer at the deal settlement between the journalist and the kidnapper."

Orla leaned back in her chair, narrowing her eyes at the man.

"I told my boss you wouldn't take this assignment. You're a thief. Rescuing is not exactly your expertise."

Orla smiled. "I take your view on my expertise as a compliment, William. Indeed, stealing is what I do best. I can steal anything from anyone . . . if paid well enough. If I consider the computer game designer as a job, I can steal her from the kidnapper. If that qualifies as a rescue—and I save her life, so to speak—then I get to be a hero. That's an added benefit."

The man put on a crooked smile. "Being a hero doesn't pay."

"As I said, it's an added benefit. What's being exchanged for the ransom?"

"That information is beyond your pay scale, I'm afraid."

"A thief like me has standards. I won't kill and I won't deal drugs."

"I can guarantee you that. No drugs and no life endangerment."

"Is that why you didn't want to do the job yourself? It's too boring for you, isn't it, William?"

"You know, if you'd reign back your sarcasm a bit, you could be quite pleasant to talk to."

"I don't get paid to be pleasant. How much?"

"Two million."

"That's not enough for me to retire on, as you claimed before."

"That's the first installment."

"Do the other installments come from other parts of the task?"

"Of course. But you have to agree on the first part before we move on to the next. You don't have to do the other parts if you don't want to. But as for the first part, if you commit, you have to go through with it."

"I have to think about this."

William stood up. "You have two hours to make a decision. There are others willing to do this. But as I said, my boss values you highly. He wants to give you the first opportunity." He grabbed the merchandise, left some money on the table for the drink, and strode toward the entrance.

Orla turned around and saw that Lorcan was no longer at his table.

Three hours later, Orla carried a bunch of shopping bags into her leased apartment. After accepting the job, she had shopped for new outfits and new gear. She changed her appearance for every new job. Experience had taught her to be cautious of everything. Taking on a new identity was routine.

She found Lorcan leaning against the wall in front of her apartment. He raised a large pizza box and a bottle of her favourite Shiraz as if they were tickets to enter her apartment.

"Perfect timing." Lorcan said.

Lorcan Brody came from a privileged family. He had a college qualification. With his family's wealth, he didn't have to work, but he chose to work as an engineer for an IT firm so that he could stay in London and be around Orla. He could have any girl he wanted. But he chose her for reasons she didn't quite understand. Regardless of how long they had been together, she never got tired of looking at him—long, lean, and well-toned body, dark hair, striking blue eyes, and a mouth that was made for kissing.

She smiled at Lorcan. She entered the apartment and left the door open. Lorcan followed her inside. Orla pulled out the envelope and removed the stash of money she had cashed. As soon as she had accepted the new job, the client had allowed her to cash the cheque. Not that she thought he wouldn't be happy with the merchandise, but she could never tell. She had done a countless number of jobs over the years, but this client was the most mysterious. She didn't even know his name or the purpose of the items he asked her to acquire. The stolen item this time was an authentic sixteenth-century antique.

She split the money in half and gave half to Lorcan without counting.

"You know I don't care about the money, right?" Lorcan jammed his hands into his pockets.

"You worked for it, you get your share. Otherwise, I can't work with you for the next job."

"You shouldn't have taken this new job. It's too good to be true . . . And it sounds fishy."

Orla arched an eyebrow, wondering how Lorcan knew. Lorcan shrugged. He grabbed her purse and peeled off a tiny spy recorder he had placed on it before her meeting with William.

"Is there a camera anywhere else?" She scowled.

Lorcan shook his head, looking sheepish.

"Not only fishy, this job sounds dangerous, Orla. Can you please sit this one out?"

"It could be dangerous, but it won't be any more dangerous than stealing the one and only White Knight's dagger out of a private collection in Paris. And we did that job easily, didn't we?" She pointed at the stash of cash.

"This is not a joke, Orla. The dagger is only an object. Now you're talking about a person. God knows what he'll ask you to do for the next installment. The guy kidnapped someone in New York and will transport her all the way to London. You can't tell me he's a small timer who picks pockets for a living."

"Lorcan, I accepted the job. You know I have to go through with it—with or without you. That's two million. I might save a life for two million. The next lot will be three times at much. That's six million . . ."

"Orla, you don't need that money. I can take care of you, of us. We can go back to Ireland and live the lives we want . . ."

"Says who? Lorcan Brody? Yeah right." Orla sneered and felt her words bubbling in her throat as she fought back tears. She did feel uneasy about the job. But the client had been good to her so far. This shouldn't be an exception. "Two million might mean nothing to you. But it means a lot to me. I need that money."

"No, you don't."

"The vase I broke yesterday cost one million."

"What? You don't deliver the job, you don't take the fee. How could that cost you a million?"

"Volkov runs one of the most notorious underground dealer networks in Europe. He missed out on a deal with his client because I didn't deliver. It cost him money, and he charged me for that."

"What the fuck?"

"He's not someone to mess around with, Lorcan. I can pay him that money. I just have to take this new job. That lump sum payout for Volkov put a dent in my budget."

"Budget for what?"

She shrugged and didn't answer the question.

"It's only a couple of million. I don't want you to take the job. I can take care of the money."

"Listen to yourself, Lorcan! I don't want you to ask for favors from your family. You can't take care of me. I take of myself and my problems. I can't go back to Ireland empty-handed."

"I don't need my family's money to take care of us. Why do you think I've hung around you all these years, working at that pathetic IT company?"

Orla waved her arms in the air. "You just want to stay in London. You want to prove to your family that you can be independent from them. Isn't it obvious?"

"And you play no role in this? You have no part in my life and my decisions? What am I to you, Orla? Your fuck buddy?"

Orla slapped him hard across the face. Lorcan fell onto the coffee table, pushing the pizza onto the floor.

"Whatever you do, you still have a family to come back to. They love you. I don't even have a last name."

Lorcan rubbed at his jaw. "That's because you didn't want your last name. You can take mine. Be a Brody."

She stared at him. "I slap you, and you propose to me. How romantic. Are you nuts? Get out."

"I . . ."

"I said get out."

Lorcan stormed out of the apartment, slamming the door behind him. Orla sat down. She felt like weeping, but she held on. She would give him ten seconds to come back.

Ten seconds passed.

Twenty.

Thirty.

There was still no Lorcan in her apartment. It was quiet except for the sound of the clock ticking on the wall. There was no sound of him clicking on his mouse or tapping on the keyboard. There was no reduced sound of all the games he watched on his computer while trying not to annoy her at the same time. There was none of his loud laughter. And there were certainly no gorgeous smiles or witty comments about the jokes she made about her clients.

Without him, her existence didn't seem to count as much. What she was doing and about to do didn't seem to matter. She ran out of the apartment, down the corridor, to the empty foyer, and outside the building, but all she found was emptiness.

CHAPTER 3

Lorcan stood in front of a small cottage outside Mortlake. It was just twenty minutes away from London, but the area already had a totally different feel to it. Lorcan was not much into cottages. Despite the fact that many people considered cottages to be full of character and cultural charms, Lorcan thought of them as enclosed spaces where people have lived and died. It didn't help his necrophobia—he couldn't handle dead things. Even the thought of them made him dizzy. Or maybe a few bottles in an empty stomach made him dizzy. He wasn't quite sure.

But this cottage was different. It's his best friend Riley's place. It was a small cottage, but it had a lively feel to it. He needed to crash right now. He wasn't much of a drinker. He didn't know why he would even go to that pub. Lorcan hesitated at the door, then thought better of it a turned around. Suddenly the door swung open, and there stood Riley with a beer in his hand. "Come on in. I don't bite."

"What kind of an idiot drinks beer at two a.m.?" Lorcan asked, glancing at the beer bottle.

"The kind that would invite you to his home at this wee hour." Riley chuckled.

Lorcan shook his head and stepped up to the patio. He stumbled and fell to the ground. Now he felt really dizzy, and that he was sure was caused by the alcohol, not his necrophobia. Riley grabbed at him. "Oh geez, you reek of booze. You drove here in this condition? I think you might be the fucking idiot!"

"I told you not to buy this cottage. People died in old houses. You know . . . dead bodies . . . corpses," Lorcan mumbled.

"All right, come on in and check out if there were corpses in this house."

Riley tried to help, but Lorcan pushed him away and reeled into the house. "Let me crash on your couch for a few hours. I'll be fine in the morning."

"Look at yourself in the mirror. You're a fucking mess. Since when did you turn into an alcoholic?"

Lorcan flopped into the sofa. "I'm not. Just tonight. I didn't think. And yes, I'm an idiot. On all accounts." Lorcan grinned foolishly.

Riley fetched a glass of water and gave it to him. "You guys fought again? Orla called earlier on."

"What did she say?"

"Nothing much. Asking about Noah and if you were here."

Lorcan emptied his glass. "What's wrong with me?" Lorcan asked.

"Where do I start?" Riley sneered.

"That's why she doesn't love me?"

"She said that?"

Lorcan shook his head. "Worse. She said nothing."

"You've got to move on, Lorcan. You're thirty-two, not eighteen. Grow up."

"Orla is the best thing that's ever happened to me. I bought her the fucking ring. I'm going to ask her to marry me, you know . . ."

"And she said no? That's why you're here, looking like shit?"

"I haven't asked her. I mean I haven't asked her directly."

"Is there an indirect way of doing it? You bought the bloody ring, how much more direct can it be?"

"There are things she hasn't told me. I don't know what they are. But until we're clear on that, she's not going to give me a straight answer." Lorcan ruffled his hair. "I love her."

Riley shook his head. "Love doesn't mean shit these days. I don't think she's good for you. I mean, I like Orla very much. But the way you two lurk around, you'll get nothing. You'll die old and lonely."

Lorcan cocked an eyebrow. "Love doesn't mean shit? Why haven't you moved on? Michelle has been gone for ten years."

"She died giving birth to Noah. It's more than love. It's a lifetime responsibility. No, I'm not the best dad on the planet. But we have decent lives. Given where I came from, this is the best it's going to get for Noah and me. But you come from a prestigious family, you have the best education available to you. You can get any girl you want . . ."

"I think we best leave it right there, Riley . . ."

Riley shrugged. "I'm just saying. You don't have many friends who are willing to kick your ass for nothing."

"Indeed, I don't . . . Listen, regarding what I said the other day, I'm serious about you taking Noah elsewhere for the medical attention he needs. If you worry about the money, I can . . ."

"It's not the money. We've been through every test possible with the technology available to date. Even if the technology is not available to the public yet, you think my colleagues won't flex their muscles for me? We've done everything we could, and we found nothing."

"Is it getting worse, though?"

Riley nodded and sank into his sofa. "Early tonight, the pain was so bad that he threw up. He told me he was okay, but I knew it was unbearable. Sometime I wish . . . I wish it were a brain tumor that he had. At least we'd know what we're dealing with."

"How can you say such a thing about your son? Oh, Jesus, I'm sorry. How could I be so thoughtless, sitting here nagging about my love affairs?" Lorcan hopped off his sofa.

"Don't worry. He's asleep now. He'll be glad to see you tomorrow morning."

Noah's scream from the bedroom sent the men surging to their feet and storming toward the bedroom wing. In his bedroom, Noah was on the floor, still clutching his blanket and screaming at the top of his lungs. His fair face was clammy, his brown hair tangled and soaked in sweat, his eyes almost blank. He convulsed with the pain and vomited. Riley scooped Noah up from the floor and carried him back to the bed. He wrapped the blanket around him, held his son in his arms, and rocked. Noah stopped screaming, but he still shivered.

"Ssshh, good boy, you're okay. We're okay," Riley whispered and kept rocking.

"You have to take him to the hospital!" Lorcan exclaimed.

"To do what? We've been through this before. I'm a doctor. Don't you think I know better? You think I wouldn't do it if it helped?" Riley's eyes filled with rage.

Noah's shiver subdued. His face gained some color, and his eyes had returned to normal. He blinked and looked at Lorcan.

"Uncle Lorcan, please don't go away."

"I'm here." Lorcan climbed into bed, took Noah from Riley, and held the boy in his arms. "I'm not going anywhere. Now if you're a good boy, you'll go back to sleep. Okay?"

"Don't go away. It's dangerous out there," Noah whispered, half asleep.

"Okay. I'll stay right here."

"They'll hurt you. I don't want you to get hurt," Noah said and fell into a deep sleep. Lorcan frowned and looked at Riley.

"What was he talking about?" Lorcan asked.

"That's what he's been saying over and over for the last five days. 'It's dangerous out there.' But the part that you'll get hurt is new."

"I'm a computer geek. How can I get hurt? Be bitten by computer bugs? Killed playing computer games?"

"You know what you're actually doing, Lorcan. You think I'm stupid? You don't take money from your family. I don't think your IT job can allow for your current lifestyle in London. Whatever it is that you're doing with Orla, I think you're wasting your life and your privilege."

"Don't start," Lorcan growled.

"I'm not starting anything. I just want to stop your nonsense. As I said, I like Orla, but not enough to watch you waste away your life and your opportunities. You're like a brother to me. If she's going to support you, great. If not, move on, Lorcan." Riley turned on his heel and left the room.

It was a rare winter day when the sun came up bright and early. Riley answered a door knock and found Orla there with a small cage and a bag in her hands.

"I thought Noah would like this little friend." She raised the small cage with the kitten inside. Riley smiled and gestured an invitation for her to come in.

"They're still as sleep. I'll give them another hour. What kind of cat is this?"

"I don't know. The poor little soul lost his mother the night before. We could have taken care of him, but we travel a lot as you know. I don't have the heart to bring him to a shelter." Orla glanced at the bedroom wing. Riley caught her look.

"He's in there with Noah."

"May I?" She gestured toward the bedroom.

Riley nodded. Orla made a beeline to Noah's bedroom. From the half-opened door, she saw Lorcan lying in bed, propped up in a pile of pillows, sleeping. Noah was snuggling next to him. Lorcan's hand still clung to a book that had nearly dropped to the floor. *He'd make a good father,* she thought. Then she shook the thought out of her head. She walked into the room and took the book from Lorcan's hand. She knew she wouldn't wake him. When Lorcan was asleep, he wouldn't wake even if she bulldozed the room. He looked so tired. She wanted to tuck away a loose strand of hair on his forehead, she wanted to give him the ritual morning kiss, but she thought better of it and let the thought pass.

In the living room, Orla found Riley had let the cat out and was feeding it. "Have you thought more about what I suggested regarding Noah's conditions?" Orla asked.

"Not until last night."

Orla narrowed her eyes. "You didn't approve of my suggestion of letting him speak to a psychic before, but last night you just changed your mind on a whim?"

"Well, Noah kept saying 'it's dangerous out there', and you suggested that he foresees something bad will happen to us. That didn't make sense because we're doing just fine except for his migraines. But early last night, Noah said Lorcan would come here. Then Lorcan *did* come. Then in another episode in the middle of the night, Noah said someone would hurt Lorcan."

The color drained from Orla's face. Someone or something would hurt him. She knew it. The hand that had grabbed her in the dungeon was no coincidence.

"Orla!"

"Huh?"

"Do you love him?"

"Of course I love him. He's only ten and he's been through so much. I only suggest what I think is best for him."

"I'm not talking about Noah."

Orla waved her arms in frustration and let them flop at her side. She didn't have the answer to this question.

"Being together twelve years isn't enough for you to answer a simple question? Do you love him?"

"Why are you pressing this? It's not your problem!"

"He's like my brother. It *is* my problem. You should have seen him last night. And if what you said about Noah's psychic ability is true, then what he said about someone harming Lorcan could be true, too. Whatever you're making him do, it's dangerous. It will harm him."

"I don't make him do anything he doesn't want to do." Orla snarled.

"He's obviously fallen hard for you. So if you don't love him, let him go."

"What are you implying?"

"Do you love him?"

"I . . . I . . ."

"See, you can't even answer a simple question. I'm not implying anything, Orla. I'm saying this straight to your face—if you don't love him, then get the fuck out of his life."

"What gives you the right to say that to me?"

"If you saw him last night, you wouldn't ask me that question. He was lucky he didn't crash and end up in the morgue after pouring that much booze down his throat. What sort of girlfriend would drive him to that after twelve years together, and after he bought you a fucking ring?"

"He . . . he did what?"

"Go and ask him yourself."

Orla stared at Riley for a moment, then she turned on her heel and stormed out of the house. At the same time, Lorcan called out from the bedroom. He charged into the living room. "What happened?" he asked Riley.

"I asked her to her face if she's serious about you."

"Shit . . ." Lorcan darted toward the door. Then he stepped backward inside the house. "What did she say?"

"Nothing."

Lorcan stormed away. Riley shook his head and went to Noah's bedroom.

CHAPTER 4

Orla stared at her empty apartment. Lorcan loved her. Not that she hadn't already known that. But he had committed himself. He bought her the ring, and that had triggered the white curse. Orla felt like crying, but it wouldn't help. She wasn't the crying type.

The white curse was designed to protect her. She remembered vividly the voice of her distant aunt. When someone loved her, the love would trigger the black curse to kill her. Thus, to protect her, the white curse would harm whomever loved her. What she'd seen in the dungeon was a sign of the black curse.

Everything came back as if it were just yesterday. The fear. The escape. The darkness. All the things she had chosen to exclude from her life were now clawing their way back in.

But she might be overreacting. The curses might be just a myth. A psychological game her family had played on her. A joke by fate. She had dated before Lorcan. Men had sworn love and devotion to her several times. None of them had died. She had been well, and her life had worked out smoothly as planned. She couldn't explain what happened in the dungeon. It might be just her, the black curse her family had placed on her. If that was the case, then Lorcan should be fine.

"Orla!"

Orla was startled and cursed. She turned around and found Lorcan at the door. He entered the apartment and raised his arms, making peace. "Can we talk?" he asked. Orla nodded. "Let's forget what was said. I'm sorry it made you feel uneasy. Let's pretend I didn't ask anything and you didn't have to answer anything."

"Would you do that? Would you do that for me?" Tears rolled down her face. She wasn't sure it was going to work that way, but it might help.

Lorcan nodded.

"We had an agreement. You'd never say the L word to me, remember? Why did you do that?"

"I didn't do anything, Orla. I didn't say it, although I totally don't understand why I shouldn't have."

"You didn't say it. But you did it. You bought the ring."

Lorcan winced, but he nodded. "I'll return it. Will that work? I'll throw it into the river? Or I'll give it to Edward the cat." He approached, tugging at her arms.

"Not Edward."

"All right. Not Edward. I'll take it back, whatever it is. Will you forgive me?"

She pulled him in to her arms and nuzzled into his chest.

"I want a deal," Lorcan said.

Orla arched an eyebrow.

"I want in. If you're taking this job with William Turk, I have to help you."

Orla shook her head. Then she looked at Lorcan's stubborn face, sighed, and nodded. He approached and pulled her into his arms. They held on to each other for a long moment.

Orla had been following Madeline for hours. Madeline Roux was the journalist from New York who had traveled to London to rescue her best friend Jo, a computer game designer. The kidnapper was Zen. *What a stupid name for a kidnapper,* Orla thought.

Madeline was hard to miss—a tall, attractive brunette, with big brown eyes and a dimple on her left cheek. The picture her client had given of Madeline didn't do the woman any justice. *Any man who didn't want to jump Madeline would have serious problems with their masculinity,* Orla mused. She'd watched Madeline spend hours at an Internet cafe. Orla sauntered into the cafe, walked past Madeline, and stuck a spy recorder on Madeline's backpack, unnoticed. Orla was as fast as a . . . thief.

Later, outside the café, Orla pulled out her phone and called Lorcan. "She's heading toward Knightsbridge. Ouch. It's going to cost her. She must love her friend very much. Can you get any audio on her yet?"

On the other end of the line, Lorcan chuckled. "Until she speaks, I can't check the audio."

It was peak hour. Orla pulled down a zipper on her tailored overcoat and peeled back the black layer to reveal a red under layer. Then she shoved her way through the sea of people and approached Madeline. "Excuse me, I'm looking for Pine Street . . ."

"Sorry. I'm not local. I can't help you." Madeline smiled then put her head down and kept walking.

Orla almost swooned at her husky voice. After Madeline turned the corner, Orla spoke into the phone, "Did you hear that?"

"Yes. Loud and clear. You could have been a bit more subtle."

"Yeah right." Orla rolled her eyes. "What a voice she has. You should see the woman in the flesh."

Lorcan laughed. "If Madeline is that attractive, shouldn't you be worried rather than enticing me to see her in the flesh?"

"I'm worried for other men. But not you. You're mine."

"Oh shit," Lorcan cursed at the other end of the line.

"What's up?"

"She must have thrown the bag down. Broke my eardrums. Why don't you get back home, and we can both listen?"

Orla smiled. "Right away. I'm picking up dinner on the way."

Orla woke in her bed, feeling the warmth of Lorcan's body seeping through her skin. All six-foot-one of him wrapped around her body like a blanket. She loved the way their bodies fit together. She shifted and kissed his sleepy face.

"Lorcan."

"Hummm . . ."

"Darling. Sleepyhead. Don't you have to go to work today?"

"Humm . . ."

She rubbed her face against his chest, traced her hand along the lean line of his body, and found one part of him awake. She chuckled, kissed him again, and rolled on top of him. He shifted underneath her so that she could straddle him comfortably. His hands grabbed at her hips. His fingers started tracing her sensitized skin. He knew where she liked his hands and how much pressure she wanted. He knew every curve, dip, and tone of her body. She groaned.

The spy device Orla had fastened to Madeline's backpack transmitted the signals. The sound of Madeline's voice came from Lorcan's computer. "Hello. My name is Madeline Roux, I'm a journalist from . . ."

Madeline stopped talking as it appeared that she was interrupted from the person on the other end of the phone.

"I understand that LeBlanc Pharmaceuticals is a private company. All I'm asking for is the information that your PR department can publicize . . . I don't have that much time . . . Look . . . I'll make it formal . . ." The conversation didn't seem to go anywhere. Madeline ended the phone call and muttered. "Four weeks, my ass."

Lorcan was already up and out of bed. He made two cups of coffee and gave one to Orla. She wouldn't get out of bed until she'd had her coffee. That was her morning ritual.

"I still think you should pass on this job, Orla."

"We've had this conversation," Orla grumbled.

"Do you know who the LeBlancs are?"

"Yes, the richest and most mysterious family on Earth. What's your point?" Orla sipped her coffee.

"I know your client said we don't have to deal with the kidnap and ransom, but we practically have to kidnap Jo from the kidnapper. That's worse. You haven't done this kind of job before. It's bad enough that we don't know Zen and what he's capable of. But when it comes to the LeBlancs, nobody knows anything."

"Rumor has it they can make gold. That's why they're so rich." Orla chuckled.

"Yes. Also the head of the family, Ciaran LeBlanc, he can make gold from his spit."

"Ew." Orla pulled a face.

"Seriously, Orla. The LeBlancs are powerful. They might be into human trafficking, drugs, or whatever. They're so powerful that they can buy out the media."

"How do you know they bought the media?"

"There's not a whiff of info about them in the media or on the Internet. What kind of money can buy that degree of silence? Even the US's top secrets have been leaked. Have you ever seen a picture of any of the LeBlanc family members?"

Orla rolled her eyes. "Yeah, I think I saw a picture of the younger brother. Was that Tadgh LeBlanc? The picture was snapped when he traveled to Australia, I think. The LeBlancs don't blend well. Very tall, gorgeous dark hair, very fair skin, and striking eyes."

Lorcan narrowed his eyes. "I get the picture. If the kidnap and ransom has anything to do with them, it can't be good . . . and . . . before you say it . . . two million or even six million is *not* worth the risk. I'm serious."

They heard Madeline's phone ring and her voice responding to the call.

"I won't say a word to you if you don't put Jo on the phone."

Silence.

Static came through the recording device and then a man's voice responded, "I can do better."

Lorcan said, "Video call, we are now capturing both voices through her speakers."

"Jo, Jo, talk to me," Madeline said. "Are you okay, Jo? Can you talk to me?"

"I'm fine and alive, but not kicking, as you can see." Jo said, her voice slurred from drugs.

Madeline let out a watery laugh.

"I'm sorry to drag you into this," Jo murmured.

"Don't say that, Jo. Can you tell me what's going on?"

"It had to do with my Mind Ripper's latest development. In theory, the program could reconstruct the mind of anyone, given sufficient information. Like how a person would speak and think. Anyone, I mean really *anyone,* including dead people."

"You've got to be kidding me!" Madeline said. "So I guess Zen wanted to talk to some dead people?"

"Okay, that's enough," Zen said.

"If she loses one hair, you won't get anything but life behind bars." Madeline growled.

"Don't act like you're innocent," Zen sneered.

"I'm not remotely close to being innocent. But if I go down, I'm sure as hell taking you down with me."

"Okay, let's not make things too complicated. Your first step is to approach the person behind White Knight for me."

"First step? How many steps are there? This isn't going to be a lifelong deal, is it?"

"Oh, no, nothing like that. Just a couple of steps . . ."

"Why don't you ask White Knight to come out yourself? I assume you know how to play these hologames given you own your own pathetic game development company."

Zen laughed. "White Knight has never played me. He only talks to Jo. Rules of the game, you know. I asked Jo to call White Knight out, but he refused."

"So what if I identify the real person? What will you do? Kill him with his own sword if he doesn't help you talk to some dead ancestors?"

"How do you know that it's ancestors I want to talk to?"

"Because no human being with a recent memory and a right mind would want to talk to a guy like you. It has to be your own kind, a blood tie, who has no choice but to give you the time of day."

"I didn't know you disliked me so much."

"Dislike is a very polite way of putting it. What exactly do you want to do with this person?"

"That's none of your business. But if you're serious about the wellbeing of your friend here, then move quickly. I am not a patient man."

"The LeBlancs! You do know it's impossible to approach them, don't you?"

"That's why you're there. I don't care how you do it. If you want Jo in one piece, then get me the White Knight."

Zen ended the phone call.

Lorcan sipped his coffee and said nothing. Orla knew he was reconsidering what he had said before. She got off the bed to get dress and leave him time to think. When she came back to the bedroom, Lorcan had a grin on his face. She winked at him.

"Got something to tell me?" she asked.

"I think I'll lend Madeline a helping hand."

Orla laughed. "I knew you couldn't help yourself when it came to the LeBlancs' computing system."

"Madeline seems to be a good person. Coming all this way to save her friend. I just want to help."

Orla rolled her eyes. "Aha . . ."

"Okay . . . plus hacking the LeBlancs' system is every computer nerd's wildest dream."

"So you're no longer worried about them trafficking humans or dealing drugs?"

"It's obvious that this deal was about computer games and technology. So . . . I'm interested. It's impossible to hack the LeBlanc's system. But if Madeline could get inside their headquarters physically, that would be something. The LeBlanc's residential addresses are unknown. There's no information about them anywhere. Their headquarters are guarded like military barracks."

"Why would you want to hack the LeBlanc's system? Wouldn't it be more challenging to stalk MI5, MI6, the Pentagon, or the FBI?"

"It would be more challenging. But hacking a government-related agency will only give me more information about what I don't want to know. Scandal. Propaganda. Politics. Wars. You name it. You could take what you see in the movies or on TV, times multiply that by ten, and you'd get what's in the government databases. Sometimes, I don't know which one is real and which one is fantasy. No need to hack for that kind of info. But the LeBlancs . . . hmmm." Lorcan's eyes sparked with curiosity.

"They're aliens?"

Lorcan laughed. "Maybe. They could be vampires, witches, sorcerers, werewolves . . ."

"Don't mention those supernatural creatures."

Lorcan raised an eyebrow. "I thought you were into the paranormal. You read those books."

"Books are fantasy. The LeBlancs are real. Let's not joke about it, okay?"

Lorcan nodded. "How about aliens? Am I allowed to mention aliens?"

Orla threw a cushion at Lorcan. "Get to work if you want to help Madeline from the goodness of your heart."

Lorcan chuckled and turned to his computer. "I'll just let Madeline know where she may be able to find the LeBlancs." He muttered.

"You said that information wasn't available."

Lorcan nodded. "Not available to ordinary people." He winked. "I'm no ordinary hacker. You should know that."

"What? You can hack their system? You know where they live?"

Lorcan grinned. "No, I don't know where they live, and I can't hack their system. But I can certainly hack the logistic control system of their guards and assistants. All of the mundane activities and movements of their minions in the company that nobody pays attention to. Then I can deduce from there."

Orla grinned widely. "You're a smart boy."

CHAPTER 5

Early morning in Hyde Park, and the fog was as thick as clouds. Orla sat on a bench with her monocular. Her phone was on hands-free. She glanced at the park to locate Madeline. She had a notebook on her lap. "What am I supposed to watch for again?"

"Birds. Look up into the trees, find a bird, and pretend to take notes. Don't point your monocular at people, or you'll get arrested." Lorcan's voice came out from the other end of the line.

"Okay, all right. I know. How do you know this will lead to something?"

"You see Madeline?"

"Yes. She's running. She's a real runner, though. Not a pretend bird watcher like me. She runs around her block every day. I can't believe she took our hint and change her routine to run here today."

"She searched for a chance to get to the executives of the LeBlancs for days without any hope. We gave her Hyde Park. What would you do if you were her?"

"I'd jump on the chance and check it out. But still, I'll bet you anything this is the location for Lindsay Freeman, Ciaran LeBlanc's right-hand man. He's practically the public face of the company. Of course, he would travel in limos and live at places like One Hyde Park. You can't get Ciaran himself with just the travel log, regardless how good of a data thief you are."

"Is that a challenge? Wanna bet?"

"All right. Bet on what?"

"Well, we missed one of our rituals yesterday morning. If I get this right, I'd like to double our activities tonight."

"Lorcan, can't you think of anything other than sex?"

"Well, men are pigs . . . but you like bacon, don't you?" she asked in jest. "Oh, my God . . ."

"What?"

In the scope of Orla's monocular, a man came out from the fog like a warrior. It was Ciaran LeBlanc. He was tall. At least six foot three. Slender build, well-toned muscles, fair English skin, long black hair that almost touched his shoulders. He had a strong face and dark, intense, smoky gray eyes. God must have been in a very good mood when he created that face. He looked like a dark angel. A god's warrior. Or maybe a wolf from Heaven. *Were there wolves in Heaven?* Orla mused.

"Orla." Lorcan's voice echoed from the other end of the line. "Orla," he repeated.

"Huh?"

"What happened?"

"I . . . I think I just saw Ciaran LeBlanc."

In the apartment, Orla stared at the computer and smiled. Lorcan narrowed his eyes. "You've got that smile on your face."

"What smile?"

"You smile for two reasons, lust and money. Given that we've just satisfied the first one, I am guessing you're using your money smile . . . Unless you've turned into a rabbit and want to go for another round?"

Orla chuckled. "Don't worry. I don't want to wear you out. The money just came in."

"What money?"

"I told the client that we located Ciaran LeBlanc. He deposited twenty percent of the money into our bank account." Orla grinned.

Lorcan shrugged as if he didn't care.

Madeline's voice came from the speaker again. She had called Zen, and it sounded like Zen had switched on the video phone.

"Miss me?" oozed Zen's sleazy voice.

"You don't have to sniff around my workplace and freak out other people. I said I'd get the information for you, and I will." Madeline fumed.

"I didn't snoop anywhere. Who else knows about this?"

Orla gasped.

It seemed that Madeline's heart skipped a beat. Then she continued. "Oh, no, I'm just annoyed. I have a few unkind readers sending nasty notes to my paper, that's all."

"You know, if you keep poking your nose into other people's business, you'll end up with something as big as a bomb—or as little a bullet. They're both lethal, though! What have you got for me?" Zen asked.

"Ah . . . not much yet. I just wanted to clarify a couple of things. So White Knight is a fictional character in a game, an avatar? The person behind White Knight only created this character? Or did he or she take on the role in the game?"

"Jesus Christ! Don't you know anything about games?"

"No, not really. I don't even know exactly how to get the information. If I get inside the LeBlanc premises, you want me just to go around asking who plays White Knight?"

Lorcan chuckled and whispered into Orla's ear "She's stalling."

Zen sounded as if he was struggling to stay calm. "No, don't ask directly and don't alarm anyone. All you have to do is to tell them that one computer on their premises was used to play a hologame. Make it up as you go. Say the game was illegal or whatever. Then, when you have the info about the person who used the computer, let me know. Don't say anything about White Knight at this stage. If it turns out to be many people, we'll narrow the list down later. But I need the real names of those who played. Got it?"

Orla asked, "Do you know what a hologame is?" Lorcan nodded.

"When will I see results?" Zen asked.

"Come on, you only gave me Hyde Park. That's a residential address, not the business headquarters. How am I supposed to . . .?" Madeline said.

"What? I didn't give you the address. I didn't know the address. Who tipped you? Who else knows about this?" Zen asked.

"Shit!" Orla exclaimed.

"Fuck, she thought Zen gave her the note," Lorcan mumbled.

"What happened? You better fucking tell me!" Zen yelled.

"I . . . I was . . ." Madeline stuttered.

"Tell me!" Zen's demonic voice sounded as if it would rip open the speakers.

"I was doing some research . . ." Madeline's voice was shaky.

Orla yanked at her hair. Lorcan pulled out his pack of cigarettes. His hands shook slightly.

"Don't you fucking lie to me again . . ." Zen demanded.

"I've got it. I've got the access . . ." Madeline begged.

There were struggling noises. Doors slamming and footsteps.

"You know why she doesn't scream? Because nobody can hear her from down here. No one can save her but you," Zen said.

"He must have put Jo on the screen," Orla said. Lorcan kept smoking and said nothing.

"I'm sorry, I'm so sorry. I'm not lying to you about anything. Please don't hurt her. Yes, I've done some research, and I got some information about a possible place of residence for the LeBlancs. I might be able to get an interview tonight with my journalist credentials. But that's all I have . . ." Madeline cried.

There was the sound of fabric being torn. Jo cried.

Orla didn't realize that tears were rolling down her face.

Madeline shouted. "Please don't hurt her. I'll do whatever I can tonight to get you the information. I'll get you the list. No one else knows about this, I swear . . ."

More sounds of struggling. Jo's cry was terrifying. It was the sound of pain, grief, and rape.

Lorcan grabbed at Orla, holding her as her body shook.

Madeline screamed into the phone. "Please, don't do that. I will get you the list."

"Then you'd better keep your promise. I'll call you tomorrow morning," Zen said and turned off the phone.

"It's my fault. I shouldn't have pushed this. I shouldn't have asked you to do this. I shouldn't have slid the note under her door . . ." Orla cried.

"Shhh." Lorcan hushed her and held her until the emotion subsided. "Madeline needed that information. It's the only way she can save Jo. It's not our fault, Orla. You see, she got an appointment with Ciaran LeBlanc. Without our Hyde Park hint, she would never have gotten that far," Lorcan said.

A couple of hours later, Lorcan finished putting together some listening devices.

"We need to hear Madeline's conversation with Ciaran tonight," Lorcan said.

"More listening in. More interference. We got Jo tortured, Lorcan." Orla's eyes welled up again.

"We don't know that."

"You want to watch video footage as well?"

"That's not helpful, Orla. We can't take back what happened. The more information we can find, the more we can help Madeline . . . and get Jo back safely."

"I'm not even sure I'd give her to the client now," Orla sobbed.

"Let's think about that later. Right now, we need more ears on Madeline."

"I don't think we'll get to listen in tonight. The recorder is in her light backpack. No girl is taking a backpack to a dinner date."

"Dinner date?"

"Well, I told you that you should see Madeline in the flesh. I know Ciaran LeBlanc is a big fish. But he's also a normal man—at least, by my gauge. If Madeline were a fifty-year-old reporter with four kids, I wager he'd give her an appointment in his office during office hours. But she's a hot cookie. So of course it's a dinner date."

Lorcan shrugged. "Well then, I'll take this chance to head into the company to grab some equipment. I'll be as quick as possible. Do you need anything while I'm out?"

Orla hesitated. "A gun."

"Orla!"

"We might need it."

"No, no. Of course not."

"If we do need a gun, can you arrange it?"

Lorcan gave Orla a blank stare.

"I guess not. You've never had to do anything like this in your life. I'm just pulling your leg." Orla smiled.

"Orla," Lorcan warned.

"Okay. All right. I won't mention it again and won't do anything silly. Happy now?"

Lorcan approached. He cupped her face in his hands. "I'm not going to let anything happen to you. I hate to break my promises. So while we're at it, can you promise to help me out by taking care of yourself?"

Orla nodded. Lorcan kissed her, long and deep. Then he left the apartment.

CHAPTER 6

Orla was stacking away her work files and doing some research on her computer when someone knocked on the door. She narrowed her eyes. Had Lorcan forgotten his keys? Not possible. She peeked behind the curtain to look outside. A stunning woman in an elegant deep red suit, exquisite scarf, and ridiculously beautiful high heels was waiting at the door. She didn't look threatening, but Orla grabbed her pepper spray and slid it into her pocket before opening the door.

"Yes?" Orla said.

"I'm looking for Lorcan Brody." The woman spoke in a half-American, half-Australian accent, with a very slight hint of Spanish.

Orla arched an eyebrow. This was her apartment. No one knew Lorcan stayed here with her. He still rented his apartment. "Who are you?"

"Mya Portman."

"I don't recognize your name."

Mya smiled. "Lorcan doesn't know me. I'm not a secret admirer, if that's what you're worried about."

Orla stepped forward and stared into the woman's eyes. Big dark brown eyes with a gold rim around the irises. She knew these eyes. "You didn't say *I* don't know you. You're looking for Lorcan in my apartment. No one knows he's here. Who are you?"

A gracious smile crossed Mya's face. "You will not like me. I wouldn't have come if it wasn't urgent. Whatever you asked Lorcan to do, don't. It will kill him. I can help, but only to a certain extent."

Mya nodded a goodbye and turned on her heel.

"Hey!" Orla grabbed Mya's elbow. As she did so, a wave of energy shot through Orla, sending her backward.

"I did say you wouldn't like me. If you care for Lorcan, and I know you do, pack up and go back to Ireland."

Orla waved her arms in the air. "Is this some kind of practical joke? I didn't make him do anything. Hell, I kicked him out of my apartment the other night."

"Did you? Not the kicking, but the intention?" Mya cocked an eyebrow in challenge.

"I . . ."

"You have no intention to let him go." Mya smirked.

"What do you mean?" Orla shrieked out the words.

"I know your kind. The Foleys. You don't let go of anything or anyone."

It had been a long time since anyone had spoken her last name. Orla felt as if she was going to implode. She wouldn't allow that. "Get out," Orla growled.

"I'm not in your apartment." Mya stood still at the doorframe and stared in challenge. "Your kind doesn't know what love is. You're lucky I am not in charge of your case. Otherwise, I swear in the name of Ishtar, I'd destroy you and all your generations."

Orla charged back into her apartment and grabbed the knife from the fruit plate on the coffee table. "Get out of here. Get out of my life." She pointed the knife at Mya.

"I come and go as I please. There is nothing you can do to me."

"Don't underestimate me."

"Oh no. I'd never underestimate your family." She fixed her scarf and continued. "If by any chance you actually love Lorcan, let him go."

"I'm not keeping him here. He chooses to stay with me."

Mya sneered. "Naturally."

Orla squealed and charged at Mya.

Lorcan exited the elevator just then and saw Orla. He darted toward her and grabbed the hand holding the knife. "Easy, easy Orla." He turned toward Mya and said, "Go."

"Be careful, Lorcan," Mya said.

Orla screamed. "Get out, bitch. I'll kill you." She tried to break free of Lorcan to charge at Mya.

"I'm Mya Portman. I'm here to protect you," Mya said to Lorcan.

"Are you nuts? Go. She's stronger than you think," Lorcan shouted, trying to hang on to Orla.

Mya turned on her heel and left.

Lorcan pushed Orla into the apartment, kicking the door closed behind them and holding Orla until she stopped screaming. The strong smell of jasmine filled the air in the room. Orla charged toward the bathroom and was violently ill.

Lorcan waited patiently in the living room. When Orla had finished in the bathroom, he handed her a mug of hot tea. When she finished, he pulled her in to his arms and cradled her on the sofa. She snuggled into his side for a while.

"Can you tell me what was going on between you and that woman?"

"I want you off this job, Lorcan. I'll do it myself."

"Orla . . ."

Images of the room because blurry in front of her. "Damn it, Lorcan. What's in the tea?"

"Something Riley gave me. I'm sure it has no side effects . . ." and then Lorcan was saying something else but Orla no longer heard him.

In the morning, Orla surfaced. She stirred and muffled into his chest, asking for coffee. He obliged, then sat on a chair waiting for the caffeine to jolt her system.

"You were wrong about the dinner date," Lorcan said.

"Huh?"

"Madeline took her backpack with her. We got her conversation with Ciaran LeBlanc along with some interesting activities."

Orla's eyebrows arched up, and the memory came back to her. "You drugged me!"

"Drugged is a strong word. I only meant to soothe your nerves. You took it like a drug because you've been overtaxing your system."

"You drugged me," she repeated and whacked him with a pillow.

Lorcan raised him arms up. "Okay, okay. I'm sorry. I won't do it again. But you missed out on quite a bit while you were asleep."

"What?"

"You were wrong about the dinner date," Lorcan repeated. "Madeline took her backpack with her, and I heard the whole conversation she had with Ciaran. The bottom line is that Madeline lied about her reason for looking for White Knight as per Zen's instruction. She said someone in the LeBlanc's headquarters had used the company's computer to hack Jo's game. That alarmed Ciaran enough to take her to their headquarters and scan their entire system. It turned out that no one had used a computer within the LeBlanc's headquarters to play any game. So Madeline came home empty-handed last night—or this morning at two a.m. to be precise."

"They did all that while I slept?"

"Yep. The recording is backed up to the computer. You can listen to it if you want. No point, though, as there is no White Knight in LeBlanc Pharmaceuticals."

Lorcan continued, "We'll wait and see what she does this morning. Zen will check in soon. But before we deal with that, can I ask about what happened when I was out yesterday? Who was that woman? Why did you want to kill her?"

Orla took a tentative sip of her coffee and looked at Lorcan. "I want you out of this job . . ."

The sound of Madeline's phone ringing made Lorcan bolt at the computer. Orla and Lorcan hunched over the speaker as if they could give Madeline extra help by doing so. Madeline let the phone ring ten times before she picked up.

"What's with the new phone number?" Zen asked.

"Dropped and broke the other one. Put the video on, I want to see Jo."

"I expect some good news, Maddieeee," Zen demanded, dragging out his pronunciation of Madeline's name.

There was a wall of silence.

"Samuel Kandinsky, that's the name."

Lorcan arched an eyebrow. He typed on his laptop and turned the monitor toward Orla. The Google search results showed a series of Kandinsky's paintings. Then he did another search and pulled out pictures from a real estate rental website, showing Madeline's apartment. He pointed at a picture. On the wall of Madeline's apartment was a Kandinsky painting.

"Give me his contact details," Zen demanded.

"That wasn't the deal, Zen. The name is all I've got. Getting that name out of the LeBlanc headquarters was hard enough. I've seen the guy, so I can lure him out as we agreed. But he didn't exactly hand me his CV and personal information."

"You were inside the LeBlanc headquarters?"

"Impressive, isn't it? I spoke to Ciaran LeBlanc myself. I'm sure Samuel is your guy. He's probably out of a job by now. So do you want me to talk to the guy, or do you want to do it yourself?"

"No, no, I'll take care of it."

"When will you let Jo go? Because as far as I'm concerned, my task is finished."

"No, there's a step two, remember?"

"The last one?"

"Yes, sure. And this one's easy. An alchemist named John Dee died in the 1500s and is buried in Mortlake. Go there and get me an artifact that was buried with him. It's only an hour or so outside of London. Piece of cake. The guy died a long time ago. Nobody will pay any attention to what you're doing."

A long pause.

"Say again?" Madeline asked.

Zen huffed out a breath. "John Dee was . . ."

"I heard you. You want me to dig up the grave of some dead alchemist?"

"Well, it's not exactly tomb raider or anything like that. You only need a shovel."

"Why don't you do it yourself?"

"I could, but it wouldn't be very efficient. I have to get Jo there, to London, and negotiate with White Knight. Once he agrees, then the artifact has to be available for him. You see, I can't be in two places at the same time!"

"Alchemists were those who squeezed gold out of steel, right? If you're after gold, wouldn't it be easier to just rob a bank or jewelry store?"

"Just like many other ordinary people, you're very short-sighted, Maddie. Get me the artifact, and then we'll talk. I might even give you some gold dust if I'm feeling generous!"

"Yeah, right, what's the artifact? And when will you need it?"

"You'll know it when you see it. I don't know exactly what it is. It has to be something of importance to John Dee. I'll need it within twenty-four hours."

"You've . . ."

"No, I'm not kidding. We'll be there in twenty-four hours. I need you to get the artifact and locate White Knight for me."

A short pause.

"The timing is very critical. If you mess this up, I'll have no mercy for you and your little friend here."

"Jo can't travel long distances without her meds. If you paid any attention at all and stopped drugging her, she'd tell you that she's diabetic and is probably overdue for her doses right now."

"All right, I'll get her the meds. Do you know where she gets them?"

"Ask her yourself. If memory serves, its somewhere in Midtown, between Park and Madison . . . I can dig up an old grave. I'm sure the dead won't mind. I can dig a new one for you, too, and I would bury you with pleasure."

"See you soon." Zen grumbled and hung up.

Orla shook her head. "She lied to a monster. Trouble."

"She lied last night to Ciaran."

"It was a white lie. What choice did she have?"

Lorcan glared at her. "So it's okay to lie. Is that what you're saying?"

The sound of Madeline's sniffling came over the speaker. Madeline was making a call. Orla and Lorcan listened. This time they couldn't hear the dialog from the other end of the line.

"You're sleeping at this hour, Stephen?" Madeline said. "London. Listen, I need your help . . ." A pause. "Really, Stephen? You don't even need to want to know what I'm asking you to do?" Another hesitation as she listened. "You know Zen, Jo's boss, right? This sounds weird, but it's serious, so please, bear with me. Zen kidnapped Jo because of some interactive role-play game Jo developed. He wanted me to be in London to find the guy who played a character in Jo's game. Zen has beaten Jo and has threatened to rape her if I can't find the guy in London." Long pause. "Stephen, I'm telling you now, and I will take responsibility for all the consequences. I committed a crime a long time ago, and Zen knows about it. If he has to deal with the cops in any capacity because of me, those will be the first beans that he spills." . . . "Serious enough to spend a lifetime in jail." . . . "Perfect. Thank you, Stephen. Thanks so much." . . . "I should have called you earlier." . . . "No, not exactly. So if Zen comes here to see me, I'll be in trouble."

The recording finished, Lorcan turned the speaker off. "Now, you were saying you want me off this job?"

Orla nodded.

"Well, it's obviously Madeline was taking the case to the next level, bluffing the criminal and all of that jazz. She also called for help from Stephen—whoever that was. I assume everything will fall into place for her, but if you want to see this case through, you still have to see if Stephen can help."

Orla nodded.

"Can you set up the listening device?" Lorcan stepped aside and gestured at the computer.

Orla stared at him. "You know damn well I can't handle your technology. I will do it the old-fashioned way."

"Ah hah. Right. So you'll be staking Madeline physically and might end up facing Zen when he comes to London. Which is fine. You're a good fighter. Now, I'm not in the case, but I'll have to follow you around because you're my girlfriend, and I don't want you to get hurt. Does that sound reasonable?"

"Lorcan!"

"I won't get involved at all. If Madeline falls dead in front of me, I won't move a muscle. I just want to keep an eye on you."

"Lorcan!" She slapped at his chest.

"Is that a yes?"

"No. That's a no. You're going nowhere with me."

"Okay, how about we meet halfway? It seems that Madeline might be able to handle the case herself. Ciaran seems like a decent guy, so he might help her. The conversation they had last night suggested that Ciaran won't be in the country today. So how about we follow

Madeline today to make sure that she's okay? When she gets back to Ciaran, I'll let you decide what you want to do next. I won't get in your way."

Orla cursed on the inside. When Lorcan talked logic, she lost most of the time. She would have to find another opportunity to drop him out of this job.

"Come on." Lorcan tugged at her arms.

Orla nodded. "All right, she's going to Mortlake now. We'd better get moving."

"How do you know?"

Orla shrugged. "Just a hunch." She went to the bedroom to get her handbag.

Lorcan went to the kitchen to grab a glass of water. He sniffed around. There was strange smell in the kitchen—jasmine. Jasmine was supposed to be a pleasant scent, but this was not. Then the smell vanished. Lorcan looked at the coffee machine. He'd bought some caramel-flavored coffee the week before. It might be causing the smell. He pulled out the bin on the coffee machine and emptied it. When he slid it back in, a sharp lever cut his fingers. He swore and sucked at the blood drop forming from the cut. He rubbed his hand on the sharp lever, making a mental note that he had to fix it before it cut Orla. Then he returned to the living room and gave it no further thought.

CHAPTER 7

Riley packed up the sandwich and put it into Noah's lunch box. He had made his son a tuna and cucumber sandwich today; Noah's favourite. More importantly, it was Michelle's favorite, too. Riley shook his head to force the memory out of his mind. The pain was raw as if it had happened yesterday. They had shoved Noah into his arms and declared his wife dead. It sounded cruel to laypeople, but in his medical discipline, he saw it every day. It was his job to deal with life-and-death matters, the well-being of others. But when it came to his family, there was nothing he could do. He couldn't help Michelle then, and he couldn't help Noah now. He wondered sometimes what use his medical skills and knowledge were.

He missed her so much, it hurt. Riley looked at the picture of Michelle and him smiling at a picnic. He didn't realize a tear had rolled down his face.

He felt a tug at the hem of his trousers. He looked down and saw the kitten, blinking its bright green eyes at him. Crouching down, he said, "The tuna sandwich is for Noah. You'll have your cat food." He saw the excitement drain from the cat's face. He picked it up and put it on the kitchen bench. "Lorcan told me you dislike the name Edward. I think he made it up, but . . ." Riley trailed off when he saw the cat's ears droop. "I like Edward for a cat." Then the cat's eyes drooped.

Riley shifted uncomfortably. "Okay, I won't call you Edward."

The cat's ears stood back up.

"Fuck me!" Riley mumbled, narrowing his eyes at the cat. "Don't you start speaking. 'Cause if you do, I'm going to freak out." He swore on his dead wife he saw the cat grin at him, but he let the thought pass because it started to weird him out.

Someone knocked on the door. Riley answered and found a woman in her fifties with white hair and a kind face looking at him with a gentle smile and mysterious eyes.

"Riley Perkins?"

"Yes. Do I know you?"

"No. But I do know you. Orla sent me."

Riley frowned. "For what?"

"For Noah."

"Oh, you're the psychic. Right. Ah . . ."

"May I come in?"

"Listen, I'm not quite sure about that. We're on our way out soon. I need to take Noah to school, and we're running late. Can we do this some other time?"

"May I come in?" the woman insisted.

"No. I mean yes. Sure. Come on in. But Noah just ran to the corner store to get some milk. We'll be on the road soon. I've have already said that, haven't I?" Riley mumbled and followed the woman inside the house as if he were the guest.

"She liked tuna and cucumber sandwich, didn't she?" The woman smiled again.

"Excuse me?"

"You wife, Michelle, she told me she liked the sandwiches. She knows you didn't, but you pretended that you liked them just to please her."

"Oh no, don't play that trick on me, lady. I think you'd better leave now. I'm not a believer."

The woman smiled. She approached Riley. He staggered back. "She said she misses you. She misses the times you took her to the Lake Districts. She visits your secret spot all the time. But you haven't been there for a while. The three stones are still there, carved with your initials and buried under the oak tree. Do you remember that?"

Riley leaned against the wall, grabbing his pounding head. He felt like it was going to explode in a moment. Then he heard Michelle's soothing voice. "You haven't been there for a while, Riley. I miss you." Riley looked up to see his wife standing in the middle of the room in her favorite summer dress, smiling at him.

"Michelle!"

He darted toward her, and reached his hands out. She withdrew. "I'm not real, Riley. You can't touch me. I'm just here for a short moment to tell you that I miss you and I'm thankful that you take care of Noah."

"I'm not exactly doing a good job at it."

"You're a good father. Noah is very special. Listen to Orla. Listen to your son. Be open minded, Riley."

"I miss you so much, Michelle. Please don't leave me again."

"I miss you too. But I don't have a choice. I have to leave now."

Riley grabbed at his wife's image, but she dissolved into thin air. His world spun out of orbit. The ground below him caved in. The walls whirled, distorted, and blurred out of their frames. His eyes rolled back. He collapsed.

From the ceiling, Riley saw his body lying on the floor unconscious. *Am I dead?* he thought. *Did I just have a heart attack?* He couldn't control his body, but his mind was crystal clear. Then he realized he was outside his body. At the moment, he was his conscious mind. "What just happened?" He landed on the floor, walking around and looking at his own lifeless body.

He looked decent, he thought, long lean body, very fit, and perfectly healthy at thirty-two years of age. If he died now, who would take care of Noah? He saw Noah walk up the patio and push at the door, finding it locked. He was confused. He pushed at the door again. The he peeked through the window and saw Riley's body on the floor.

Noah became panicked. He pushed at the door again and instantly knew that it wouldn't work. He called for the cat. Then the cat, sitting in the corner watching everything, used its teeth to pull the bunch of keys out of Riley's pocket and toss them through the cat door Riley had just made for him last night.

Noah stormed into the house. He inhaled deeply. That was a sign of him trying to stay calm. Calm and collected, he checked for Riley's pulse. *Damn it.* Riley cursed to himself as he couldn't even check his own pulse. But he was proud of his son. Noah was doing everything right at the moment. Noah wasn't crying, so Riley wagered he wasn't dead.

He shook Riley's shoulders. "Dad!" He shook again. "Dad, you're scaring me." Noah's breaths caught. He was going to cry. He was going to lose it. Riley had to help his son. Noah grabbed the phone. His hands shook. Tears rolled down his face, but he wiped them off.

Riley concentrated and tried to reach out to his son. *Noah.* Riley used his mind to speak. *Noah,* he called again. Noah stopped dialing the phone. Riley couldn't believe what was happening. He continued, *Noah, is my pulse okay?* Noah panned around the room, then nodded. Noah could hear him. Riley felt delirious. He continued, *That means I'm going to be okay. I'm just a little out of myself at the moment. If you can hear me clearly, nod.*

Noah nodded.

All right. Don't panic. Just call uncle Lorcan.

Noah called Lorcan.

Ten minutes later, Lorcan and Orla stormed into the house.

"Jesus Christ, call the ambulance!" Lorcan exclaimed.

"No," Noah said. "Dad said he'll come around soon."

"What? When did he say that? He might have had a stroke, Noah. How long has he been out?"

"I went to the store, so it might be around ten minutes. Since I called you, it's been another ten," Noah said calmly.

"I'm calling an ambulance."

"Dad wouldn't be happy about that," Noah said.

Damn right. Riley thought. *Just shake me, you idiot. I didn't have a stroke. Why are you letting a ten-year-old tell you what to do, Lorcan?* Riley thought. But Lorcan couldn't hear him the same way Noah could.

Orla pulled Noah into her arms. "Your dad will be all right. How do you know he wouldn't want to be in the hospital?"

Noah bit his lips. He said nothing. Then a tear rolled down his face. And another one. Then he cried. Orla embraced him. "Don't cry darling. He'll be okay. You'll be okay. You can hear him, right?" she soothed. Noah nodded.

Bitch. You sent that woman here, Riley thought. He wanted to trash something, whack at something, but apparently he couldn't do that with his mind.

"Let me try this." She put Noah aside and kneeled next to Riley. Holding his head in her hands, she rubbed at his temples with her thumbs. She closed her eyes and mumbled something to herself.

Suddenly Riley felt weakened. Then he found himself dissolved and sucked into a black hole.

His eyes flung open, and he gasped. Orla released his head. Riley sat up, dazed. Noah darted over, wrapped this tiny body around his father's, and let out all the tears he had withheld. He ruffled his son's hair and said, "Come on, Noah, you're a good boy. Don't cry. I'm okay. You did very well."

"Lorcan crouched. "What's going on?"

Riley leaned against the sofa. "I don't know. I was in the kitchen. A woman came, claiming to be the psychic Orla sent . . ."

"Me? I didn't send anyone!"

Riley stood up. "Well, that's what she said. Next thing I know, she put a whammy on me. Then bam, I'm on the floor."

"She put a whammy on you! I can't believe that word came out of your mouth, Riley!" Lorcan laughed.

"Why not?" Orla asked.

"Psychic? Magic? Are we going to talk about aliens next?" Lorcan exclaimed.

Riley shrugged. "That's what happened. That's what she said. And as you can see, I'm in one piece. I didn't just black out for no reason."

"It might have been a stroke, Riley. You're such an idiot not to let Noah call an ambulance. If Orla and I hadn't been doing some business around the area, it would've taken us at least half an hour to get here from London. By that time, you would have been dead!"

"What business are you doing in Mortlake?"

Lorcan shrugged. "Private business. We have to go back there, but we'll take Noah to school on the way. Call in to work, take a day off."

Lorcan grabbed at Noah's shoulders. "Come on buddy, go get your gear."

Noah scurried to his room.

"I'm taking Noah to school. That woman might come back for him. She said Orla sent her for Noah," Riley said.

"The psychic I referred you to is a he, not a she."

"You referred him to a psychic?" Lorcan asked in disbelief.

"What's wrong with that?" Orla responded.

"So who was the woman?" Riley asked. "What did she look like?"

As Riley described the old woman, the color drained from Orla's face. A tear rolled down her cheek.

"Orla?" Lorcan called out.

Orla covered her mouth. She ran to the bathroom and vomited. If she wasn't mistaken, Riley had just described her late aunt, the one who had set up the white curse before she died. Orla had been a kid, but she remembered the experience vividly. Her aunty had loved her very much and had promised to take care of Orla wherever she might be. When she was ten, Orla felt lucky to have her aunt's love and care within a family full of dark secrets, but she didn't feel too lucky right now.

Lorcan waited outside the bathroom door. Orla pushed the door open and flung her bag over her shoulder.

"Where are you going?" Lorcan asked.

"Back to Madeline at church," she mumbled.

She sidestepped Lorcan to walk away.

Lorcan snatched the car keys from Orla's hand.

"Seriously, Lorcan, I told you to go away."

"We talked about this—one more day, and I'll let you do whatever you want. You promised me."

"I'll call a cab." She mumbled and kept walking.

"Hey." Lorcan grabbed Orla's arms. She shrugged him off. They scuffled for ten seconds before he pinned her to the wall. "If you can't tell me what happened between you and the woman called Mya at the apartment, if you really have to lie to me about that, I'm fine. If you have to withhold the information about the woman who came to see Riley and what you did to fix him just now, I'm struggling here, but I can live with that too. But I won't leave you, and I won't let you go out there by yourself. If you can say to my face that you don't love me and you don't want me in your life, then I'll leave you alone."

She closed her eyes and said nothing.

"Passive-aggressive isn't your style, Orla."

She opened her eyes and looked straight at him. "I . . ."

Lorcan muffled what she was going to say with a bone-melting kiss. Then he released her and raised his arms up, surrendering. "Okay, I bluffed. Please don't say anything. I don't have the confidence that you won't say it. I don't want you to make me leave." Then he let his arms flop down by his sides. He simply stared at her.

Her throat hurt. Before the tears bubbled out, she said, "There's a curse . . ."

"A what?"

The device in Lorcan's pocket buzzed. "Someone called Madeline," he said, then he listened to the recording. "Stephen got shot in New York," he relayed. "Madeline's plan was fucked up. Zen knew she sent Stephen, and now he's after her. Let's go." Lorcan grimaced. There wasn't time for Orla to say anything else. She merely followed him.

CHAPTER 8

Lorcan turned the Bluetooth tracking device off and slid it into his bag. "We can see her from here and hear what she says from the speaker." Orla nodded. Orla and Lorcan had planted themselves in the front yard of a house a respectable distance from Mrs. Hanson's. Gauging from the overflowing mailbox and overgrown garden, they speculated the house was uninhabited. But to be sure, Orla knocked on the door. There was no response.

A hoarse female voice croaked out from their speaker, "I've convinced Woody to forgive your intrusion this morning, but he's still upset!"

They heard a dog barking.

"Mrs. Hanson, I'm sorry I was rude this morning, but I . . ." Madeline said.

Lorcan winced at the old woman's voice. It was unpleasant and oddly spooky—it gave him goose bumps.

"All your kind are the same," the hoarse voice continued.

"My kind? Mrs. Hanson . . ." Madeline raised her voice in defense.

"You want to find John Dee's grave, right?" Mrs. Hanson said.

Wait. No. That wasn't Mrs. Hanson's voice that Lorcan heard. The voice was right next to him. He turned and saw Orla's empty eyes. The voice coming out of her mouth wasn't her own.

"Orla!" Lorcan grabbed Orla's shoulders and gently shook her. "Orla." She didn't respond. He didn't pay attention to what was coming out of the speaker. He was focused solely on Orla. He shook her harder. She looked right through him and didn't respond to his call. "Orla, come on baby, come back to me."

The voice came out of Orla again, "What you want to find in the grave is not my problem. I knew you were coming. Like all the others. Greed doesn't do anyone any good."

"But I didn't . . ." Madeline's voice protested via the speaker.

Lorcan shook Orla hard. She skipped a sentence and went silent. She paused and stared at him blankly.

"Oh baby, come on, fight this." He pulled her into his arms as she swayed.

"Where can I find the grave?" Madeline's voice said.

The old voice continued via Orla's mouth. "Fossey Way. It's guarded by Roman soldiers. And I have to warn you, young lady, these soldiers cannot tell the difference between greed and grief. They judge you by your actions. So be careful."

"I'm not Madeline, and you're not Mrs. Hanson." Lorcan shook Orla again and again.

"I'll kill you, little bird. Like I killed the others. Go to Fossey Way. There are lots of bones for you to find. Today is a good day to die," the old voice rasped from Orla's mouth.

"Please, Orla, please. Come back to me." Orla suddenly snapped back. She swayed and collapsed into his arms. Lorcan scooped her up to carry her to the car. Shortly after, she shifted and opened her eyes. "Oh, thank God." He put her down on the ground.

"What happened?" Orla asked, still slightly dazed.

"We were listening to the conversation between Madeline and Mrs. Hanson. The next thing I know, I heard Mrs. Hanson voice's coming out of your mouth. Do you remember anything?"

Orla shook her head.

"Why are you lying to me?" Lorcan snarled.

"I'm not."

"You have that 'I'm lying' look on your face."

Damn her pathetic failure of a poker face. "Okay, okay. I remember. I don't know how. But I remember the words coming out of my mouth. Someone was speaking through me, and I couldn't control it."

"Since when have you been able to do this?"

"Never. This is the first time."

Lorcan stood up and ruffled his hair, trying to control his temper. But this time, he failed. "I can't tolerate your lies anymore, Orla."

Orla saw the fury in his eyes. "If you can't tolerate me, then go away."

Lorcan waved his arms in frustration. "You want me to leave, this is your plan, isn't it?"

"If you won't leave, I will." She pushed up to her feet and walked toward the car.

At the school, Riley jumped out of the car he parked illegally in the loading dock and charged toward the principal's office. He almost ran into Mrs. Abbey, Noah's teacher, on her way out.

"Mrs. Abbey, where's Noah?"

"In there with the principal. He's all right now. He didn't want to go to the hospital. He just asked for you," Mrs. Abbey said, her lips pressed into a thin line. Riley knew she thought he didn't take care of Noah well, but he didn't have time to explain. He couldn't care less what people think about him and ignored them as long as they weren't accusing him of negligence and sending in a social worker.

"Dad." Noah stormed out. He darted over and clung to Riley. He held his son, lifting the boy up.

"I'm sorry, Noah. I can't help you with the pain. Would you like me to take you home?"

In tears, Noah said, "It's not painful anymore. But I don't want to go home. Could you please call Uncle Lorcan?"

"What? Why?"

"I need to talk to him. Right away."

Riley frowned. "What did you see, Noah? You had a vision, didn't you?"

"Blood. I saw Uncle Lorcan and a lot of blood."

Riley nodded. "All right. Let's get out of here, and we'll call him on the way."

The principal walked out from his office and was about to say something. "I'm sorry, we have to go now. I'll arrange a meeting with you when I have a chance. I promise."

Riley put Noah down. They darted down the corridor before the principal could say anything. Fifteen minutes later, Riley left a voicemail for Lorcan. He crouched down next to Noah. "He might be using his phone to do some of his spy work. If that's the case, he won't even check his messages. Noah, what did you see exactly?"

"We have to find him. I know where he is. He's heading toward Fossey Way."

"Noah, do you even know where Fossey Way is?"

Noah shook his head. "I heard his voice in my head. He's going to Fossey Way." A tear rolled down Noah's face. Riley wiped it off.

"All right, son, we're heading toward Fossey Way."

Back in Mortlake, Orla sat in the car, staring at the dashboard. She could drive away and let Lorcan call a cab to get back to London. But just then, Lorcan banged on the car's window.

"Orla, we need to warn Madeline not to go to Fossey way."

"We can call her."

"Sure. But I need you to stay with me for a bit."

Lorcan pulled out his phone, "Oh no, you've got to be kidding me." The screen of his phone was blank.

"This is a sign. We have to go back to London, right now. You're getting out of this job!"

"Sign of what? Crappy technology? We can't let her go to her death, Orla. You heard what that woman said."

"I heard her. I'll warn Madeline myself. You're not going with me."

"The hell I'm not! Until you can give me a proper explanation, I won't let you do this job alone."

"Don't even hope, Lorcan. She doesn't have the guts to tell you," Mya's voice came from behind them, sending Lorcan and Orla jumping out of their skins.

"You again?" Lorcan exclaimed.

"Go away," Orla growled.

"Why? Afraid I'm going to tell your lover what a liar you are?"

Orla jumped out of the car and leapt at Mya, teeth bared and prepared to fight. Mya was as quick as a cat. She sidestepped out of Orla's path. Orla dropped to the ground, rolling, and stood up. The two women circled each other, each eyeing the other.

"Hey, ladies!" Lorcan shouted, but neither woman paid him any attention. He darted toward Orla, grabbing her from behind.

"Let me go, Lorcan!" Orla shrieked.

"I have to hold off one of you. Would you prefer I held onto her?"

"I told you if you keep doing this, you're going to get him killed, Orla," Mya said.

"I don't believe you!" Orla screamed.

"Then use your own senses. You have talent. Use it and figure out how you're killing him."

"Don't talk like I'm not here. We have a woman driving to her death right now, and you two are ranting about nonsense. If there's some inexplicable reason that we can't save Madeline or go after her, can we at least call the police?" Lorcan exclaimed.

"No." Orla and Mya chorused.

Orla and Mya started at each other. Lorcan swung his gaze back and forth between the two.

"Why not?" he asked.

"What will you tell the cops?" Orla asked. "Tell them that a woman is driving to Fossey Way, which tourists do all the time, and that the woman might be in danger because your girlfriend told you so?"

"You're more than just a girlfriend," Mya snarled.

"Who are you to say?" Orla squealed, threatening to charge at Mya again.

"And why do you think I'll be killed? Why should I believe you?" Lorcan asked Mya.

"You don't have to believe me. Ask her. She knows." Mya pointed at Orla.

"How am I supposed to know if the gypsy was right?" Orla snarled.

Lorcan stared at Orla while Mya smirked. Lorcan approached Orla and put his hands on her shoulders. He looked straight into her eyes. "Orla, how do you know Mrs. Hanson is a gypsy? We haven't even seen the woman."

"I . . ."

"You can't tell me?" Lorcan released her, letting his hands flop to his sides. "I'm not sure if what Mrs. Hanson said is true or not. I can't call the cops because I don't know exactly what to tell them. So I'm going to do what any normal person would. I'm going to Fossey Way to tell Madeline to go back to London. I'll tell her I'll help her find what she needs to save her friend." Lorcan turned on his heel and walked away.

"No!" Orla and Mya chorused again.

Lorcan turned around and arched an eyebrow.

Orla huffed. "Okay. I'm telepathic. Somehow I connected to Mrs. Hanson and heard her thoughts. She had some pretty scary thoughts about what she had laid out at Fossey Way. So I don't want you to go there."

"They're just thoughts. But if it's true, we can't just let Madeline go there without warning. Anyone with half a conscience would try to stop her," Lorcan said.

"I'm a thief. I don't have the moral grounds that you do. I'm telling you not to go to Fossey Way—for your own safety . . . and for me."

Lorcan stared at Orla, then he turned around and walked away.

"Lorcan!" Orla called out. "I'll drop everything. I'll go back to Ireland with you right now."

Lorcan kept walking.

"Okay, okay. I'm a deity," Mya said. "I know you're destined to die if you go to Fossey Way, Lorcan."

Lorcan slowly turned around. "Say again?"

"You heard me. If you have a wholehearted desire to die, then go. I can't stop you."

Lorcan laughed. "A gypsy, a telepathic, and now a deity. Any more surprises?"

Orla stared at Mya. Mya raised an eyebrow in challenge. "Unlike thieves, good deities have high moral grounds. I revealed my identity. What are you going to do?"

"I don't care if you're a god. Don't challenge me," Orla snarled.

"Actually, I'm a goddess."

"I'm going. You're staying. She's going to protect you," Orla pointed her finger at Lorcan and then Mya as she talked, then walked away.

"Hey, no, you're not going anywhere. And I don't need protection." Lorcan grabbed Orla's arm. She shrugged him off.

He spoke to Mya. "Let's say I believe that you're a deity, and for reasons that only God knows, you can see my future and feel obliged to protect me, how am I going to die?"

"A stab wound to the heart," Mya said bluntly.

Orla thought she heard something about stabbing and death. Her limbs went numb. There were buzzing noises reverberating in her head. She forced herself to remain upright and swallowed her tears.

Lorcan shrugged. "Wait here." He strode toward the car, opened the car trunk, took something out, then came back to the yard. He lifted his jacket to reveal a gun.

"You arranged that?" Orla gasped.

"You said we might need it." Lorcan smiled. "Mya, between a knife and a gun, my money's on the gun. I'll see how the Roman soldiers handle it, but I think we have a slight advantage. We're going after Madeline."

"You're an idiot, Lorcan. You're both idiots." Mya turned on her heel and left.

CHAPTER 9

Later, sitting in the car, Orla mumbled, "It's not working." She slapped the screen of the portable tracking device without mercy.

"Gentle, baby. Not everyone would make love to you after you slapped him across the face." Lorcan chuckled.

"It's an object, not a person. I don't make love to an object, and I can hit an object as much as I want." She slapped at the device again.

"Give it to me." Lorcan reached for the device.

"No, you're driving. I don't want you to turn us into corpses."

"Want an IT solution to the problem?"

"What?"

"Turn it off and on."

Orla rolled her eyes and turned the device off. Then she turned it on. It made a 'bing', sound and a blue dot appeared on the screen.

Lorcan laughed. "Don't worry, I won't tell anyone."

Orla slapped his shoulder. "It's your device, and it's stupid."

Lorcan shook his head and smiled. "That's debatable. Where's Madeline?"

"Heading toward Roman Road."

"All right. We'd better get to her before it gets dark." Lorcan accelerated.

The road was bumpy, and clouds were creeping across the blue sky. A storm was brewing. "Great," Lorcan muttered.

"Anyone with common sense would have come back to the highway by now," Orla said. "And for your information, your stupid device is dead again. And I've turned it off and on three times already."

Lightning slashed through the distant horizon, and thunder rumbled somewhere in the sky. The road in in front of them blurred into the rain and darkness. Strange chanting sounds hovered in the air behind their necks. Water fell from the sky, streamed from the creek nearby, and trickled from the long stone walls tracing along the narrow country roads, almost as if the stone itself was weeping.

"I don't have a good feeling about this," Lorcan mumbled.

"If we turned around now, what about Madeline?"

Lorcan eyes darkened. "You're right. We've got to find her. If we're uneasy about the strange weather and this strange place, how will Madeline handle it on her own?"

A lightning bolt slashed through the sky, and thunder exploded in the distance.

Something hit the car hard, making it veer to the side and scraped along the stone wall. Lorcan's lips formed a thin line, and his jaw clenched as he tried to control the car. "What the fuck was that?"

After a short distance, they could see Madeline's car outlined by the flash of the lightning bolts.

"She's veering off the wall," Orla gushed.

"Her car's rolled. Fuck." Lorcan hit the accelerator.

There was a loud bump on the side of their car and a few more bumps on the road that almost lifted the car. "What the fuck?" Lorcan clenched his teeth again and hung on tightly to the steering wheel.

A lightning bolt struck a tree right next to the car, nearly exploding their eardrums.

There was another bump. The car almost jumped into the air.

Lorcan drove faster. Something hit the car again from the side and pushed it off the road. The car landed on a slope and rolled. It hit a large rock and stopped, motionless and upside down. Orla and Lorcan dangled by their seatbelts. After regaining his bearings, Lorcan reached over to Orla.

"Are you okay, Orla?"

"Yes," she muttered.

They freed themselves from the seatbelts and landed with a thud on the ceiling of the car. The crawled out, stood up, slid in the mud, and rolled down a little hill. In the dark, two large shadows charged at them. Lorcan knocked down his man quickly and snatched at the man on top of Orla. Lorcan pounded on him. Another man charged at Orla, and she squealed and fought.

A male voice came out from the dark. "Not that woman, you idiot," said a tall man darting out from the bush.

The fighting men stopped. "What?" one of the two men asked. "Ugh." And as he was distracted, he earned a knuckle punch from Orla. He roared and charged at her again.

"Not that woman, I said, you dumb ass," the tall man commanded. "Over there. She's out of the car already, you useless idiots." He pointed in Madeline's direction.

The rain kept coming down. More lightning and thunder, and then loud, confusing noises echoing through the darkness around them. Orla continued to hear the strange chanting sound.

The two men who had been attacking Lorcan and Orla turned and ran toward Madeline. "You're attacking a defenseless woman!" Lorcan growled at them as there was nothing else he could do to stop them.

A few more men had arrived. The tall man suddenly turned back, looking at Orla and Lorcan. "They've seen us. Kill them," he commanded the new men.

Two men brandished knives and charged at Lorcan and Orla. Lorcan pushed Orla behind him, but when two other men approached, they were pulled apart.

Orla fought one man. She didn't have a weapon, but she was quick. The other three were on Lorcan quickly. She lost track of him in the stormy night. She gave her attacker a few good hits and dodged around his knife swings. She suffered some minor cuts to her arms, but he couldn't get close to her.

She stumbled on a piece of rock and fell. It was raining heavily now. She couldn't see Lorcan. She knew it was the end of her when she saw the man leap at her with the knife.

Then she heard a loud bang. The man's head exploded in front of her, and his body dropped down on her like a two-ton sack of potatoes. His dead weight squashed her into the ground. There were a few more loud bangs, and in the haze of pain, blood, and confusion, she saw something hovering in the sky like a big bird. She heard people shouting. And then it went quiet. She passed out.

Moments passed. Orla opened her eyes to find Mya shaking her shoulders.

"Can you get up?"

"Where's Lorcan? Big bird. They had knives. You were right." Orla's voice slurred with the effects of a concussion.

"Only the last part of what you said counts. Snap back and get up, or you'll lose your man."

Orla's eyes flung wide open. Lorcan. Loud bangs. They were gun shots. She pushed herself up, forced away the dizziness, and looked to the side of her. Lorcan's body was sprawled on the wet ground, lifeless.

"Oh no. No . . ." she cried and bulldozed over the dead body lying next to her to get to Lorcan. "Oh no." It had stopped raining, but his body was soaking wet and as cold as steel.

"He's not dead. Yet," Mya said. "Will you help me get him to the car?"

Orla nodded. She was still dazed, but she moved as quickly as she could. They put Lorcan in the back seat of the car. Orla jumped in and cradled him in her arms.

"Guess that means I have to drive," Mya muttered and got into the driver's seat.

Orla was fully awake. "Oh God." She moaned and checked the blood stains on Lorcan's shirt. His pulse was extremely weak. Mya glanced at her in the rear view mirror.

"He killed for you. He gunned down four men and copped two bullets himself. And he's not dead. Not bad for a man with a desk job."

"He doesn't have a desk job," Orla snarled. "You said he'd be killed by a stab wound. These are gunshot wounds. That means he won't die, right?"

"The information was relevant at the time we spoke. With interferences from other forces, things often change."

Orla didn't realize that tears were rolled down her face. "Can you drive faster?"

"It's a car, not a helicopter. The LeBlancs rescued Madeline using the chopper you called a big bird. But my resources don't stretch that far."

"They rescued Madeline? So she's fine now?"

"Yes. It was a full-on search and rescue. The LeBlancs don't do anything on a small scale. They didn't know about you, lying there in the mud."

"If you saw them, why didn't you call them and ask them to help us?"

"I can only interact directly with my subject—Lorcan, in this case."

"You're a deity. Can't you heal him or beam us to a hospital rather than crawling along in this car?"

"You watch too much TV, Orla. I thought you knew better than that."

"So what do deities do exactly? You said your job is to protect Lorcan, but how can you do that?"

Lorcan groaned and shifted.

"Oh darling, open your eyes for me, please." Orla shook him slightly.

Lorcan opened his eyes and saw her teary face. He smiled weakly. "Are you okay?" he asked. Then his head lolled back, and he passed out again.

"Oh no, no," Orla cried. His body was too cold. His pulse was too weak. She didn't need to be a doctor to know this wasn't going to end well. "Stop the car," Orla snapped.

Mya stopped. Orla lay Lorcan down. She jumped out of the car and yanked the driver's door open, suggesting Mya to get out of the car.

"Don't boss me around." Mya grimaced.

"Please," Orla said.

Mya slid out of the driver's seat.

"How exactly is it that you're going to protect Lorcan?"

"I have to switch back to my deity form, which basically just gives me a vision of what will happen within the very near future and whether the subject can be saved. But I have to save the subject as a human. So apart from warning him against idiotic actions and driving him to a hospital, I can't heal him. I have no such magic."

"So you can do less than what a witch can."

"It's not what I *can* do. It's what I *will* do for people."

"So do it. Switch on your vision and tell me if he can be saved." Orla shifted. "Please."

Mya nodded. She closed her eyes, clasped her hands in front of her chest as if she were praying, and concentrated. Shortly, she returned as Mya, except her eyes were darkened and shone with tears.

"Oh no." Orla saw the look on Mya's face and gasped. "You promised to save him," she snarled.

"I warned him, and I warned you. It's out of my control now. People die. That's just how it is."

"No. Not him. Not like this," Orla growled.

A jasmine smell thickened the air. Not only could Orla smell it, she could feel it brushing against her skin. Mya smelled it too.

"Orla, I know what you are capable of. But it's too late now. Let him go."

"No, not in a million years. Not after what we've been through," Orla's voice croaked.

"No, Orla. You will regret this, and it can't be undone."

A car zoomed out from the dark and braked just behind them. From the car charged Riley and Noah. Noah made a beeline to the car.

"Uncle Lorcan." He shook Lorcan's bloody shoulders.

"Let me see." Riley put his medical kit down on the floor of the car and gently nudged Noah aside. From a distance, Mya frowned at Noah.

"Can he make it to the hospital?" Orla asked Riley. The doctor looked at Orla, then shook his head.

"Oh God. Oh no," Orla cried. Noah held his father and cried. The sob dissolved into thin air like a plea to God for help. Mya looked up to the sky.

"You're a deity . . . now you tell me, is God going to help me this time?" Orla asked. Silence. Orla nodded. "All right, I'll have to call for help elsewhere," Orla muttered.

"Don't do it, Orla," Mya said.

Orla returned to the car and asked Riley to take Noah away. Riley didn't know Orla's intention, but he picked Noah up and walked toward where Mya stood. It had stopped raining, but the strange chanting sound echoed out from the brush nearby.

CHAPTER 10

Orla waved everyone away. The jasmine smell was thickening by the second. Noah cried and tried to run to Lorcan, who was lying in the car, blood seeping out of his wounds along with his strength, his life force. It took both Mya and Riley to keep Noah away.

Next to the car, Orla had traced a triangle in the mud. She remembered the ritual as if it had just been yesterday when she learned it. Regardless of how painful the memory was, regardless of what happened next, Orla had to do this. She couldn't lose Lorcan.

She mumbled the sorcery curse and then used the knife she had taken from the dead body of the attacker to cut off a bit of her hair. Then she chanted the curse a few more times. The wind started to blow. The scent of jasmine wafted into the wind and whirled about like a small tornado. Orla cut her arm with the knife, dripping her blood into the triangle. The triangle attracted a lightning bolt, and Orla was blown a few feet away.

From a distance away, Mya shook her head. Noah screamed for Orla to stop. Orla got to her feet and went back to the triangle. She chanted the curse again, the black curse her ancestor had created. The smell of jasmine engulfed the entire area and a swirl of black mist seeped up from the ground, forming a funnel.

Mya moved toward the car, but a lightning bolt suddenly struck directly in front of her, sending her skidding backward and flopping into the mud.

"Get out of my way." A deep demonic male voice hovered in the air.

Orla's eyes were darkened and empty. She stood still, her black hair blowing in the wind. A smile spread across her face. More lightning bolts struck the ground, and the air sparked liked fireworks. Mya felt as if she was in the middle of an explosion.

The form of an eight-foot-tall ancient man appeared out of the mist. He snaked a hand out of his black robe and reached toward Orla's heart while she stood still and waited. Noah broke out of Riley's hold, pushing Riley to the ground. Riley looked at his son and saw that Noah's eye were blank and white. Noah charged at the ancient man, hitting him from behind.

"He's possessed," Mya said.

"He's telepathic. For God's sake, do something about it!" Riley yelled.

The ancient man fell forward when Noah hit him. He released Orla and turned toward Noah, furious. Noah staggered backward. His eyes had gone back to normal, and at the moment, he looked like no more than a scared kid. The ancient man reached out his arm to grab Noah, but Riley jumped in front of him and held his arm to prevent him from approaching his son. The ancient man pulled back, staggered, and looked at Riley. He reached for him, but as soon as he did, he shrieked as if in pain and exploded into nothingness.

Lorcan awoke, finding himself tucked comfortably in bed in Orla's apartment. He shifted, his body ached everywhere. He closed his eyes and tried to recall what had happened. They'd fought in the dark, in the midst of rain, storm, lightning, and thunder. Three men had been on him and a big one was chasing Orla with a knife. They had left him no choice. Lorcan remembered pulling his gun and shooting at the guy launching himself at Orla. Then he'd swung the gun to fire at the three others racing toward him. And the tall man who seemed to be the boss shot him.

He remembered the sensation of the bullets hitting him. There had been very little pain. A bit of pressure. And then he was drowning. He remembered nothing else.

Orla walked out of the kitchen with a mug of coffee. Seeing that Lorcan was up, she darted to the bed.

"How are you feeling?" She cupped his face. He was the same, her Lorcan with the striking blue eyes and the mouth made for kissing. And that was exactly what she did. She kissed him. Deeply and possessively.

He shifted again and tried to sit up. He looked at his chest, remembering where the bullets had hit him. The wounds were completely healed. Astonished, he straightened more and looked again. There was no trace of the wounds save for two new faint scars.

He stared at Orla for a long moment. She looked different.

"What happened to your hair?" He asked. Her long black hair was a foot shorter.

She smiled. "It got muddy and tangled in the fight last night, so I had it cut this morning."

He smiled. "Pretty." He pulled her into his arms and embraced her. He could feel her body shaking a bit, and then settle. She gave him her coffee mug. He smiled and took a tentative sip. From the moment he had woken, he felt his body recovering at an amazing speed. He could literally feel the cells in his body regenerating and healing. A sea of energy and strength washed through him. He felt incredible.

"What happened last night, Orla? I mean, after I passed out. I remember being shot. I couldn't have recovered this fast from those injuries. I feel as if I could knock out two bouncers at once now."

Orla bit her lips and hesitated.

"I'm asking for the facts, Orla. If you're taking this long to answer, that means you're plotting your lie. I don't want you to lie to me. Just tell me the truth."

Orla cleared her throat. "Mya came for us. She used her abilities to heal you. Otherwise, you wouldn't have made it to the hospital. I hesitated telling you because Mya said the healing might have undesirable side effects. She doesn't know what they might be. It's different for each person."

Lorcan gazed at Orla's face, searching for what she was leaving unspoken.

She regretted lying to him, but she continued. "I don't have an 'I'm lying' face right now, if that's what you're looking for. Are you feeling any different?"

"Apart from an amazing strength surging through my body, not much different really. I still love you the same."

"Not more?"

"Much more." He smiled. "What about Madeline?"

"Mya told me that the LeBlancs rescued her."

Lorcan narrowed his eyes. "Is that all you're going to tell me?"

Orla nodded and pushed up to her feet to go to the kitchen. Lorcan mumbled a curse. He knew she was lying. Suddenly, there was static as the spy device activated. Mrs. Hanson's voice resonated from it, making Lorcan leap from the bed and dart toward his desktop computer.

"It's good to see you again, Ciaran. What has this old woman done to deserve a visit?" asked Mrs. Hanson.

Orla charged out from the kitchen. "Shit, Ciaran and Madeline beat us there. They're at Mortlake now," Lorcan said. "We have to let Madeline and Ciaran know the old woman planned that attack last night."

"Lorcan!" Orla had her arms waved in the air.

"Yes."

"The guys yesterday were willing to kill for whatever they're looking for. I don't want to have to handle another episode like last night."

"Based on what you said, Mya saved me, right? She might be able to do it again. She's a goddess. Why worry?"

"Can't you just call Ciaran?"

"There's only one person I know of who can hack Ciaran LeBlanc's phone number. And that's God," Lorcan deadpanned and grabbed his jacket.

"It's half an hour to Mortlake. They won't even be there by the time you get there," Orla protested.

"That's when you drive." As Lorcan finished the sentence, he was already halfway out of the door. Orla cursed and followed him.

Fifteen minutes later, Lorcan and Orla were hiding across the street, close enough that they had a good visual of Mrs. Hanson's place. From their vantage point, they could see Ciaran and Madeline standing in Mrs. Hanson's front yard.

Madeline's shaky voice came over Lorcan's spy device. "Her earrings, the jingle of her earrings caused my hallucination at the walls. Don't listen to it."

"Your magic—if I can call it magic—won't work on me, Mrs. Hanson. I believe you know that," Ciaran said.

Mrs. Hanson grunted out the words, "Greedy people are supposed to die!"

"Madeline's not greedy, Mrs. Hanson. She was blackmailed into this, and I'm going to help her sort it out. I believe you've mixed with dark forces. I've lost a man because of this. A dear friend of mine. I need to know who asked you to send those seeking information about John Dee to Fossey Way," Ciaran asked.

Mrs. Hanson laughed, a crooked laugh that pulled at the muscles on her face and made it look as if she was in pain. "You think I'm going to tell you that?"

"I just wanted to give you a chance to tell me in person. I still have respect for you for what you did in the past. But if you don't tell me now, I will find out, and I'll trash your Rose Powder," Ciaran said.

"Don't you dare," Mrs. Hanson screamed, but it came out more like a croak. She swung her head so that her earrings jingled loudly.

Madeline grabbed her ears and stepped back.

Mrs. Hanson shook her arms so that the bells dangling on her beaded wristbands sang as well. The sound from the earrings was the worst, though. Mrs. Hanson gyrated as if doing some macabre dance. She laughed.

Next to Lorcan, Orla grabbed at her ears. "Oh no no, baby, block her out of your mind. Please. Don't do that to me again." Orla nodded. She closed her eyes, concentrated, and brushed Mrs. Hanson's voice out of her head.

In the yard, Ciaran stepped in front of Madeline.

"Go to the car and wait for me there."

"No."

"Go, Madeline!"

Mrs. Hanson swung her earrings harder and the noise increased. Madeline grabbed her ears and slumped to the ground. Ciaran called Madeline, pulling her up and backward.

Lorcan felt sorry for Ciaran. He knew what it felt like when the same had happened to Orla. He didn't know how to help Ciaran.

Madeline shrugged off Ciaran's arms and charged toward the old woman. She grabbed the dangling earrings and pulled hard. The woman screamed in pain. Blood poured from her ripped ear lobes. The old woman grunted, and the sound coming out of her was demonic and deep. She pulled out a knife and charged at Madeline. Seeing the swing of the knife, Madeline stepped back, and Ciaran darted toward her from behind. Madeline tripped on a small stone, tumbled, and fell on her back. The old woman growled and jumped atop her, swinging the knife in a downward arc.

Ciaran grabbed the old woman's hand. The old woman looked at him as if she had been waiting for just that moment. She did not jerk her hand free, but turned the knife on herself, along with Ciaran's hand, and plunged it into her chest.

Lorcan and Orla gasped.

From behind of Mrs. Hanson's house, the gardener walked out, and what he saw was Ciaran's hand still on the hilt of the knife, stabbing Mrs. Hanson.

"Oh, God! Oh, my God, Mrs. Hanson!" He stumbled backward, fell, and then stood up and ran.

Madeline rolled away. Mrs. Hanson lay on the ground, still evilly grinning at Madeline and Ciaran.

"Keep the powder. You and your bitch will never get away with this, she said. "I'll see you in hell." And then the old woman stared into nothingness with dead eyes.

Madeline pulled at Ciaran. He stood there with blood on his hands. Madeline wiped the blood from his hand with the inside of her jacket and pulled Ciaran away.

Lorcan put his listening device away. He stepped out from their hiding place, and Orla pulled at his elbow. "Nothing more to listen to here, Lorcan. Let's go . . ." She trailed off when they saw the gardener come back to look at Mrs. Hanson's dead body. He took her necklace and ran away again.

Lorcan clenched his teeth. "Low life scumbag. Do you think he's going to come out as a witness when the LeBlancs are framed for this murder?"

"Why do you think they're going to frame Ciaran for this?"

"That's quite obvious," he grumbled and darted in the direction in which the gardener had disappeared.

Orla puffed as she tried to chase after Lorcan. She was sure he just wanted to beat the gardener up and dissuade him from going to the cops as a witness. They skidded to a halt a safe distance away as they saw a man pulling the gardener into a limousine parked at the corner of the street. They waited. And waited. Then the gardener was kicked rolling out of the car. From the back seat, a tall man stepped out.

Orla gasped. "That's William Turk."

William stepped forward as the gardener staggered back. When they got into position beside a dumpster, William pulled out a dagger and swung at the gardener's throat. As the man slumped to the ground, William wiped the dagger's blade on the gardener's shirt and walked away. A couple of William's goons stayed behind to clean up the mess.

Orla was shaking in Lorcan's arms and tears were streaming down her face. She could feel his body shaking with anger as well.

"He used the White Knight's dagger I stole for him," Orla cried.

"Shhh." Lorcan kissed her forehead, and held on to her for a long moment. After a while, they walked solemnly back to their car.

CHAPTER 11

The cell phone in Orla's purse buzzed before she reached the car, on the screen was William Turk's caller ID. She almost dropped the phone.

"He just killed a man, and now he's calling me. What could he possibly want?" Orla hissed.

"Just pick up the phone and stay calm, baby," Lorcan soothed.

Orla blew out a breath and picked up. "Hello?" she greeted.

"Orla, I've changed the plan now . . ." William said at the other end of the line.

"I've changed my plan too," Orla cut in firmly.

"What? You know you can't back out of the job, right? You don't want to upset me, Orla."

"What do you want?" Orla asked.

"I need to speak with you in person. Same place. In half an hour."

"I'm not even in the country," Orla raised her voice.

"I know where you are, and I need to speak to you. Be there or else." William hung up.

Orla swung her arm to heave her phone at the ground, but Lorcan grabbed at it. "Calm down, baby. We're down to one phone now. Let me hold on to it." He slid Orla's phone into his pocket.

"Where's your phone?" she asked.

"Lost in the fight last night. Let's go."

They sat at a corner table in the restaurant where Orla had met with William Turk before. This time, Lorcan remained with Orla. They saw William appear at the entrance of the restaurant.

"Stay calm and play it through, Orla. You'll be fine."

She nodded although her stomach quivered.

William approached reluctantly. Lorcan sat still, his arm protectively around the back of Orla's chair. He extended his hand for a shake, which William reciprocated after an awkward pause.

"He's not part of the deal," William snapped.

"He's my partner. He's been in on all of my deals, including the White Knight's dagger. But that's not relevant. We want out of the deal. I'll return the client's deposit."

William shook his head. "It doesn't work that way."

"How does it work?" Lorcan asked dryly.

"Why do you want out of the deal?"

"Change of heart. We have bigger and better fish to fry." Lorcan gave William an icy stare.

"You want more money?"

Lorcan let out a dry chuckle, but the amusement wasn't reflected in his eyes.

"I'll take that as a no to more money. Well, you can opt out of the next step. But you have to deliver Jo to me as the completion of this job."

"What will you do to her when you get her?" Orla asked.

"That's none of your business. You'll rescue her from Zen. You'll be a hero, as you said. What else do you want?" William smirked.

"You said before that there would be no killings in this job." Orla raised her voice.

"Have you seen anything different?"

Lorcan squeezed Orla's hand under the table. She bit her lip and said nothing.

"She's just seen a lot of incidents involving violence and death in kidnapping cases in the news lately. She's a bit worried. That's all," Lorcan said and absently rubbed the back of Orla's hand.

William sneered. "Get a clerk job if you're scared. But with the crime rate these days, even checkout chicks are killed as collateral damage. Hell, bystanders were killed at a bank robbery yesterday. Why don't you wrap her in velvet and make her a housewife?"

"I asked. She thinks it's too soon to make such a commitment to me. But a positive step toward it is that she takes no more jobs from you. So what'll it cost for you to release us from this job?"

"As I said, that's not how it works. You have to deliver Jo to me. It's a done deal."

Lorcan arched an eyebrow. "And if not?"

"If not, S . . . my employer isn't going to be happy. When he's in a bad mood, people tend to encounter a lot of unfortunate incidents—some of them fatal. You don't want that to happen to your loved ones, do you?"

Lorcan laughed. "All right. If you insist. I want fifty percent of the money in our bank account by tomorrow."

"That's not the deal."

"You have that deal with Orla. This is *my* deal. Jo is a computer game designer. You need more than just to rescue her. You need her talent. You need that as much as the LeBlancs do."

William arched an eyebrow.

"Oh, and I forgot to mention . . . I can provide you with the exact locations of the LeBlanc's whereabouts. If you can find anyone who has my kind of skills that will work at this rate, I'll give you the info for free. What do you say?"

Silence.

"I'm sure this is beyond your pay scale, so if you need to consult your employer . . ." Lorcan said, withholding his smirk.

"All right. I'll take the deal."

"Fifty percent in our account by tomorrow morning," Lorcan confirmed with a smile.

William cast a stern look toward Lorcan and Orla. "You know what will happen if you two fuck me over."

Lorcan winked. "Of course, we do."

"Why did you call me here?" Orla asked.

"I need to push the plan forward. Zen will arrive with Jo tomorrow. I want you to get her right at their hotel. The address is here." William pushed a piece of paper toward Orla. "This should be easier than getting her when Madeline and Ciaran make the exchange."

Lorcan smirked at William. "You want to fuck Zen around, or your boss around?"

William stood. "That's none of your business," he said and turned on his heel, striding along the lush corridor toward the entrance.

Orla slammed the apartment door behind her, and threw her purse against the wall. "More money? Finishing the job? Didn't you see what William did today? He killed a man in cold blood. Let me guess, the only reason he didn't kill the guy in his limo was because he didn't want blood stains in his car."

"What choice did we have, Orla? He wouldn't let us out of the deal. The deal that *you* made. The one that I told you not to take before we had a proper discussion."

"Oh, so now that's my fault." Orla waved her arms in frustration.

"Blaming doesn't help the situation. Just in case you didn't notice, I killed four men yesterday. So I've got William beat on the killing chart," Lorcan growled.

"I didn't notice?" Orla snarled, jabbing her finger at Lorcan's chest. "You bled in my arms. You almost died in my arms. Do you know how hard it was for me to keep you alive yesterday? Do you know how much it hurt seeing you die, knowing that it was my fault? Do you know what I had to do to trade for your life?"

Lorcan narrowed his eyes. "What did you trade for my life?"

"It doesn't matter!" She waved her hands absently, exhausted after her rant. She headed toward the bathroom.

Lorcan grabbed at her elbow. "It does matter. What happened yesterday wasn't your fault. I've never said it was your fault. We're in this together. I just want you to trust me. What did you trade? And with whom?"

"There's nothing you can do about it anyway."

"Then tell me. Please." Lorcan rubbed Orla's arm. He nudged her gently so that she sat down on the sofa. He cupped her face and gazed at its every curve and line. "You know what I feel about you, Orla. Whatever you're going to say won't change that. I want you to trust me."

She shook her head. "No. I can't lose you, dead or alive. I can't. I can't even handle the thought of losing you." Tears rolled down her face now.

Lorcan pulled her in to his arms. "Orla, how could even think of that?" He kissed her hair and left her sitting on the sofa as he went to the desk. He pulled out his computer bag, opened the zipper of a small compartment at the side, and pulled out a tiny velvet bag. He put something in his palm.

"You never look in my computer bag, and that's why I put it there." He opened his palm revealing a thumbnail-sized rusty yellow stone.

Orla stared at the stone. The stone looked back at her. It was an ordinary stone she had picked up at the riverbank in Ireland. Emotions poured out of her like a storm. He gathered her into his arms and let her weep.

"I keep my promises, Orla. Until the end of my time, that stone is not going to turn into gold. Until then, I will love you no matter what. It was my vow to you, and I'll live up to it."

"Damn you, Lorcan. You were nine when I picked up that stupid rock."

He lifted her chin, "And you were six. A six-year-old girl who believed she could turn that piece of ordinary rock into gold. That's the girl I love. Not because she might be able to turn rock into gold, but because she had the crazy and idiotic belief that she could."

He kissed her forehead. "As long as the rock is not turning into gold, you're mine. So as long as the result of whatever you traded with whomever is not turning that rock into gold, I can take it. I will still love you. Nothing will change." He smiled. "Now, hit me with the truth."

She shifted. "I'm supposed to be a sorcereress."

There was silence.

Lorcan released her.

"God damn it. I knew this would happen!" she exclaimed.

He stood up and looked at her.

"Lorcan . . . never mind . . ." she sighed.

Lorcan jammed his hand with the rock into his pants pocket and stepped back. "What do you mean by you're 'supposed to be'? Are you or are you not a sorcereress?"

"That's what was expected of me . . . but no, I'm not a sorcereress . . . I don't have the training."

Lorcan let out a sign of relief. "So you're not turning my rock into gold?"

She let out a watery laugh. "No. I'm not going to turn that stupid rock into gold."

"But can you?" He frowned.

"No."

"Promise me even if you can, you won't, okay?"

"I promise I won't. Is that all you're worried about? Me turning that rock into gold?"

"Yeah." He nodded solemnly.

She laughed, tears rolling down her face. Then she narrowed her eyes at him. "You weren't surprised. You were pulling my leg."

Lorcan smiled. She flew at him, slapping at his chest. "Damn you, smart ass."

He let her hit him for a while. Her beating had no real heat in it. Then he snatched her hands and looked into her eyes. "I met a deity. I saw your telepathic reaction. I wouldn't be surprised if I saw unicorns walking down the street right now. So knowing you're a sorcerer or a witch doesn't surprise me. It doesn't change a thing. I thought you'd say you traded my soul for a demon in exchange for my life."

"Hmmm."

Lorcan's smile faded. "Is there a second half to the sorcerer reveal?"

She shook her head. "I didn't trade your soul or anything." She blew out a breath. "I did, however, let you receive a life force . . ."

"Life force? Like in *Star Wars*?"

"No. I don't know any Jedi Knights, I'm afraid." She shrugged and looked at him. Her eyes darkened. "The life force that you received is a bit like qi in Chinese medicine, which is supposed to be a natural source of energy. What I used on you was a qi created by dark magic from a special branch of sorcery."

Lorcan arched an eyebrow, waiting for what was coming next.

"The dark qi in your body won't change you. It makes you stronger in mind, body, and spirit. You don't have to do anything about it."

"What did it cost you?" Lorcan asked.

"The special branch of sorcery that gave you the dark qi, they're my family. They've been performing dark magic for more than a thousand years. Five hundred years ago, we were one of the strongest branches. Then everything fell apart because the leader violated a fundamental rule. We aren't allowed to have positive emotions. The emotion of the light, they called it. Love, happiness, enlightenment . . . All of those are not allowed. The leader at that point let himself love a woman, and that emotion corrupted his magic. The branch was ruined until . . ." she paused and looked at Lorcan.

"Oh no . . . ," he muttered.

She nodded. "Until me." She sighed. "The telepathic ability makes me one of the strongest Alphas since the incident five hundred years ago. I was raised to believe I would one day be the leader and revamp our branch of magic. I could have anything and everything I wanted. Money. Power. Hell, I could turn that rock you have into gold if I wanted to."

Lorcan approached, lifting her chin up so she looked him in the eye. "But you're not allowed to live as a normal person. You can't love. So what's the point of all that power?" He wiped a tear that trickled down her face. "That was why you never let me see your family. All that time we spent at the river, picking out rocks, playing children's games, you never told me. Then you ran away without a whiff of warning."

"But you found me."

Lorcan smiled. "It's not hard to find the second half of your soul. We're soul mates, Orla. How could you even think of losing me by telling me about your family?" He kissed her again.

"For years, I just wanted to make a lot of money, be successful so to speak. Then I could go back to my family and tell them we could have the life we wanted without using dark magic. I thought it was that simple. After I ran away, my uncle took over and built it up further."

"They still want you, I assume?"

Orla nodded. "At Fossey Way, I couldn't let you die. So I called them for the dark qi. In exchange, I have to go back to the family. They still want me to lead."

"What if you break the deal with your family? If you don't come back, what will they do?"

She blew out a breath. "It's not that simple. There were curses. When I ran away, a black curse was placed against me. When I am loved by someone, the black curse will kill me. My late aunt, she loved and raised me. She placed a white curse on me to protect me. So if I am loved by someone, the white curse will kill that person."

"Nice work," Lorcan muttered.

"I didn't know how much to buy into until . . . until you were going to die at Fossey Way." She cried again. "It was my fault," she said.

"No, Orla. No . . ."

Orla's phone buzzed. She looked at it and picked it up. "Riley? . . . No, don't cry darling, tell me what happened . . ." Orla hung up and phone and rushed toward the door. "Noah just called. Riley's in trouble," she said as she flew out the door. Lorcan followed her.

CHAPTER 12

Riley saw Lorcan and Orla charge into the house. Noah cried again, darting over to hug his uncle. Riley wanted to gather his son into his arms and take all of his fear away, but instead, he could only stand still, looking at his lifeless body and the people panicking around him. He regretted causing the look on Lorcan's face. Lorcan was like his brother. The only family he and Noah had. Riley wanted to help, wanted to stir and give them some signal so that they would stop worrying.

He wasn't blown up when the ancient man had exploded at Fossey Way. Riley hope he didn't actually kill the guy. He had looked like a ghost, so Riley assumed he was already dead. He couldn't kill a dead man, could he? Then Mya took him and Noah home. Riley had only had a few cuts and bruises, so he'd assumed everything was fine. That was why Mya left him and Noah and went about her business. If something were going to happen to him, a deity like Mya would know, wouldn't she? That was what she said before she left. Then he'd had another episode. It was like someone had pulled the rug out from under him. He fell into a coma again. But unlike what had happened when the old woman was here, this time, it hurt. His entire body felt as if it was on fire.

But what hurt him most was the fear on Noah's face. He had tried, but this time, he couldn't communicate with Noah. Riley needed to know what happened and how to snap out of this. He concentrated. From a distance, he saw a light. He walked toward it and moved through the light gate.

In front of Riley was a stone chapel. He walked into the hall of the long chapel. A cold breeze brushed across his skin. The stench of mud and rotten meat oozed up from the damned floor, covered in broken stones, bricks, and something that looked like broken bones. He didn't know what this place was, but he was certain it wasn't Heaven.

He saw an empty altar and the shadow of someone praying.

Hearing Riley's footsteps, the person turned around. At the same time, large candles on the stone base and torches on the wall lit up. The woman at the altar was stunning. Her sandy hair cascaded to her waist. Her milky skin shone in the flickering light. Her slanted blue eyes, although intense, looked at Riley with affection.

"Michelle," Riley whispered, thinking she looked like an angel.

As much as he wanted to, he didn't run toward her. Instead, he stopped with caution. There was something missing in her eyes. When he'd seen her before at their place, he had reached out, wanting to embrace her. But now, he wanted to withdraw from her. Something was wrong. He was fully aware that he was dreaming or operating at a subconscious level. This incident wasn't supposed to be real. But the danger he felt now was as real as it had ever been.

Michelle stepped closer to Riley, her long dress sweeping the floor. She reached her hand out. "Come here, darling," she said.

Riley staggered back.

The smile on Michelle's face faded. "Why won't you come to me? You always wanted this."

"You're not my wife," Riley said, feeling a lump in his throat. "What did you do with my wife?"

The woman smiled, and her face cracked, turned pale, and then darkened. Her skin and hair, dried up and tangled up like straw, turned black. Her eyes became bloodshot, and her lips blackened. "You're right," she said. "I'm not your wife, but I'm the death of her."

"But . . ."

"Yes, I know what you're thinking. She's already dead. But she couldn't pass to the next plane because of your stupid love for her. Not that I care about any of that. But it hurt my brother when he came claiming a sacrifice for a black curse. So I ought to fix it for him."

"I don't know what you're talking about."

"Someone was giving a sacrifice for a black curse. My brother was supposed to claim it, but then somehow you jumped into the process. He touched you without knowing you hold onto that love for your dead wife. That's lethal to my brother, and he's now stuck between worlds."

"Well, I didn't know. He was going to hurt my son. So I did what a father should."

The woman stared at Riley. "And you think I care about that?"

"But you care about your brother."

"You are mistaken. I don't. He's the head of the family. If he finishes, the power comes to me. But if he's stuck between worlds, I can't get the power, and no one can do anything about it."

"What do you want me to do?"

"Release your wife."

"How? Just say I don't love her anymore? Not only is that a lie, but I also don't see how it will free your brother."

"You have to say the reverse spell for the love your have with your wife."

Riley narrowed his eyes. "So in your world, it's an official statement, like a divorce."

The woman smiled. "Ah, you're smarter than I thought."

Riley shrugged. "All right then. I suppose it wouldn't hurt to say it. It might matter in your world, but not in mine. I need to get back to my son. So if I say what you want, you'll let me go back to my world?"

The woman smiled. "Of course. You and your son can live happily forever after."

"How do I know you'll keep your promise?"

"You have my word."

"Well, verbal conversation, even in a form of a spell—or maybe especially when it's a spell—doesn't work as an official record in my world. I need proof. A guarantee."

"How do you propose I do that?"

"I need something in writing."

The woman nodded and waved her hand. A scroll of paper appeared. She opened it. "I'll sign it with my blood," she said, signing. Then she held out the scroll to Riley. He smiled and approached.

"If my love for my wife bound your brother in a spell, it would most likely do the same to you," Riley said, and before he finished the sentence and the woman had a chance to react to it, he reached out and grabbed her hand instead of the scroll. The woman screamed in pain and tried to shrug off Riley's grip.

"Let me go. Let go of my hand." She tried to cast Riley away, but couldn't. She was weakening by the second. "Why?"

"My love for my wife can only get stronger. I refuse to physically or spiritually divorce her. Living or dead, she will always be my wife. You think I would ever believe that a simple reverse spell would release her from our ritual commitment? I don't know you, and I don't know your world, but I do know that the spell would do a lot more damage to my wife than that."

"It's just a release spell, I swear," the woman cried. She slumped to the ground and started to burn. The heat transferred to Riley, but he wouldn't let go.

"I'll burn you, bitch. Even if I die with you, I'll burn you now."

"Please don't . . . what do you want?"

"Let me go back to my world, and I'll release you there."

"I don't know how. Please don't kill me."

"How did you get me here?"

"You walked through the light yourself. Please let me go."

The woman burned like a torch. She swung harder and threw Riley against a wall. He slid to the floor. The woman screamed and raised her arm as if to strike him. He looked in the distance and saw the light gate. He used whatever strength left in him to charge at it. A force struck his back. He rolled on the floor, and then stood up to dive through the gate. Behind him, he could still hear the burning woman's screams.

Riley rolled out onto the floor of his house. He saw his body convulsing as if he was having a seizure. His nose and mouth bled. Lorcan grabbed the car keys and said he was taking Riley to the hospital. Orla stopped him, saying that this was a supernatural thing. They scuffled for the keys. Noah wailed and held on to his father.

There was a bang on the door. Lorcan yanked it open and saw Mya. "Just in time! Get in here and tell Orla that this has nothing to do with your spooky stuff, and I have to take Riley to the hospital. In fact, I'm calling an ambulance right now."

"No, you're not." Orla grabbed the phone. "He'll die if you do that. You have to let me perform a ritual."

"He's dying, and you're going rely on magic?" Lorcan yelled.

Mya walked into the house and glanced at Riley.

"Mya, tell me if he's going to die. I know you can't do magic. But it's the least you can do." Orla asked.

"I'm not supposed to say. It's only natural." Mya stared at Orla.

"Oh my God," Orla whispered. "He's really destined to die. That's why you aren't doing anything."

Noah cried out loud. He ran to the door. The kitten jumped up, clinging to Noah. The young boy ran out into the darkness of the night.

"Noah!" Lorcan called out and chased Noah. Orla followed. Mya was about to follow, but decided to stay with Riley.

CHAPTER 13

In the darkness, Noah ran as fast as his tiny body could tolerate, the kitten on his shoulder. He had turned into a quiet part of the national park. As much as the area was peaceful and serene every morning when he took walks with his father, now the darkness distorted the shapes of the trees and bushes, making them look like demons reaching out to grab him. An eerie wind howled around him, blowing the sounds of hell's chanting into his ears, a melody of death.

Lorcan called out and raced after him. He caught up and grabbed the boy. "Noah, please, don't do that. It doesn't help your father." He wiped the tears from Noah's cheek. "He'll be just fine. I'll make him better. Don't worry."

"How?" Noah cried.

"I'll find a way. You have to trust me. Your father's very strong. He'd never give up. He'd never leave you behind. You know that, right?"

Noah didn't answer. Tears kept streaming down his face. Orla caught up with them. "This isn't the place for talking. Let's get back inside the house." They didn't even have a chance to turn around when there was a demonic roar from behind a tree. From a dark corner, two shadows came toward them. Lorcan pushed Orla and Noah behind him. The kitten hissed profusely, teeth bared, eyes wildly green. They withdrew.

The two shadows approached—a woman and a man. They appeared human except for their deathly pale skin and blazing red eyes.

"Are they demons?" Noah asked.

"No, but worse. Much worse," Orla whispered, then raised her voice, "I'll break your curse. You know I'm good enough. I'll send you back to where you came from. You have three seconds to disappear."

The woman looked at the man, then both of them cast menacing looks at the group of humans and a cat. They laughed. "Nice try," the woman said. "But we aren't the ones who placed the black curse on you. You can't reverse it on us."

"What do you want?" Lorcan asked, stepping in front of Orla.

The woman looked Lorcan up and down. "Well well, this is the one she ditched the white curse for . . ." She made a purring sound. "Delicious!"

"I don't strike women. But if you keep pushing me, I'll make an exception," Lorcan snarled.

"You intrigue me. Let's try this," the women whispered and advanced.

"Lorcan!" Orla called out and pulled Lorcan back. The woman let out an eardrum-piercing shriek. In the blink of an eye, they appeared to be standing in a different world. The dark black sky was scarred with blood red cuts that looked as if they had been caused by claws or fangs. The cold wind brought bizarre sounds from the distance, the sounds of demons crying from Hell. Wolves called for their pack from somewhere among the trees.

"Let's play, shall we?" the woman smiled, showing her shiny fangs.

"Don't harm us. I swear I'll cast a spell on you," Orla whispered.

"You're out of practice, I'm afraid." The woman continued to advance.

"You've forced me to make an exception," Lorcan said and gave the woman a hard kick, sending her skidding backward. She regained her stance, furious. She waved her arm and sent a lightning bolt at Lorcan, striking him and sending him to the ground.

"There's no point in fighting. What do you want?" Orla asked.

"Nothing you could offer. We're here for the boy." She pointed at Noah.

"Then the fuck I'll let you," Lorcan swore and scooped Noah up. The woman swung her arm for another strike. Lorcan turned his back and copped the hit. He fell but still hung on to Noah. He stood up and said, "Run, Orla."

"No, we can't run. They'll strike us from behind," Orla said.

The man now moved forward, wearing a crooked grin. "Enough play. Let's get to business. Give us the kid, and we'll let you live."

Lorcan pushed Noah behind him. "We don't need your permission to live. And you can't have Noah," Lorcan said firmly. The man opened his mouth to speak, and a fireball shot at him, exploding on his chest.

He roared. "Bitch!" he said and jumped to his feet, charging toward Orla. Lorcan put Noah down and grabbed for the man. The man turned and, with a supernatural power, threw Lorcan several feet away. The woman darted for Noah, and Orla hurled another ball of flame in her direction.

"I said there's no need to fight," Orla demanded. "Your kind has never beaten us."

"You're not with your family anymore. You don't even speak of them. You summoned the dark spirits, and you will have to pay for it. We don't want anything to do with it. We just want the boy," the woman said.

"Why?" Orla asked.

"His father sent our brother to the between-worlds. We need an innocent soul to get him back," the man said, pointing at Noah.

"Riley? How the heck did he do that? Good for him," Lorcan said.

The man ran at Lorcan again. Lorcan figured he had the advantage because he was a lot faster. He grabbed a nearby tree branch and whacked him with it. The man staggered a bit, but continued toward him, reaching his thick arms out to grab him. Lorcan hit him again, but the tree branch cracked with the impact.

The man kicked Lorcan hard, sending him into to a fence on the side of the road. In the meantime, the woman ran at Orla. The women scuffled. Like the man, the woman had an incredible supernatural strength. She caught Orla with her forearm and sent her skidding into a tree trunk. Orla was dazed by the impact and lay on the ground as the woman turned to Noah.

Lorcan saw her movement, surged to his feet, and ran toward Noah, but the man gripped him from behind. Lorcan punched him in the face, but he might as well have punched a stone wall.

Noah staggered back as the woman moved toward him. Tripping, he fell to the ground, scrambling backward with his hands and feet. The woman came closer, and the kitten jumped straight into her face, biting and scratching violently. She shrieked in pain.

On the ground, Lorcan yanked a board of the fence loose. He gave the man a hard kick, making him stagger back. Lorcan leapt to his feet and swung the board at the man's neck. It turned as hard as metal in his hands, and he could feel the weight of it changing. With the momentum of his swing, the bar hit the man in the neck, cut through it and decapitating him.

At the same time, the woman screamed in pain as a tiny wooden stick Noah had found on the ground to stab at the woman to free the kitten pierced through her throat. Noah dropped the stick and moved back, and Lorcan dropped the piece of wood bar, staring at the head on the ground with horror.

From a dark corner, Orla was sitting on the grass, her eyes now back to normal. It was just now registering what had just happened. "Oh God, oh God, what did I do?" She started crying. Her body shook. Lorcan hurried to her and pulled her into his arms.

"It's okay, darling. You didn't do anything. Stay calm. We have a kid to take care of." Then he rushed to Noah, who couldn't even cry. He wiped a blood smear from Noah's face. "Noah, talk to me. Come on, say something."

A tear rolled down the boy's face. "I killed that woman," he sobbed.

A chant came floating through the air. A shriek cried from Hell. In front of everyone's astonished eyes, the man's head rolled back to his body and merged with it and the bodies turned into two black snakes and slithered away. Haunting female laugher echoed out from the trees into the darkness.

"Orla Foley, congratulations! You have shed blood on the black curse," the voice came from the trees.

Orla jumped to her feet and whirled around. "They weren't human, and I didn't curse them. They didn't even die. I'm sure it's not going to work that way."

"You know how it works, Orla. It's your intention that counts. There is no way to come back now. I'm looking forward to seeing you on the other side. Say goodbye to your man."

"Who are you? Why are you doing this to me?" Orla cried.

The laughter faded away, and the voice echoed from the distance, "You should never have left your family, you should never have loved a man . . ."

And then everything became silent as if nothing had ever happened. Orla whirled around. "Don't go away! Come out here, whoever you are! Come out! Don't do this to me!" She screamed and then she blacked out.

CHAPTER 14

Orla woke to find herself in Lorcan's arms on a couch at Riley's place. As she tried to sit up, he pulled her back into his arms. He kissed her forehead. "Rest a few more minutes," he said.

"I'm not tired. How's Riley?"

"No more seizures, but he's still not up."

"Noah?"

"With the cat! Now tell me what the voice meant when we were out there."

"I told you about the curses."

"Yes, but what just happened was new, right?"

She sighed and snuggled into Lorcan's chest. "I'll take a few more minutes," she said and closed her eyes. She needed time to figure out how to deal with this new situation.

"The black curse is unbreakable now," she muffled into his chest later. "When I called for the dark spirit at Fossey Way, the one that held the black curse, I effectively broke the white curse. The white curse will never again be placed on you."

"That leaves you with the black curse?" Lorcan asked.

She nodded. "The black curse is hard to break. But as the voice said, it was all in the intention of the people. Because the curse was placed by my family, I can always go back to them and ask for compassion. There are people in my family who actually love me."

"Like your late aunt. What was her name?"

"Siobhan. Yes, Aunty loved me. But family can't help me now. When I saw you and Noah I trouble, I wished . . . I mean, I cursed . . . I asked the dark spirit to bring me a metal element, and as you saw, it caused bloodshed. Although the creatures you and Noah killed weren't human, my intention—and the summoning of the dark spirit for such purpose—was close to a blood-letting sacrifice."

"But you were provoked to do that!"

"My reaction was provoked, but the decision and the intention to kill were a matter of choice. I didn't actually have a choice, but there's no point arguing with dark magic. It's a double-edged sword, and I got cut."

"So how do we get out of this? Don't tell me there isn't a way."

"Bloodshed."

"What?"

"Not my blood. I have to kill someone and sacrifice the person's soul to the dark spirit to break the spell. The matter is no longer with my family, it's with the dark spirit who holds the curse."

"And if you don't kill someone to break the curse, what will happen?"

"I don't know for sure. The most optimistic scenario is that I'll die. The worst one might be that it would take me and turn me into a dark spirit like itself. I'll become a monster. Like I'd let that happen . . . uhhhg."

Lorcan kissed her to stop her from talking. They hadn't yet finished when they heard some throat-clearing behind them. They turned to see Mya with her hands on her hips.

"All right, if you two are finished, I'll leave you take care of the boy and his father. It won't take long. I have things to do," Mya said as she strode toward the door.

"Wait, what do you mean by it's not going to take long? Riley doesn't have a fever or anything. He'll just get a little rest, and then he'll snap right back like he did the last time, right?" Lorcan said.

Mya sighed. "I've got to go."

Orla got to her feet and grabbed Mya's elbow. "I know this has nothing to do with you. Your only focus is Lorcan, and now that he's safe and sound, you have every reason to leave. But if you're half the deity you claim to be, you'll tell me what's going on."

"You'd listen?"

"Yes, I would. I tired of the black curse. I'm done. Noah doesn't deserve this. The boy needs his father," Orla pleaded.

"What do you mean, you're done? You thought I wouldn't believe in the supernatural stuff. All right, I admit it—I didn't. But now I do. So perform your ritual to help Riley, and then we can figure out how to deal with the curses. Don't ever say you're done with this, or with me!" Lorcan exclaimed.

Mya walked toward the door. "Do whatever you want."

"No, no." Orla grabbed Mya's hand. "You know my rituals won't help. You saw his death. Am I right?"

Mya shrugged. "I can't tell you."

Lorcan slammed the door shut. "What kind of a deity walks out and lets a man die?" Lorcan asked.

"Don't you dare judge me!" Mya snarled at Lorcan. She reached for the doorknob, and he blocked the door. "Let me go!" she exclaimed.

"After you tell Orla what she needs to know," Lorcan said dryly.

"You don't know what you're doing, Lorcan."

"And you do?"

"I've seen it all. Do you have any idea how old I am?"

Lorcan cocked an eyebrow. "You're asking me to guess a woman's age? Might as well ask me to jump in front of a bus! Why can't you just tell us? What's it going to cost you?"

She stared at Lorcan. "I can't tell you for your own best interests."

"Now that I won't take. If you help Riley and his kid, you can take whatever you want from me," Lorcan said.

"I don't want anything from you. What happened to Riley is only natural. It's God's will. Manipulating that isn't going to bring anything good."

"But Riley manipulated it. He sent the fuckwitz to the underworld—or between- worlds, whatever that means. If that's not fate manipulation, what is?" Lorcan exclaimed.

"What? He sent whom to where?" Mya asked.

"Ohhh, so there *are* things we know and you don't. One of the creatures that attacked us before said Riley sent its brother to the between-worlds. That's why it wanted to claim Noah."

Mya frowned, contemplated, and then nodded. "All right, then . . . if a mortal man can do that in that situation, I should help him. I just want to let you know that whenever I interfere in what is considered natural, things change. It's the law of cause and effect. Action and consequences. I don't know what will come next or what effect it will have on you both. Can you accept that?"

Orla nodded. Lorcan shrugged.

"Do you accept, Lorcan?"

"All right."

Mya opened her mouth to chastise Lorcan's attitude and asked him for a firm answer, but then she decided to let it go. She went to the bedroom, and Lorcan and Orla followed. Approaching Riley's bed and tilted his head to the side, she pointed to a puncture mark on his neck close to his left ear.

Lorcan gasped. "There's nothing supernatural about his coma this time!"

Mya said nothing. She on her heel, leaving Lorcan and Orla standing there in shock.

Lorcan left the bedroom and sat down on the sofa. "There was no point rushing him to the hospital. Mya could have let us know that before. What she saw suggested that even if we got him to the hospital, he would have still died. That means whatever we do to help him has to be done differently . . ." Lorcan said.

"And it's important to know what was pumped into him and who did it. Those two pieces of information might lead to decisions that will change our current situation regarding the curses."

Lorcan nodded. "It can't possibly get any worse regarding the curses, so I guess we need to focus on Riley first. Lorcan went to Riley's medical cabinet and pulled out his medical box. He unwrapped a syringe and took a blood sample from Riley.

"Are you taking that to Simon?" Orla asked. Simon was a mutual friend of Riley and Lorcan and was a medical doctor. Lorcan nodded. When he finished drawing the blood, he carefully put the syringe into its container and slid it into a bag.

"I won't be long. Be careful. Take care of Noah, and please be right by the phone," Lorcan said. Orla reached up and kissed him.

An hour later, sitting opposite Simon, Lorcan stared at the report he had silently pushed across the table. Simon leaned back on his sofa, holding a coffee mug in both hands, turned it around about a dozen times before taking a tentative sip. After many years knowing Simon,

Lorcan noticed that habit had never changed, especially when he concentrated.

"You don't look surprised," Simon said.

"About this gibberish? No. I have no idea what it is, but as long as it's not poison, I'm okay."

"It's not poison. It's sedative. A very special kind of sedative, and Riley was given a very strong dose."

"Will he snap out of it?"

Simon stared at Lorcan for a brief moment. "Medically, no."

Lorcan put his head in his hands and ruffled his hair. Then he looked at Simon. "Can you give me a bit more than that?"

Simon sipped his coffee again. "What happened to Riley?"

"What?"

"Come on, man. Riley asked me to take care of medical matters for him and Noah if anything were to happen to him. I have his files."

"He asked you?"

"Don't be offended. I'm sure you're the guardian of Noah for everything else in the boy's life, and you might be in Riley's will too. But when it comes to medical matters, he trusts me. Don't you think I come in handy in situations like this?"

"Not too handy when the answer you give me is a no. Man, what I am supposed to do? The kid's cried his eyes out already. And now you expect me to tell Noah his father is going to be in a coma forever?"

"I said *medically* no, not just a no."

Lorcan stared at Simon, waiting for him to give more information.

Simon put his coffee on the table, flipped the report to the next page, and pointed at the table. "Look, the base of this sedative is pretty standard. But there are twelve weird ingredients in it that make no sense. They're mainly herbs and plants and organic agents I don't recognize. The point is, they don't add anything whatsoever to the sedation aspect of the drug, they're just there in the mix. Why?"

Lorcan raised his hand, requesting silence, and made a phone call. When Orla picked up at the other end, he gestured Simon, pointing toward the list. "Hey, there's a list of ingredients here. See what you can make of them." Then he repeated after Simon. "Garlic, sage, lilac, aspect of oil . . . some unrecognizable organic agent . . . Hey, Simon, that's not helpful, just give me those you can recognize . . ."

"It's a preparation for a spell or a curse. It could be of any nature—black curse, white curse, reverse spell. It depends on how the ritual is performed, the purpose, time, date, and the location," Orla cut in. "Where did you find this?"

"Long story. Talk to you later." Lorcan finished the phone call and stared at Simon. "Is that what you mean by 'medically no'. You know this?"

Simon shook his head. "I don't know anything of the kind. It's just a hunch."

"Now the fact that you, a medical doctor, is open to a combination of scientific sedative and supernatural practice is beyond me. But let's set that philosophical debate aside for the moment. Is this a hard-core sedative? I mean, a real one that has to be properly produced and manufactured, not one that can be made by hand or cooked up at home?"

"No, the sedative is industrial rate. Not homemade. And I know what your next question is—there's only one company that might be making this . . . LeBlanc Pharmaceuticals."

"You have evidence of this?"

"No. And it's not an accusation because this drug is not illegal or harmful. It's just a sedative with exotic ingredients. The only basis for my wild guess is that the LeBlanc Pharmaceuticals have a reputation for using unusual ingredients. That's it. We and the rest of the world really don't know much about them."

"So because you know nothing about them, you blame this spooky drug on them?"

Simon shrugged. "As I said, the drug is legit. Someone might have stolen it from their labs."

Lorcan nodded. "Good point. So what are you suggesting regarding Riley?"

"Medically, with the strong dose he was given, it could keep him in a coma for a very long time. But given the spooky ingredients—to use your terminology—why don't you ask Orla to try a spell or something to wake him."

"Excuse me?"

"I said . . ."

"I heard you. Why Orla?"

"She's into this supernatural stuff, isn't she?"

"Now I'm offended."

"Jesus Christ, don't tell me you've been with her for twenty years and . . ."

"Twelve years."

"Yeah, whatever. You can't tell? Everyone can."

"Now I'm *really* offended."

"Anyway, that's my suggestion for now. Try it. If it doesn't work, get back to me, and I'll try some other things. But to snap out of this, Riley needs some miracles! It's ironic, but it's the situation. Deal with it."

CHAPTER 15

As soon as Lorcan reached the patio, Noah and Orla ran out to greet him. Noah's eyes were wide with anticipation and anxiety. Lorcan could see tears welled up and ready to roll down his face. He ruffled Noah's hair. "Uncle Simon said your father is going to be okay." Lorcan glanced at Orla and said nothing. Orla could read the sign—he didn't want to talk in front of Noah.

Later, they tucked the boy into bed. In the living room, Orla sat and played with the cat. "Now can you tell me what Simon really said?" Lorcan told Orla what was said at Simon's place.

"Do you know what to do?" Lorcan asked at the conclusion of the story.

Orla nodded. "Sort of. In theory, at least. I told you before, I haven't practiced for a long time. I had a good understanding, but that was about it. Because of my psychic abilities, my practice is very different from the rest of my family. I work with the subconscious level of the mind, and not so much in conjuring mythical creatures or summoning spirits."

"You mean, you can hypnotize people?"

"Well, that's the best way to describe it, I suppose."

"Could you . . . I can't believe I'm saying this . . . Can you somehow communicate with Riley?"

"I can try. But I have to perform the ritual and keep an eye on the surrounding environment just in case things go wrong, or we're interrupted. I have to be here and awake. But I can send you."

"Send me? Into Riley's subconsciousness?"

Orla nodded. "I'm not physically sending you anywhere, but I can find a channel so that you can communicate with him."

"Like tuning a radio?"

Orla smiled. "Yes, just like tuning a radio. Do you want to try?"

Lorcan nodded. "Sure."

Orla laughed. "You don't look so sure."

He smiled. "I'd like to be in control of my own body."

"Do you trust me or not?" She kissed him on the cheek.

Lorcan shrugged and nodded. She pushed him down on the sofa and put her thumbs on his temples, rubbing gently. "Close your eyes for me. Just relax. What do you see?"

"Nothing."

"Is it dark or light?"

"Dark."

"Go to the light. You know where it is. You and Riley took Noah to a picnic once. Where was it? Think about the places that Riley wants to take Noah. He'd be there. Has he told you about the places he loved to go with Michelle? He might be there too," Orla's soothing voice whispered. Soon Lorcan was no longer responding to her questions.

He was at the edge of a forest in a fairy tale land, where green grass carpeted rolling hills and flowers danced happily in the gentle wind while birds sang among the trees and the sun smiled down on a peaceful meadow. Lorcan saw Riley standing next to a gigantic and colorful mushroom. As Lorcan approached, Riley turned and smiled.

"Really, Riley! Fairy land? *This* is your favorite place?"

Riley chuckled. "When you have a wife and a kid, you'll understand."

"I don't think you understand Noah as well as you think. The boy would much prefer a water pistol, a White Knight sword, or maybe some Star Wars gear . . . not Bambi or unicorns." Lorcan gestured widely at the surrounding scenery.

Riley nodded. "Agreed. This is more like Michelle." Then he looked down, pressing his foot to the grass.

"Right, Michelle it is. So that's the reason you're here, letting your son cry his eyes out in the real world? And she's not even here."

Riley shook his head. "She was here. I saw her."

"You can't see her. She passed away ten years ago."

"No she didn't. She was waiting for me. She lingered. That's what the witch told me."

"What witch?"

"Witch or demon, I don't know. I saw a woman in a temple. She was trying to trick me. She said if I wanted to go back to Noah, I had to let go of Michelle. Sort of like a spiritual divorce. Like I would do that to Michelle. Dead or alive, she's my wife, and nothing's going to change that."

"Nothing, including Noah?"

"What are you talking about? I'm going to say goodbye to Michelle here, and then I'll come back to Noah. I made the witch explode. I sent her to where her brother was. What are you worried about?"

"All right. Okay then. So just say goodbye and come back. Where is she?"

"She was just here."

"We don't have forever."

Riley walked around. "I saw her here."

From the corner of his eye, Lorcan saw the sky darken, black smoke creeping up from the ground and forming into strange shapes. Evil chants hovered in the air. Riley whirled around. "What is this? Why is this happening? I swear I saw Michelle here."

"I don't think you sent the witch to where she should be. She was outside your house, back in the world that you abandoned, trying to claim Noah."

"What are you talking about?"

"What did you do at Fossey Way?" Lorcan asked as the wind grew stronger by the second and the stench of dead bodies engulfed the air.

Inside the house, a strong and strange wind smashed the glass windows and swirled around the living room. "Oh no," Orla muttered. "Lorcan, come back to me. Whatever you and Riley are doing, wrap it up and come back right now." She touched Lorcan and felt him burning with fever. "Oh God." She ran to Riley's bedroom. Riley started seizing again. The wind broke the window in Riley's room. She tried to hold Riley. He wasn't responding.

"Noah!" Orla yelled, and Noah rushed in from his bedroom. "Hold your father." Riley calmed instantly at Noah's touch. "He responds to you. So just keep him calm, okay?" Noah nodded. Orla hurried back to the living room. On the sofa, a stream of blood ran from Lorcan's mouth.

In the field, the forest and the meadow had caught on fire. Lorcan stood after rolling on ground from the impact of a hit. He wiped the blood from his mouth. In front of Lorcan and Riley were a dozen creatures from hell, and they heard the rumble of more footsteps. "More are coming. Do you know how to get back to reality? You won't see Michelle now. It's better to stay alive," Lorcan said.

"Get the hell out of there, Lorcan." Orla's voice sang in Lorcan's mind.

"Orla called" Lorcan said to Riley. "We have to go back."

"I don't know how," Riley said.

"How, Orla, how?" Lorcan wasn't sure if it was going to work, but he spoke it out loud. A creature that looked oddly like a buffalo charged at Lorcan, knocking him to the ground once again. Riley grabbed a nearby rock and threw it at the creature.

"How, Orla? We're being attacked from all sides by creatures from Hell!" Lorcan shouted.

"How do you know they're from Hell?" Orla asked.

"Because they're fucking ugly."

Another creature knocked Riley down as Lorcan jumped to his feet.

"Ask them what they want," Orla said.

Lorcan wasn't sure if they could speak, but he asked anyway. As soon as he did, the creatures stopped. A large demon with horns cast its red eyes on Riley. Then it pointed at him. "If he releases what belongs to us, we'll let you go."

"What? What is it you want?" Riley asked as his blood ran cold.

"You spell bound our brother and sister. We want a soul in your family to release them."

"Hell if I will give you that," Riley said.

The creature swung its arms, and Riley was flung several feet away, crashing down onto a rock. The creatures approached him. Lorcan grabbed a tree branch and attacked them. They threw Lorcan away like a rag doll. He crawled over and dragged Riley away from the crushing foot stomp of the buffalo-like creature.

"You'll have to let Michelle go, Riley. If you die here, Noah will be on his own. Do you think that's what Michelle would want?"

A small army of creatures approached in the distance.

"It's not just releasing her. It's killing her. They'll drag her to hell for eternity. She waited for years because of me. She couldn't pass on to the next plane because of me, and now you expect me to send her to Hell?"

The creatures moved closer.

"I know this is hard. But it's between her and your son—which one will you choose?"

"They can take me. Don't make me choose."

"That's what they're doing. They're forcing you to be a coward. But are you sure they won't go after Noah after they take you? Can Michelle protect Noah? You know he's special. He has a gift. They will all want him."

A thought dawned in Riley's mind. Michelle knew Noah was special. She had asked him to take care of their son. Riley nodded. Tears rolled down his face.

The creature with horns croaked out its demand, "Repeat after me. I shall release the spell I placed. I shall denounce the love I have for my wife. I shall take back what I had given her before. If anyone prevents me from doing so, I will curse that person."

Riley repeated. They heard a scream tearing through the air. Michelle was dragged by the demon into a bottomless fiery hole, her white dress tattered, her face smeared with blood. She looked at Riley. Amid the pain and desperation, her eyes were full of love. Michelle and the creature vanished into the Hellhole.

CHAPTER 16

Both Lorcan and Riley gasped and woke at the same time. On top of his being completely dazed by the experience, something in Lorcan's eyes bothered Orla. Noah called out from the bedroom, letting her know that Riley was up as well. She touched Lorcan's face.

"Darling, talk to me. How are you feeling?" she wiped a strand of hair from Lorcan's forehead and a teardrop fell from the corner of his eye. His striking blue eyes looked at her, and she saw pain, fear, and a tangled web of inexplicable emotions. She kissed him, and he kissed her back lightly. But he didn't pull her into his arms and deepen the kiss as he always did. He touched her face, and looked into her eyes, gazing at her as if storing every plane and angle of her face, as if she might vanish right in front of him.

"What's this?" she asked. Lorcan didn't say anything. He got to his feet, but his body swayed, so he sat back down.

"Give me a couple of minutes," he said.

Noah's horrible scream reached them from the bedroom, sending Orla and Lorcan racing to it. Riley sat up, squeezing his son in his arms, tears streaming down his face. "I'm sorry, I'm so sorry, Son," he whispered into Noah's ear as the boy cried. Riley looked up at Lorcan and Orla when they entered the room.

"He saw what we saw. He hugged me, and he saw what I saw. He heard what I said." Riley looked at Lorcan, devastated. Lorcan withdrew from the room. He went back to the living room, flopped down on the sofa, and put his head in his hands. Orla came sit next to him.

"Can you tell me what happened?" she asked. For a while, Lorcan looked up at Orla. He pulled her into his arms and rocked with her.

"Oh God."

"It's okay, Lorcan. Just tell me."

Then he told her. He told her about how he had talked his friend into sending his wife to Hell, about the look on Michelle's face before she disappeared into the flames, and about the sound of Michelle's scream. Now Noah had seen and heard all of that. Lorcan wasn't sure how Riley was going to be able to live with himself.

"There's no point beating yourself up. The same goes for Riley. Noah will understand. You didn't have any other choice."

Lorcan stood up, looked around, and saw the damage the wind had done to the house. He stared at the broken windows, at the broken glass on the floor. "How am I going to handle it when it's your turn to be dragged into Hell? Isn't that what the curse is going to do to you? Isn't that what you said before—that death would be an easier solution?"

"Lorcan!"

"Tell me. Don't lie to me, Orla. Is that what you meant?" Lorcan grunted out the words, his eyes sparking with fury.

Orla nodded. Lorcan ran his hand through his hair. Riley stood at the door way.

"How's Noah?" Lorcan asked.

"Asleep now," Riley said. "Thanks for being here, for helping out."

"You're thanking me?" Lorcan exclaimed.

"Lorcan!" Orla growled.

"Orla's right. It's not your fault," Riley said.

"Do you know how you got that puncture mark on your neck?" Lorcan asked.

"What?"

Lorcan pointed. "A puncture mark on your neck. Do you know how you got it?"

Riley touched his neck, then shook his head. "I don't remember."

"All right. Call Simon. He'll tell you. Orla, I'm taking you home."

Riley nodded, looking around at his trashed house.

"Talk to you tomorrow. Take care, Riley," Orla said and followed Lorcan. All the way home, Lorcan said nothing. His expression suggested that conversation was not a good idea. Orla said nothing and went to bed.

A strong wind flung open the door, smashing it into the door frame and sending a vase crashing to the floor. Orla sprung up from the bed, panting. The apartment was empty. She looked around the room. Lorcan was nowhere to be found. She didn't know if he'd been gone all night or not. It was five in the morning. Where was he?

She sat down, trying to stay calm, and waited. Two hours later, Lorcan walked through the door.

"Where have you been? Why . . ." Orla trailed off when she saw his face. He was as pale as a ghost. He pulled her into his arms and hugged her. A strange smell lingered on his clothes—the smell of wood, trees, wildflowers, and ashes.

She nudged him down onto the bed. "Take an hour or so." Lorcan didn't need an invitation—he was already halfway to a very deep sleep.

Three hours later, Lorcan surfaced. He sniffed and awoke to the mug of coffee Orla put in front of him. He grinned up at her. As he sipped the coffee in bed, she asked. "Where were you all night?"

He shrugged. "Out for a bit of fresh air. Thinking. That's all."

She arched an eyebrow. She knew he was lying, or at least withholding information from her. But unlike him, she wouldn't throw a tantrum and pry for the truth. If he had decided to lie to her, forcing him would merely give her another lie on top of the previous one. Then there would be too many lies to keep up with. He'd tell her the truth when he was ready.

Orla left for the kitchen to make her coffee. She spoke from the kitchen. "The computer beeped while you were asleep." She took a long time making her coffee and drank almost half of it before she returned to the living room. If he needed time and space, she'd give him just that.

Back in the living room, she found Lorcan hunched over the computer. His fingers flew on the keyboard.

"The money's in. I'm going to trace and figure out the name of William's boss. Once I have it, I'll give Ciaran and Madeline the name so they know who they're dealing with. Zen is just a pawn in this, and the kidnapping is a decoy," Lorcan muttered and worked at the same time.

Orla's phone rang. She picked up, took notes, and hung up the phone. She said nothing and sat down next to Lorcan. Then she got up, taking her on-the-job purse out of a cabinet. It looked like the other purses she owned, but this one had specially-designed compartments and levers that she needed for her jobs.

"William call?" Lorcan asked, his eyes still glued to the computer screen.

"We got the location where Zen is keeping Jo. He changed hotels a couple of times, but he seems settled now," Orla said.

Lorcan finished a command on the computer and let it run. He turned toward Orla. "Before we do this, I want you to promise me one thing."

"And what would that be?"

"We don't know Jo, Madeline, the LeBlancs, William and his gang—they might *all* be bad guys. We need to settle your curse."

"You want me to kill one of them to free myself?"

"I can't lose you. I can't let you be dragged to Hell the way Michelle was."

"But I can't just kill . . ."

"I'm not asking you to kill someone just to save yourself. I'm asking you to consider it should the opportunity arise."

"I'm not sure. I don't think I can do that."

"You can't, or you won't?"

"I won't."

Lorcan nodded.

"What, you're not mad at me?" Orla asked.

He smiled. "If you had said yes, I would probably doubt myself for loving you for all these years and not knowing you were capable of killing in cold blood. Let's just do this job, then we'll figure out how to get out of this. Deal?"

She smiled and nodded. Lorcan darted at her, lying her back on the sofa. He kissed her. He trailed his lips along her jawline, his hands busy on her body. Her blouse was on the floor now, followed by his shirt and jeans. Their bodies tangled on the sofa, moving to the rhythm of love until they were both sated.

She snuggled into his chest, feeling the virility of his body, hearing the beat of his heart, and she wished they could stay like this forever. She shifted. "We'd better go."

"Just a few more seconds," he whispered and held onto her for a little longer. Then he released her, and they left the apartment, leaving the computer running.

CHAPTER 17

It had been two hours, and they had not been able to locate Zen and Jo. "Unless you can see through walls, I don't think staring at the building will help," Lorcan teased.

"Do you have a better idea?"

"I think we should go straight in and ask."

"Ask whether they have a guest who appears to have kidnapped someone and hidden said person in their room?"

"Well, the building is in the middle of Soho. Anything can happen here. But we can be a bit more subtle than that. Let's go."

Lorcan left the rooftop of the building. Orla muttered an objection but followed.

The receptionist looked up from his computer. "May I help you?"

"What do you have available? We don't have a reservation," Lorcan said.

The receptionist glanced up and down at them. "We're fully booked. I'm sorry."

Orla knew the receptionist hadn't even checked his database. She slid a bill across the desk. "Well, we only need an hour, and it's okay if you haven't had time to make up the room." She smiled and snuggled into Lorcan's neck, feeling him stiffen. She slid another bill across the desk and said, "We'll also need a meal delivered. You can deliver it, say, next year . . . And keep the tip, by the way." She smiled again.

The receptionist glanced at the bills and smirked. "I'll find you a room. Would you like to pay by cash?"

"Of course," Lorcan said, scowling at the way the receptionist eyed Orla.

Orla opened her purse. She tipped it over, spilling the contents. Her lipstick fell to the floor and rolled to the other side of the reception desk. She cursed and chased after it, pushing the purse over. More contents poured from her purse, dropping everywhere. The receptionist got down on all fours, picking up bits and pieces for Orla.

Lorcan took advantage of the receptionist's distraction, jabbing a device into a USB port on the keyboard on the counter. Before he could pull it out, the receptionist stood up. "Oh, what a mess," Lorcan muttered and bent over as if to help pick up the runaway contents of Orla's purse. He pushed the keyboard over, but before it dropped and dangled by its cord, he pulled out his device.

"I'm so sorry," Orla said.

As soon as the receptionist put the room key on the desk, Lorcan snatched it and ushered Orla toward the elevator at the end of the dimly lit corridor covered in stained carpet.

In a dingy hotel room, Lorcan looked up from his device. "Zen registered for one night only. He didn't go by Zen—not a surprise—but he wasn't smart enough to go for anything too creative either. He's in 25B."

Orla nodded. "We're in 32A, so if we go out, left, down the stairs, and right, we'll be there," she spoke while tracing her finger over the building map on the wall.

A short moment later, Orla, attired in a room service uniform, knocked on the door to 25B. "Room service," she said.

"I didn't order anything," Zen's voice came from inside the room.

"You have a package, sir," Orla said.

Zen cracked the door, the inside chain lock still engaged. "From whom?"

Orla looked at the handwritten note. "Madeline, sir."

Zen frowned. "Give it to me," he said and reached his hand out through the gap only wide enough to fit his fist. The package was too big to fit through. "Put it on the floor," he said.

"Of course, sir." Orla put the package on the floor and disappeared from Zen's sight.

He waited for a few seconds. The corridor was quiet, so he opened the inside lock and opened the door wider. Before he could step outside, Lorcan kicked the door in hard. It smashed into Zen's head. Before he could register any more information, Lorcan pushed him inside the room and knocked him down.

Orla darted inside and glanced around. No Jo.

She ran to the wardrobe.

"You've got to be kidding me," Lorcan muttered.

Yanking the door open, Orla saw Jo curled inside the cabinet, tied up and drugged. Orla untied her and helped her to the bed.

Lorcan pulled Zen up so that he stood on his wobbling legs and punched him. "I won't hit a man while he's down. Stand up and take it like a human, you fucking lowlife scumbag woman beater." He punctuated each word with a punch. Zen slumped to the floor.

"You'll kill him, Lorcan. We don't get paid for cleaning up his mess." Orla gave Jo a glass of water and a dampened washcloth. Then she picked up the desk phone and ordered a feast delivered to the room. Lorcan tied Zen up and squashed him into the cabinet with a pair of his underpants stuffed into his mouth.

Orla raised an eyebrow at Lorcan. "I had my gloves on when I touched them," he said.

Orla paid for the meal using Zen's cash, gave the delivery man a two hundred percent tip, and shoved the rest of Zen's cash into her pocket.

With some food and fresh air, Jo recovered. She was a petite beauty in her late twenties with long black hair, a foxy face, and huge green cat eyes.

"Thanks for the rescue," Jo said. She looked at Orla and Lorcan with a measured stare. Then she continued. "You're not with Madeline. You're Irish. Madeline doesn't know anyone from Ireland."

Orla and Lorcan stared at Jo blankly. She grinned. "I'm kidding. I design characters for hologames. I've done a lot of people profiling, and I'm very good at picking up accents. You're doing very well, by the way.

Most people wouldn't be able to pick up your Irish accent. Not like I'm abnormal or anything . . . I'm talking too much, aren't I?" she trailed off.

Orla smiled. "Saves us asking you questions."

Jo shrugged. "Zen made a call last night to Madeline. He put me on the phone. So I got to talk to Madeline and Ciaran. They made a deal with Zen to make an exchange for me later today. That is, Madeline and Ciaran were to give Zen the information he wants, and Zen was to let me go. I don't think you're in this deal at all. Who are you working for, and what do you want from me?" Jo polished off the last bit of pancake on her plate.

Lorcan raised an eyebrow and leaned back in his chair. Jo cast him an intense look, then she smiled. "You're a hacker."

"I'm sorry?" Lorcan asked.

Jo pointed at Orla. "She does the sweet talking, and you do the tech and muscling jobs. You're contractors for hire. So what's your service exactly? And don't say rescuing kidnapping victims because I won't believe you."

Orla stood up. She walked to the window and stared outside. Lorcan cleared his throat. "You're too smart for your own good, Jo. She does more than sweet talking, and I hardly ever use muscles unless I have to punch up scumbags. You're right about the tech job. She hates computers. Yes, we were hired to provide a service, and part of that the service involves rescuing you. Tell us why they kidnapped you, and we'll tell you the rest."

Orla turned back from the window, looking at Jo, waiting for an answer.

Jo shrugged. "I designed a hologame called Mind Ripper. It can profile people's minds and simulate their thought processes. Effectively, it means you can pry information out of people without even asking them. Zen wants to simulate the mind of a dead alchemist named John Dee. I think Zen believes John Dee could make gold. Anyway, I was lucky. I only handle one part of the program. The other half—the more difficult half—was programmed by a game partner in London called White Knight. That's why Zen snatched me out of my apartment and blackmailed Madeline. He wanted her go to London to lure out the real person behind White Knight."

Lorcan and Orla looked at each other. They'd been spying on the conversations. They knew Jo was telling the truth.

"You think Zen will let you go after he knows who White Knight is? Wouldn't he need your part of the program?"

"He's already got my part. He stole it from my computer. Not that he knows how to run the program. So that's my story. What's yours? To whom am I being delivered?"

"Why do you ask that?" Lorcan asked.

"Obviously, someone paid you to rescue me. And that person isn't Madeline or Ciaran."

Orla and Lorcan looked at each other, saying nothing. Then Lorcan nodded.

Orla took Zen's cash from her pocket and gave it to Jo. "Take this. Don't run straight to Madeline or Ciaran. Go to the police."

Jo stood up to leave.

"Can I at least know your names?" Jo asked. Tears welled up in her eyes.

Lorcan smiled. He kissed Jo in the cheek. "You take care. I hope we meet again. I like hologames."

After Jo left, Lorcan locked the door and yanked Zen out of the cabinet. He threw him on the floor.

"Please don't kill me," Zen moaned. Lorcan pressed a pillow against his head and pointed the gun at it.

"Orla, one bullet and you'll free yourself from the black curse." He gave Orla the gun. Zen kicked, struggled, and cried underneath the pillow. Orla held the gun, her hands shaking. She aimed at Zen's head while Lorcan held him down.

"We're so close, Orla. No need to worry about the curse anymore. No need to run. We'll be free to live the life we deserve. Just pull the trigger. For me. For us." Lorcan's eyes were pleading, desperate.

Orla pointed the gun. Her hands shook more. She pulled at the trigger. Tears rolled down her face. Zen begged and cried. Lorcan looked at her. She let out a cry and lowered the gun. Lorcan pulled her into his arms and squeezed her tightly. "Oh God. I'm so sorry. I don't know why I asked you to do that. I'm so sorry." Orla could feel his body trembling with emotion. They were so close to freedom, and yet too close to demonize themselves.

Lorcan dragged Zen back into the cabinet. "Today's your lucky day. One more scream before we leave the building, and you won't be that lucky."

He slammed the door closed and escorted Orla out of the hotel.

CHAPTER 18

They walked from Soho toward the river in silence. Hand in hand, they walked along the river, breathing in the cold breeze blowing in across the water. They turned into the park and went to the riverbank where they watched the water flowing peacefully. Lorcan cradled Orla in his arms. He cupped his hand behind her neck and kissed her. His kisses always sent shockwaves through her system. She tilted her head back, stood on her tiptoes, and reached up to give him more access.

"Marry me," he whispered.

Orla looked at Lorcan, a tear rolling down her face. "After all that we've been through, you still want to marry me?" she asked. "Knowing I might be a sorceress using dark magic or be dragged down to Hell, you still want to marry me?"

"As long as you don't turn the rock you gave me into gold . . . I still love you and want to spend the rest of my life with you, however long or short our lives are going to be. I keep my promises. I want you to keep your promises to me too." He lifted her chin. "Please say yes."

She smiled. Lorcan put on a pretend scowl. "Still not a yes." He pulled out the ring box from his pocket and flipped it open. A square sapphire stone looked up at her. She smiled again.

"Do I need to kneel? It's a bit embarrassing in public, but if that's what it takes . . ."

"Yes." Another tear rolled down her face. He hitched her up, kissed the tear off, and they kissed. The phone in her pocket buzzed. He groaned. "Ignore it," he said. He kept kissing her. The phone buzzed again. He shoved the ring box back into his pocket and let her answer the phone. "It's Riley," Orla said looking at the Caller ID. The smile faded from Lorcan's face. "Okay. Be right there." Orla hung up. "It's Noah. Trouble," she said. Lorcan grabbed Orla's hand and pulled her toward the parking lot.

Twenty minutes later, they stormed into Riley's house. Riley spoke too fast, stuttering. "His teacher called. He sneaked out of the school in late afternoon just before the day finished. The teacher said he left during the day as well. I don't know where he is. He hasn't called me. You said before that those Hell creatures might still want Noah, right? Where did you run into them?"

"But I thought they got what they wanted," Lorcan said.

Orla shook her head. "No. I don't think this is their doing."

"What do you mean? Something else out there wants Noah?" Lorcan asked.

Orla looked around the house. She crinkled her nose. "You smell that?" she asked. Lorcan and Riley shook their head. Orla walked around. "The smell of ritual. Incense. Potion. Someone performed a ritual here. As to what it was, I don't know."

"Someone got my son . . ." Riley flopped to the couch.

Orla said, "He's not in danger. Or not yet."

"Please tell me how to find him. I'll do anything," Riley said.

"He can't go too far by himself . . ." Lorcan said.

"Hush, shhh. Listen," Orla said. They heard a hissing sound, scratching, and something moving in the corner of the room. Then the kitten climbed in from the little door Riley made him. "Oh, there you are. You know where Noah is, right? Show us." The kitten stared at Orla, then turned and went back out the cat door.

"You've got to be kidding me," Lorcan grumbled but followed Orla outside. The kitten headed toward the park behind the house. "You can't be serious. We got attacked here, and now Noah's coming back here by himself?"

The kitten kept walking. At the far end of the park, they could see the flicker of candles. Even from a distance, they could see Noah's tiny shape, wearing a black jacket and walking barefoot in a circle with a book in his hands. He chanted words he read from a small piece of paper.

Before Riley could call out for his son, a whirl of black smoke seeped up from the ground around Noah. They heard the painful roars of demons from Hell. The wind gushed out from behind the trees, and the candles flickered rapidly.

"He's summoning the dark spirits to free his mother," Orla muttered. "This isn't going to work. It doesn't work that way." The three of them ran at Noah, calling out to him. He didn't seem to hear them but continued to chant as if he couldn't stop. His eyes rolled back in his head.

The wind grabbed at Orla, Riley, and Lorcan, throwing them in the opposite direction. It whirled around Noah like a small tornado, forming an invisible wall. They couldn't penetrate it. Riley called out for

Noah again, but he didn't answer. He dropped the book on the ground and kept chanting.

"It's the wrong spell. They're going to take him," Orla said.

They could all hear the roaring sound of hundreds of hungry demons from Hell.

"Do something, Orla." Lorcan said. "You can't let them."

The heard a shriek from behind them. Spirits raised up and marched toward the circle. Orla dropped to the ground and drew a triangle on the grass. She mumbled a spell to release hexes and curses. The ground rumbled, and they heard cracking sound. "Look out!" Lorcan charged at Orla, pulling her out of the way just before a tree fell down where she just sat.

Orla kept muttering her spells. Noah's eyes came back to normal. He saw the army of creatures and demons approaching him. In the distance, he could see his father, Lorcan, and Orla. The creatures penetrated the wind wall and approached Noah. Lorcan and Riley tried again to break through but couldn't.

They heard a 'meow' and saw the small shadow of the kitten throwing itself at the wind wall. The wall shattered and the wind stopped. Lorcan and Riley rushed over to Noah. The creatures ran toward Noah as well. The cat stood in front of the boy, ears perked up, green eyes sparkling, fur bristled, tail straight up, teeth bared.

These gigantic Hell creatures stopped in their tracks, halted by a cat and a kid.

"A symbol of the innocent," Orla whispered. She smiled and continued to chant her spells. The ground beneath the creatures suddenly caved in and swallowed them. The ground underneath Noah also dropped out, and he disappeared from sight. Orla swung her arms, and the earth in front of them cracked open. She dove in, followed by Lorcan and Riley.

They dropped into a dark place.

Hell.

In front them and at a distance, Noah stood with the kitten in his hands. The long and dark hallway was flanked by holes and cells with creatures, demons, and shackled people. Blood and gore was everywhere, and Noah walked straight ahead, ignoring Lorcan and Riley's cries.

"He's going to get his mother. Until he does, he won't come back," said Orla.

They raced after him, but no matter how fast they ran, they couldn't catch him. Noah strode through the narrow corridor, ignoring the creatures that reached out to grab him. Riley, Orla, and Lorcan ran and ran, called to him. Nothing seemed to work.

While the adults were being attacked left and right, Noah seemed unstoppable. The creatures and demons hissed at him but withdrew as he passed. He finally reached the last cell where he found Michelle shackled to a wall.

"Mother!" Noah called.

Michelle looked up, blinked, and recognized her son. "Noah! Run!" she cried out.

Two demon gatekeepers stepped out in front of the boy, gigantic axes in their hands. Orla screamed out her spells. Fireballs flew at the gatekeepers, but they caused no damage. Instead, they bounced back at Orla. Lorcan could see them coming, but they were too fast, and there was nothing he could do except watching them rain down on her. But suddenly, a white shadow shot out in front of Orla and wrapped the fireballs up in a ring of white light. The shadow turned around.

"Aunt Siobhan," Orla gasped.

The old woman glowed. She smiled at Orla. "You owe me the white curse again." She cast a glance at Lorcan, and then she vanished.

"No, no aunty. That's not what I want!" Orla cried but her aunt could no longer hear her.

Michelle continued to beg Noah to go away. The two gatekeepers approached him. Riley yelled out for Noah. He and Lorcan were attacked and held back by other creatures.

"I command you to release my mother," Noah said.

The gatekeepers snarled, teeth bared, and swung their axes. Noah hung on to the cat with one arm, swinging his free arm at the gatekeepers. Their two axes bounced back, sending the gatekeepers reeling. They roared in anger.

"I command you to release my mother," Noah repeated and swung his arm again. The barred doors at the side of the corridor collapsed. He swung again, and the barred door of this mother's cell flew away and her shackles broke loose. The wall behind her exploded, revealing a lighted pathway—the way to Heaven.

Michelle turned around, looked at Riley, and smiled.

"Thank you, Noah," she said and vanished into the light. Behind Michelle, if Orla was not mistaken, she saw the small shadow of the mother cat following her into the light.

From the dark corners, the gatekeepers and other creatures had recovered. Orla and Noah swung their arms at the same time and chorused their spells. Then the entire world exploded into white light.

CHAPTER 19

Orla opened her eyes in the hospital to see Lorcan's striking blue eyes looking down at her. Then Riley came in, sitting down next to him. She wished Noah and the cat would come in as well, so she'd know she was the only one lying in a hospital bed.

"How's Noah?" she asked groggily.

"He's fine now, in the children's wing," Riley said. "He doesn't remember what he did, though."

"I'll look into it when I'm up," Orla said, pushing herself to a sitting position. Lorcan helped her. He tucked a large pillow behind her back for support.

"I just want to say thank you," Riley said.

"For what? I didn't exactly help Noah or anything. The boy saved himself—and his mother. That's unbelievable."

"You took us there." Riley said.

"How did we end up in the hospital, and how did we explain to people what happened?" Orla asked.

Lorcan spoke now, "We were having a picnic, and our gas canister exploded. You and Noah had concussion. Riley and I only have cuts and bruises. The doctor bought it."

"Did we destroy the park?" Orla chuckled.

Lorcan nodded and smiled. "Freak accidents happen," he said.

Orla's phone buzzed on the table. Lorcan picked it up and showed the caller ID to Orla. It was William Turk. He hit the ignore button. Five seconds passed, and William called again. Lorcan picked it up. "We're busy," he snarled.

"Where's Orla?" William's voice came out from the speaker.

"I'm part of the team. You can talk to me."

"Oh I forgot, you bullied your way into the team. How did it go with the merchandise? Did you get the job done?"

"Yes. We got the job done. And for your information, Jo is not merchandise."

"Whatever. When will you deliver her?"

"Soon."

"How about tomorrow?"

"That's too soon."

"It's not your call. Put Orla on the phone."

"She's busy."

"Busy blowing up public property? I watch TV, Lorcan. Look, I know you guys are working for other clients, too, but I paid you half the money already, and I want my merchandise."

"It's your boss who paid us, not you."

"I have the rest of the cash. Can you deliver tomorrow?"

Lorcan looked at Orla. She nodded.

"All right. Tomorrow. Text me the when and where." Lorcan put the phone aside. He came back to Orla's bed and caught the look on her face, gesturing toward Riley. Riley stood leaning against the wall, his face was pallid, and he was taking deep breaths as if trying to take control of himself. Sweat trickled down from his forehead into his face.

"Riley, you don't look well," said Lorcan. "Why don't you sit down? It was very hard to yank you back here, so don't you dare have another episode on me." Lorcan pulled a chair over and pushed Riley down onto it.

Orla got up from bed. She crouched in front of Riley. "Riley, look at me. Open your . . ." She reached up to hold his hands, but as soon as she touched them, they both jerked back and fell onto the floor. Orla's eyes rolled back. She couldn't see and hear anything. She was sucked into a dark tunnel, moving backward, and then she was on the floor. Orla concentrated, focused. No, it wasn't her on the floor, but she was looking up from the floor in Riley's house. She was seeing the vision via Riley's eyes.

The man standing over Riley was one of the goons working for William Turk. She had seen him getting out of the car to take care of the gardener's body after William had executed him. He was speaking on a cell phone, and William's voice was responding to the questions.

"Boss, I don't think this guy knows anything. And I don't see a kid in the house. Are you sure he gave you the right address?"

"We've got the right address, and you've got the right guy. He was at Fossey Way. How can you be so sure he doesn't know anything?" said William.

"I don't know. If he'd gotten your paper, he would have reacted when I showed up at the door. It's just a hunch. But better safe than sorry. I'll put a bullet in him, and I'll do the same with the kid. That way we don't have to worry about whether they know anything. Okay?"

"No, don't make a mess. People will notice. Just stick the needle in him. He won't remember a thing after this."

"Are you sure? A bullet would be a lot easier. I can make it look like a robbery gone wrong."

"People rob banks, not medical doctors with kids, you idiot. Just do what I say."

"Okay . . ."

Lorcan's voice sounded in the distance, "Orla, wake up, honey." He shook her shoulders. Orla opened her eyes and saw Riley sitting on the chair, looking a bit dazed but awake. Lorcan pulled her into his arms. "Don't keep doing this to me." He rocked her in his arms. Orla whispered into Lorcan's ear, "Riley's remembering what happened to him. He doesn't know about our job for William. William lost something at Fossey Way and thought Riley had gotten it." Lorcan turned and looked at Riley.

"What just happened to Orla?" Riley asked.

"Ah, she still has the concussion. What about you?" Lorcan asked.

"I'm okay. Just a bit dizzy. I remember that voice."

"What voice?"

"You just talked to him on the phone. I remember his voice."

"All right. I'll take you back to Noah. And then you stay there. Okay?"

Riley nodded. When Lorcan and Riley left the room, Orla got up and changed out of her hospital gown.

Later, Orla told Lorcan what she had seen in her vision. They went back to her apartment where Lorcan spent a few hours on his computer searching for information. Orla went to the kitchen to make coffee for Lorcan, and she heard his voice from the living room, "The coffee machine has a very sharp lever at the side. Don't cut yourself on it. I'll fix it later." She checked the machine and found the sharp edge. Orla smiled to herself. Lorcan would make a very caring lover, husband, and even father. Her smile faded, knowing it was wishful thinking at the moment. She made the coffee and took it back to the living room.

"The guy is Sam Windsor. He doesn't have a residential address, but I knew where he is now," Lorcan said.

"Why do we need to do anything about Sam Windsor? We have a plan. We'll go back to William, trick him to a location, and call the cops on him."

"Well, that was the plan. But the money William wired to us using his boss's account? He closed the account. Disappeared without a trace. We can't tie him to the murder of the gardener."

"But we did receive the money. It's in our bank account."

"Yes, but the name on the sender's account now is Stephen Marshall. He's an American cop and has nothing whatsoever to do with what we're doing here. He's never been to England. Let alone a cop of his rank having a million to throw into a job that obviously has nothing to do with him."

"Is he a real cop or just a profile?"

Lorcan turned the monitor around to show Orla the picture. "New York cop, shiny record. Look at him. I bet he doesn't even have a speeding ticket."

"How can William change the record just like that? And why?"

Lorcan shrugged. "I think he's jerking his boss around. They're all gold diggers at the end of the day. Looking for John Dee, computing, data mining. It all leads to that. Everyone wants a piece of the cake. Whatever his boss is looking for in Jo, William wants that too. We let Jo go. Gotta make up something by tomorrow for William. Sam Windsor seems to be the guy who does dirty jobs for William. Find him, we might find whatever it is William was afraid that Riley knew."

Orla nodded. "Fair enough."

Lorcan frowned. "If it's fair, why are you still scowling?"

"I'm just copying the look on your face right now."

Lorcan exhaled. He put his head in his hands. "We triggered the white curse again. Which is fine. The white curse is just against me. But we have the black curse against you that we have to take care of, and now . . ."

"Now we don't know how to break the curses." Orla smiled. "The white curse against you is not fine. It triggered everything. The black curse is unbreakable now, so adding another curse doesn't matter anymore. People are going to die eventually."

"That's not the point. You saw Michelle. That's no way to die."

Orla sat down next to Lorcan. "I have you. We have each other. As far as I'm concerned, we're luckier than a lot of people. If we were to die soon, would you rather spend the rest of our days sad and angry?"

Lorcan turned Orla around and looked into her eyes. She had changed a lot, matured a great deal in a short period of time. This sort of statement would most of the time come from him. He knew he was a sentimental fool. Many would consider him weak when it came to her. He didn't mind. Couldn't care less. Lorcan Brody had never cared what people thought about him. Never cared about the way people were supposed to live. Love and freedom was what he lived for. Now the love that came from Orla shook him to his core.

He lifted her up and carried her and walked over to the sofa. Her legs wrapped around his waist. She unbuttoned his shirt, her mouth busy on his. He put her down on the sofa, but she flipped him over. They both dropped on the floor with her on top, straddling him. Before he knew it, his jeans were tangled at his ankles. He kicked them off. He tore off her blouse. His hands roamed over her body. She took his arms by the wrists.

"No, let me." She pinned his arms to the floor and used her hips to drive him. She kissed him slowly, so slowly it was torture. She savored the moment. He responded. They ravished each other. His body bucked underneath her. He closed his striking blue eyes.

"Open your eyes," she whispered. "I want you to watch me, I want you to watch us." Then she kept driving, pushing, loving until they were both sated.

CHAPTER 20

In China Town, Lorcan and Orla weaved their way through the crowded streets, heading toward an Asian grocery store. The small shop sat on a corner street. A small rusty door sagged open on one side, and the flickering neon sign was not inviting. Inside the shop, stacks of goods were piled everywhere.

Lorcan walked inside, pulling Orla behind him. An Asian man standing at the back of the shop glanced at him. "We're not open," he said. Lorcan approached the man. At six foot one, Lorcan towered over him. But the man certainly didn't act as if he had any physical disadvantage. "I said we're not open," he repeated.

"We're looking for Sam Windsor."

"Don't know him."

Lorcan lowered his voice. "You might want to rethink your answer. I'm in a good mood, and I don't want to have to hurt anyone."

"What did he do?"

"He owes me money. Serious money. Unless you want to pay me, you call him here right now so we can have a chat. I'll be waiting upstairs." Lorcan walked toward the back of the shop where there was a small set of stairs tucked in a corner.

"I told you . . ."

"And I heard you. But as I said, I'll be waiting for him upstairs. Tell him that the money he lost at Fossey Way is mine. I want it back."

The man grabbed a steel bar used to lock the door and swung at Lorcan. Lorcan grabbed the bar in mid-air, yanked it away from the man, and leveled it at the man's kneecap. He screamed. Lorcan followed with a kick and dragged the screaming man up the set of stairs. Orla locked the shop door.

As soon as they got to the top of the stairs, a bullet hit the man's head, exploding onto the wall behind them. Lorcan fired in the general direction of the shooter. He dropped the dead man and charged at the silhouette of his adversary as it fell to the ground.

On the floor was Sam Windsor. Lorcan gave him another kick and tied his hands behind his back. Lorcan's bullet had hit Sam in his shoulder. "What do you want?" Sam grunted. Orla charged up the stairs and stood behind Lorcan.

"You know who I work for?" Sam asked.

"What did William lose at Fossey Way?" Lorcan asked.

"Do you know who I work for?"

"I have the gun. I get to ask the questions."

Sam smirked. "He's an idiot. He bluffed you about the money. And he wanted to cheat his boss."

"Who's his boss?"

"I can't tell you."

Lorcan pointed the gun at Sam's head. "Even if I threaten to blow your brains out?"

Sam stared. "Go ahead. There's no easy death for betrayal. I'd rather eat your bullet right now than betray my master."

"Your master?" Orla frowned.

"I work for God," Sam said.

Lorcan whacked Sam in the head with the gun barrel, pounding on him with the rage he'd withheld all afternoon. "No God is going to ask you to kill a defenseless man and a kid," Lorcan screamed, railing the man with kicks and punches. Orla had to pull him off.

"You'll kill him, Lorcan."

Lorcan exclaimed, "He would have put that bullet in Riley's head and killed Noah without a second thought. If William hadn't say no, he would have executed them without blinking. What kind of monster is he? Why does he get to live, and people like Michelle have to die and be sent to Hell. And now he claims he's working for God!" Lorcan waved his arms in frustration. "What kind of justice is that? What kind of world are we living in?"

Sam chuckled, "That's why we're working our way out of here."

"Let me help you." Lorcan pointed the gun at Sam's head, but Orla pulled him back.

"That's too easy, Lorcan. Listen to me. We have a problem to handle here. He and William are the same kind, cold-blooded killers. But if you kill him now when he can't defend himself, you're no different than he is. We talked about this, Lorcan."

Lorcan nodded, and he lowered the gun. "All right. You work for William, but I guess you're just a mole in his company. I don't care who you really work for. But if you're not on William's side, then tell us what he lost at Fossey Way."

"A formula."

"What kind of formula? Drugs?"

Sam stared at Lorcan. "Do I look like the kind of guy who can make sense of gibberish on paper?"

"Guess not," Lorcan muttered.

"It's got to have something to do with medicine. That's why he freaked out when he thought the doctor had it," Lorcan asked.

"Does this have anything to do with the drug you injected into the doctor?" Orla asked.

"How the hell should I know? Look, William's a nasty son of a bitch. He's ambitious too. He stole the formula from my boss. He only wanted to copy it. But then some guy snatched the paper. He got his right hand man to get it back. But you killed that guy at Fossey Way. When William asked me to go there, the bodies were gone, as well as the paper."

"Does William want Jo as well? He's not giving her to his boss?"

Sam nodded. "Look, if you want to nail him for whatever reason, I don't care. I'm not his buddy. I have no ties. I can show you where he stocks his smuggled drugs right here in this warehouse. You can use that against him. One call to the cops, and he'll be done."

"He hides the drugs here?" Orla asked.

"Is there anything we can use to tie him to the drugs? Finding the drugs doesn't do anything if we can't link him to them."

"I can show you, and then you can decide what to do."

Lorcan nodded. "All right." He untied Sam. Sam stood and moaned then pointed at a side door. He led, and Lorcan and Orla followed him. The door opened to another wing of the building. Stacks of sealed boxes were piled high against the wall. Sam shuffled through piles of paper for a few minutes and then opened a drawer.

Lorcan saw a flash of metal in Sam's hands. He pushed Orla backward and pointed his gun at Sam. They both fired at the same time. Sam's head was shattered as the bullet pierced it. Lorcan staggered back with a bullet in his shoulder. His gun fell to the floor.

Orla grabbed him before he fell. "Oh God, so much blood."

"It's okay. Just a flesh wound."

"Let's get out of here," Orla said. They exited the building by the back door.

The next morning, Lorcan snuggled in bed next to Orla. She had tended to his injury, and he was trying to recuperate as much as possible. He stirred.

"Hey." She kissed his cheek. "Take another hour, then we have to go to William's office."

Lorcan nodded.

"Is all of your wiring gear ready?"

"Yep. I can do it with my eyes closed." He smiled at her. "It should be okay. We'll bug him and then hand him over to the cops. Then we can get out of here."

"Have you thought of where you want to go?"

"Anywhere with you is good with me. Is there a place where the curses won't follow us?"

"Unfortunately not. Until I can kill someone to feed the black curse, and you can stop loving me to free yourself from the white curse, we won't find a place on Earth where we can be free."

"How about off the planet?" Lorcan grinned.

Orla rolled her eyes. "Sure. Let's take the spaceship. Have you reserved the tickets?"

Lorcan chuckled. "Yes, of course." He rolled over and buried his face between her breasts.

"I certainly don't sell any tickets in there." She giggled, pulled his face out, and kissed his lips.

CHAPTER 21

William's office was located on level forty-six of the Century Tower. Directly outside of the bank of elevators, a corridor led Orla and Lorcan to the sumptuous but deserted entrance of The Connector Group. The door swung open as they approached. There was no receptionist at the counter. The open planning area with more than twenty desks was empty. The lights were dimmed and the computer screens were idle.

"In here." William's voice echoed out from an office wing.

Lorcan pushed Orla behind him and walked toward the door.

The massive office had no furniture except for a gigantic desk at the far end where William sat. This was the corner end of the building where the glass walls allowed open views of the city. William gestured to the seats in front of his desk.

"We've just moved in. It will take time to settle," William said and glanced at Orla. "Obviously, you haven't brought the merchandise with you."

"We're not stupid," Orla said dryly.

Lorcan put a piece of paper on the desk. "Here's where we put Jo. You have the money?"

William put a briefcase on the desk. "As you requested, this is in cash."

Before reaching for the suitcase, Lorcan attached a bug under the seat of the chair in which he was sitting. Orla dropped her purse on the floor.

"Excuse me," she bent down to pick up her purse and attached a bug underneath the desk. When she sat upright, the exchange continued. The briefcase and the piece of paper were both pushed to the midpoint of the desk. William stopped, saying, "I can't let you take the money before I check on your delivery."

"I can't give you the address without having the money first," Lorcan said.

"As you can see, I have no assistance here. None of my staff are around. I couldn't go against the two of you if I wanted to keep the money. I can make a call from here. You wait for my people to check out the address to see if Jo is there. Once they confirm, you'll get the money."

"What if they confirm, and then you kill us right here. It would only take a couple of bullets. I bet you have guns close at hand," Orla said.

"And you don't have a weapon?" William smirked.

"Indeed we do, but there's no need for bloodshed," Lorcan said.

"Are you sure the address is real?"

"Of course," Orla said.

"And my people will find Jo there?"

"They will. But as I said, I can't let you check it out before we get the money," Lorcan said.

William leaned back in his chair, contemplating. Then he nodded. "You won't walk out of here with the money before I verify at my end."

Lorcan shrugged. "Okay." Then he pushed the piece of paper further toward William, while William pushed the money toward Orla.

Then they heard a faint clicking sound.

Lorcan sprang to his feet and threw his body over Orla. They dropped to the floor.

Bullets sprayed the room.

Machine guns.

The glass wall behind William shattered. His body was riddled with bullets. His body, propped up in his desk chair, rolled over to the shattered wall and fell out of the building.

Wind blew through the office via the broken glass wall. Lights flickered. A hand snatched the piece of paper with the address before it flew away. Someone grabbed the briefcase of money. And then footsteps clicked on the polished floor.

Someone flipped Lorcan's body which lay on top of Orla's, flopping him onto the floor.

The footsteps walked away. And further away. Then it was quiet.

Darkness.

Orla could hear the wind and feel the cold. She could hear herself drawing her last breaths. They were heavy, filled with bubbling blood flowing into her lungs.

She promised Lorcan she'd marry him when this was over. Now here she was, unable to fulfill her promise. She had unfinished business. She couldn't let it end like this. She was special. She'd been born and raised to lead. She had spent her life as a thief because she didn't want to kill. She'd sacrificed her access to power. And it wasn't all to end her life on a cold floor, unable to protect her lover.

She heard herself chanting the ancient vow—the vow of devotion, the vow of herself—to her ancestor. The smell of jasmine rose up from the floor and thickened in the air. Whorls of black mist hovered around her. Strong spirits, she thought. But nothing was as strong as her vow, the vow she meant to make to her ancestors.

The jasmine scent increased. Energy washed through her body as she chanted the ancient spell. More energy. Waves of energy. Oceans of energy poured into her. Her wounds closed. Her body was healed.

She sat up, gathering Lorcan's body in her arms. He stirred and opened his eyes.

"Orla." As he spoke, blood bubbled from his mouth and ran down his chin. She wiped it away. Tears rolled down her face. "Orla, please don't use the black curse to save me. I don't want it to hang on you."

"I can't let you die."

"The ring. It's in my pocket."

She took the ring box out of his pocket. "Lorcan, please don't do this to me."

"I'd like to see you wear it," he whispered.

She put the ring on. Her vision blurred with tears. The sapphire stared up at her. In her arms, Lorcan smiled. He closed his eyes, and then he stopped breathing.

"Oh, no, no. You're supposed to propose to me properly. You're supposed to marry me." She rocked his body in her arms. She knew he was gone. The white curse was too strong this time. But she couldn't let it take him. Nobody, nothing, could take him away from her.

She respected his wish, but she loved him more than any wishes on this Earth.

Then she chanted the black curse to summon the dark spirits.

She kept chanting, murmuring the ancient tune and the promises to the spirits and to her tribe, to the dead and the alive, and to her branch of sorcery. She called to everyone and everything she remembered from those short years of training in her childhood. She called. She promised. She'd turn around the planetary chart of the world if she had to.

He shuddered in her arms. She felt a hint of warmth. She could feel the blood flow again in his veins and his heart resume its steady beat. She heard bullets clank on the floor as they were pushed from his body. She felt his life return.

Lorcan coughed and opened his eyes. He jerked up, panting, and looked around. Orla cupped his face. "It's all right. You're all right. Calm down." His blue eyes pierced her, striking and focused. He looked at her. Her eyes were dark. He glanced around, taking stock.

"What have you done?" Lorcan asked.

A tear trickled down her face. Lorcan could smell the jasmine. It was so thick it burnt. He knew it was the smell of spirits, the dark spirits. She had used the black curse again. But this time, it was more serious than before. This was the point of no return for her. He could see it in her face.

In the room was something beyond his control, something that would take her away.

"No." Lorcan sprung to his feet. "No," he repeated. "I won't let this happen." He could see the black mist whirling now.

"I'm sorry, Lorcan." Tears rolled down her face. "I have to go now."

More wind blew into the room. It got colder by the second.

"No, you're not bringing me back here and then leaving me, Orla."

"But we live. Once we stay alive, we can figure things out."

"Now." A hollow male voice echoed in the room out of nowhere. "Orla. Now."

"The whisper of an ancient sorcerer," Orla mumbled in fear. Lorcan had never seen her afraid.

The black mist formed into the shape of a man in a black robe. "Now," he said again.

Lorcan pushed Orla behind him. "Old man, she's not going anywhere with you."

The figure croaked out something in an ancient tongue that made no sense to Lorcan. Realizing Lorcan didn't understand a word, the old man rumbled in English. "I can take back what I gave." He blew out a stream of cold mist. It swirled and shot at Lorcan. Lorcan slumped to the floor as the energy was evaporated from him.

"No, ancestor. Whoever you are. Please don't take him," Orla cried.

The door of an elevator opened. Mya strode in. "These shoes aren't made for walking, let alone running. You owe me this one, Lorcan."

On the floor, Lorcan looked up at Mya. She was stunning. Her skin radiant, her hair flowing, and gorgeous in those high heels. She looked different from the day he'd met her in the backyard in Mortlake.

"I won't touch your subject, you won't touch mine," the old man croaked. He released Lorcan. Lorcan stood up and grabbed Orla.

"You made it, Mya. Do we have the deal?" Lorcan asked her.

Orla frowned.

Mya nodded. "Yes, we've got it. You've got what you asked for." Lorcan grinned.

The old man growled.

"Where and when?" Lorcan asked.

"Down below. Now." Mya pointed at the broken glass wall. Lorcan cautiously peeked over the edge and looked down. Orla followed. From level forty-six, William's body sprawled on the cement of the empty parking lot looked like a broken toy.

"Can we do it on the ground floor? Or I can maybe tolerate jumping from level one. But this is a bit high, don't you think?" Lorcan asked Mya.

"What? Jumping out of *here?*" Orla gasped.

The old man growled louder. His body glowed.

"Coahm Foley, I'm a deity. Do you really think that old spirit of yours can do any more than scratch me? Stop your infernal howling," Mya chastised.

"Caohm? You broke our rules five hundred years ago. You used to be the leader," Orla exclaimed.

Mya interrupted. "This is your one and only chance, Lorcan. I can't control the gate. It'll open on the third thunder strike and remain that way for exactly thirty seconds."

The first wave of thunder rumbled across the sky.

Caohm roared and glowed so brightly he looked as if he would burst into flames. "Orla, come with me now. You have made a vow." He advanced on her.

Mya swung her arm. A blade of cold air pushed Caohm backward.

"That's going to cost me, damn it," Mya muttered.

A second thunder crash.

"The gate will open on the next one, Lorcan," Mya said.

Lorcan looked down, there was nothing in the air below.

"What gate, Lorcan?" Orla asked.

"The Daimon Gate," he said.

"So we jump and die, and then end up at the gate to Heaven?" Orla asked.

Lorcan shook his head. "You promised to marry me when this is over. So follow me. I love you."

The third thunder blast exploded in the sky.

Coahm roared in anger, "Orla, come back to your family." He reached out. Mya blasted him with another wedge of icy air.

Lorcan stood at the edge of the floor. He turned around and looked at Mya.

"Thank you, we owe you this life," he said. Then he spread his arms like wings and let himself freefall.

"Lorcan!" Orla screamed. She charged at the edge of the room, and she jumped after him.

The fall was long.

They fell. And fell. And kept falling.

Lorcan looked down and saw William's body in the lot. He looked up and saw that Orla had followed him. Lying, body crushed, next to William in an empty parking lot was not the most desirable way to die. There was really no good way, Lorcan thought. He'd always considered the saying that your life flashed before your eyes before you died as a cliché, yet here he was, recalling the moments of his childhood with Orla at the spring in the Irish countryside. If his life could be summed up by short moments, those were the ones he was remembering as he fell. Not that his adult life with Orla wasn't good. But it certainly wasn't innocent. He was happy, but he craved the feelings they had for each other as childhood sweethearts. He was a sentimental fool after all.

The night after he saw Michelle dragged to Hell, Lorcan left Orla. Not for forever, but the thought did cross his mind. He would have preferred that they live apart but hold onto the love they had for each other rather than live together in a place where she had to block him and their love out of her mind because of her idiotic commitment to her family. Leaving her wasn't a solution, but he was confused, desperate, and in need of a way out for both of them.

Then Mya came to him with a proposal he couldn't refuse.

The brilliant and beautiful deity—who for reasons he didn't understand and didn't have time to find out—was bound to save his life. After Fossey Way, she told him that he was to die by gunshots if she didn't interfere. He *had* died tonight, but Orla had cheated their way out of death again. In an effort to save him, Mya had negotiated for him to take a test to be a Daimon Gate gatekeeper.

Daimon Gate was a dimension that connected the multiverse. It was like another world, Mya said. The description seemed appropriate. A whole new world. In reality, it was a dimension that curved in time, space, mind, and world view. It was the connecting passage between ninety other dimensions. It was a tunnel that helped screen travelers between the participating universes. In a nutshell, in order to pass through the Daimon Gate, passengers had to pass tests designed by gatekeepers. The Daimon Gate was recruiting for new gatekeepers with the skills that Mya believed Lorcan had—data thievery for auditing and reinforcement.

If he became a gatekeeper, he could live in the Daimon Gate—a dimension and a world independent of any universe, Earth included. He would be free from life, moral debts, and lingering strings which attached him to Earth. He would be free.

That night, he took the tests. It was only a few hours Earth time, but in the gate, he suffered through three months of life and death tests that cut him to the bone. His body, his mind, and his spirit were tested to their limits. But he passed the tests, and they wanted him. He was offered a position that he never have dreamed of in his life. They wanted him, and they wanted him badly. It was at that point that he lay down his cards. He wanted a package deal. He wanted Orla there with him. He let Mya negotiate the deal for him. As far as he was concerned, it was all or nothing.

That morning, he returned to Orla in the apartment, not knowing whether the deal had gone through or not. The smell of wildflowers and forests lingered on his clothes. He saw her pulling him into her arms, not asking questions, and he knew that he had done the right thing for both of them.

And here he was, jumping to another dimension—or maybe not.

The gate was wide open on the ground, somewhere right in front of him. But this time, he knew they were testing him for courage by opening it mid-air.

He looked down and could still see William's dead body. He looked up, and Orla was still freefalling with him.

How long was thirty seconds? It felt like a lifetime. As the important moments of his life played out in his mind, Lorcan had a feeling that he might have been jumping to his death. Even worse, he had asked Orla to come with him. And she had.

He looked down again.

As they reached a point nine floors up from the ground, a hollow ring of air with a red rim of fire and sparks of electrical current opened up and swallowed them.

Epilogue

Lorcan and Orla dropped down onto soft grass and rolled a bit before they got their footing. He stood up, darting toward Orla to help. She huffed. "Did we die?"

Lorcan chuckled. "Apparently not."

"Where the hell are we?" Orla asked.

In front of them were rolling green hills, the scenery of the Irish countryside. Lorcan smiled. He had requested the setting. On top of a nearby hill, a stone castle perched. Lorcan kissed Orla.

"We're home," he said. "This is the Daimon Gate, a whole new world, *our* new world. It's independent from any other world in any dimension, including the supernatural. This is a world where our curses can't follow." Then he told her about the night he had left the apartment and had come back exhausted. He told her about the tests he had to pass to gain them entry to this completely free and virtuous world.

"You said virtuous?" Orla asked.

"Yes. The Daimon Gate recruits only the most virtuous to be gatekeepers."

"Like saints?"

Lorcan laughed. "No. They recruit men. Good men."

"What does being virtuous mean? Exactly how did they test that?"

Lorcan frowned. "I had my own way to pass the tests. I'm good at what I do."

He held her hand, leading her to the castle, imposingly located on top of the hill. They stood at its entrance, and her jaw dropped. "You named the castle after me?"

Lorcan grinned. "Orla means the golden princess. Didn't you know that? It's a pretty name for a castle." He verified his palm print on a lock control panel at the door. A robotic voice announced from the speaker, ""Welcome home, Mr. and Mrs. Brody. Your household has been prepared for you, and your dinner will be served in ten milles."

"What's ten milles?" Orla asked, confused.

The voice answered, "Ten milles is equal to one hour Earth time; one point twenty-five Eudaiz time; zero point six Xiilok time; five . . ."

"Stop," Lorcan said. "We get the idea. Thank you."

"I am at your command, Master Brody."

"Master? They call you master?"

"Would you prefer prince? I think that's a bit cheesy. How about boss? Nah, that sounds like a TV show." Lorcan chuckled. "They're robots. Machines. They'll call you whatever you program them to. It's nothing personal. There is no ego here." He grinned.

"This is perfect," she whispered. He spun her around and pinned her to the wall. He savored her lips.

"There are many more perfect things upstairs. Everything is just the way you like it."

"This is too good to be true, Lorcan. What did you have to do to get it? What did you trade for all this?"

"I traded nothing but my talent." He kissed her again.

"Tell me please. How did you do this?"

His striking blue eyes locked on hers. "Do you like it here?"

She nodded.

"Are you happy?"

She nodded again.

"That's all that matters." Then he planted a bone-melting kiss on her mouth so that she completely forgot what she had been asking him.

PART TWO
BLUE FOX

The course of true love never did run smooth.
A Midsummer Night's Dream , 1598
William Shakespeare

CHAPTER 1

The cold breezes seeped up from the ground, whirled into a small funnel, slashed at her skin, blew and tangled her beautiful long black hair. The gusts came from nowhere, carrying with them a strange chanting sound she didn't care for. It was the hovering sound of Hell— the sound of the dark magic. It was not supposed to follow her to the Daimon Gate, a universe far away from Earth. She had escaped from the haunt of the dark magic seventeen years ago, fleeing from a remote village in Ireland to London. She ran again a month ago, this time not by herself but with Lorcan, the love of her life, exiling themselves from Earth to the Daimon Gate. She assumed they had found their Heaven here.

Now she couldn't make it home—to the small castle Lorcan had named after her. She stood at the corner of a dead end street, beneath a gothic dome—a place Lorcan had told her several times not to take the short cut through. But she had taken this route several times in the last month. It was quiet and easy. It only took a few hundred yards around the corner, and she could go up the hill to their place. It should be perfectly safe based on what she was told.

The Daimon Gate was a virtuous universe— everything here was governed by righteousness. Orla couldn't help but roll her eyes when she thought about it. Being righteous was the very reason this whole universe was governed by machinery and a wicked computer system called the EYE. Only machines could tell right from wrong with no exception. It was perfectly normal for her, a human, to make mistakes, wasn't it? The fact that she wasn't good at following the rules was only a minor issue.

"All right, wallowing is a stupid thing to do, Orla," she muttered to herself. She had developed the strange habit of talking to herself since they had moved here. She didn't want to admit that it could be the result of loneliness and isolation. She shifted her stance and felt a tingling sensation on her toes and fingertips. It was just the chill, she thought, as she stared at a black brick wall in the place where she had seen her usual route home just a few seconds ago.

She had charged at it three times. When she stepped back, the path revealed itself; but when she approached, it closed up on her. Orla was certain if she turned around to go back to the main road, that path would close as well. In this universe, the physical rules were strange. She didn't understand them, nor did she appreciate them. She knew someone or something had to be playing a joke on her, and if this was a prank, it wasn't remotely funny. Her psychic ability was telling her nothing at the moment. Her palms were clammy and, even in the freezing air, a bead of sweat trickled down her forehead.

She shoved her right hand into her pocket to grab her cell phone and almost laughed at her own reflex. There were no such things as a cell phones here. In fact, the computer geniuses in the Daimon Gate considered her earthly technology primitive. She merely wanted to call for help, but there was no time to fumble with the thing they used in place of a cell phone—a wrist unit. It was a funky type of watch to her, and a useless object that she had never bothered learned how to operate.

The wind grew stronger, and she thought she heard a howl echo from somewhere in the air. A dried tree branch on the ground flew up, whirled in the wind, and then aimed at her left arm, slashing into it.

"Oww," she yelped and grabbed at the cut. A small stream of blood oozed through the gaps between her fingers. A brick wall on her left cracked and collapsed. Orla just had enough time to jump out of its way. She turned around, glancing in the direction of the main road. A wall, coming from nowhere, slid across and blocked her view. She was being closed in. She turned back, looking at her usual corner path, open now. She made a small step forward, and the path closed up right in front of her.

She remembered what Lorcan had said—there were invisible networks of dimensional holes that only gatekeepers had access to and could control. She was sure these walls had come from those holes. More walls slid out from dimensional holes, surrounding her like a maze. A wall came in close proximity to where she stood and hit her from behind. Orla fell to the ground. She stood up immediately, her hands balled into fists. "That's enough, you coward. Wanna play with me? Show your pathetic face!" There was no response save for the sliding sound of black brick walls. Soon they would sandwich her, and she wasn't in the mood to be anyone's meal.

She swirled her palms in a circle as if making a ball out of thin air. A ball of fire formed. She smiled as if she couldn't believe what she had learned from her childhood had worked. She threw the fireball at the wall that blocked her way home. It crashed into the wall and burst into hundreds of pitiful fire particles. Another wall hit her from behind. Orla fell again onto the cold dirt road.

She stood up, created a bigger fireball, and hurled it at the wall. Again and again, she threw them. The sound of the balls hitting the walls was as loud as thunder. The wall cracked and shattered into a pile of dirt and then vanished. The cold wind still whirled, but it was not the icy breeze sending the chill to her spine right now.

A clapping sound came from a dark corner, followed by a man. He looked like a dark prince Orla had read about in gothic novels—tall with slightly long black hair framing a sinfully handsome face. His clapping and his smile sent a chill from her spine to her brain. Her blood ran cold. If her psychic ability was at work right now, it gave her only one word: *shit.*

Orla pasted a smile on her face.

"Impressive," the man said. "It took a considerable amount of time and effort on my end to get to witness your dark magic." A faint accent penetrated his voice, but Orla couldn't make any sense of it.

"There was no dark magic. Just a trick to fool kids who still believe in Santa Claus." Orla stepped backward slightly, sizing up the man. He was at least as tall as

Lorcan, so he had a height advantage over her. He seemed as agile as a cat with movements of an experienced fighter. It was obvious now that he controlled the walls that blocked her way home, and that meant he was a gatekeeper. Taking all that into account, Orla wagered that her chance of winning this fight was nonexistent.

"Who are you? And what do you want?" Orla asked.

"I am a gatekeeper."

"I figured as much. I can tell that by the way you're playing with the dimensional holes. But being a gatekeeper doesn't guarantee your safety when harassing an ordinary citizen like me. I'll report you."

The man chuckled. "I was only trying to protect the gate from intruders—and from those who cheated their way in."

Now her blood ran ice cold. The only person who knew Lorcan had cheated the system for them to come to the Daimon Gate was Ciaran LeBlanc. But Ciaran had promised not to tell anyone. Lorcan had never told the authority of the Daimon Gate that Orla was a trained sorceress who had used dark magic to cheat his life back, not once but twice. In this universe, if they were caught cheating the system for personal gains, they could face the death penalty.

"I don't know what you mean. But at the moment, as far as I'm concerned, you're harassing me."

"Let's cut to the chase. I don't have much time, and I don't think you and your lover have much time, either. You used the dark magic to throw fireballs at my walls. That's evidence of using it inside the Daimon Gate. I don't need to explain the consequences of that to you, do I?"

Orla shrugged. "Well, if it's in the system, we'll have to face the consequences. Usually, there's no way out of a severe penalty. So what's your ulterior motive for giving us a solution?"

The man laughed. "If all the people from Earth are as smart as you are, I could be in trouble." The man smirked. "Lucky for me, there aren't many of those around here. Yes, the evidence of your magic was captured within my system. At the moment, it's internal and under my control. That explains the number of walls I had to use to shield the view of the EYE. But I can report the evidence to central at any time—unless you do one simple thing for me."

"And what would that 'simple' thing be?"

"Ciaran LeBlanc used the system within your castle to cheat the system. I want you to get your man to report Ciaran to the central." His voice was as smooth and calm as still water. He locked his gaze with Orla.

"Ciaran LeBlanc, the king of Eudaiz?"

The man sneered. "Not for long."

"Why? Who are you? What did he do to you?"

"Come on. You don't owe him anything. But you owe your life to yourself. And don't you want to live happily ever after with your lover at your castle?"

Orla nodded. "I suppose so. But what if the council has already recorded my use of magic? If that's the case, I don't have to do anything you ask."

The man laughed. "Aren't you a skeptic?"

"I'd call it brain power."

"Right." The man approached Orla. "I'm not a big-time gatekeeper, but I can assure you, I am in total control of my limited world inside these walls. Each gatekeeper has a private zone into which even the EYE cannot intrude."

Orla arched an eyebrow, then as quick as lightning, she threw a fireball right into the man's chest. Taken off-guard, he staggered back, grunting in pain. Orla smiled. She might not have any physical advantage over this man, but she refused to go down easily. "If that's the case, then nobody will see me kill you," Orla said under her breath, hurling another ball. He dodged it and threw his dagger at her. She threw a ball at his hand, but missed.

As the wall behind him moved, the man was distracted. Seizing the opportunity, Orla threw another ball. The man dodged her fireball once again, and it sailed past him toward the wall behind him that had slid open.

Lorcan stood at the opening wall, holding a portable device. He ducked as the fireball flew past, missing his face by inches. The man waved his arm. Orla couldn't see anything except Lorcan yelling and pointing at her, and then the wall behind her hit her head. She slumped to the ground, and the whole world turned into darkness.

A large, gothic-looking arch stared down at her, making her blood run cold. There was something wrong with the air around them—her skin felt charged, almost like she was conducting electricity. Lorcan stood in the center of the arch, dancing away from the lightning bolts chasing him. Orla couldn't believe how many of them there were! There had to be at least a few thousand. She stood there, rooted to the spot, unable to help her lover. She kept trying to run out to help him, but he yelled at her to stay away and save herself. As he shouted at her, he stopped moving, just for half a second, barely escaping the next lightning bolt. Fighting her way free from whatever was holding her prisoner, she started to run to Lorcan, not heeding his warnings to stay away. She was getting frustrated because no matter how fast she ran, she didn't seem to be getting any closer. Tears started streaming down her cheeks as the hopelessness of the situation started to sink in. She watched helplessly as one of the lightning bolts hit Lorcan, causing him to burst into flame like a Roman candle. As his ashes fell into a neat little pile, Orla screamed in agony. Her heart was dying along with him.

"Orla! Orla! Come on, honey, you need to wake up now." Lorcan was trying to shake Orla awake, but so far it wasn't working. He had seen a gigantic wall hit her from behind, and then the man that she seemed to be fighting with fled the scene. He didn't understand why this was happening. The Daimon Gate was supposed to be the safest place for them, a self-contained world that was the entrance between universes. Who was the man she had been fighting with? He looked like a gatekeeper. Lorcan wanted to look the man up on his computer system, but at the moment, he couldn't leave Orla.

"Orla! Come on, baby, wake up for me now, okay?" He went back to shaking her gently, hoping she would open her eyes. Her eyelids fluttered, and she groaned. He swept her up in a tight embrace.

"What happened?" she asked groggily.

"I should ask you that."

She blinked, and then the encounter with the man came back to her. "We're in serious trouble, Lorcan."

CHAPTER 2

Lorcan helped Orla sit up, leaning her against the head of the bed, then he went to get her some water. While Orla took tentative sips and looked at him over the rim of the glass, Lorcan sat at the side of the bed and checked the cut on her arm that he had secured with a bandage. He tried not to look into her eyes because all he saw in them was the trouble that would put to an end the short happy month they'd been living in the Daimon Gate. "What kind of trouble are we in, Orla? Who was the gatekeeper you fought with?" he asked when he thought any further delay on his part would seem odd to her. She told him about the man's demands. Lorcan said nothing for a long moment. He went to the window and stared silently outside. After a while, he turned to her. "You'd agree with me that we won't report Ciaran?"

"Of course. There's a dark side to Ciaran, and he must have created a lot of enemies along the way because of that, but he's an important man. People in his universe—their lives—depend on him. If we did anything to harm him, we wouldn't find a place in Hell."

The sorrow in Orla's eyes cut at Lorcan's heart. He wondered whether the universe Ciaran was ruling, the Daimon Gate, Earth, and anywhere else that had living creatures shared the same Hell. He had seen Hell on Earth when they fought to bring Riley back and tried to free Riley's late wife, Michelle. If he and Orla committed a sin now, would they return to that same Hell? Or did Daimon Gate have its own version of Hell?

"Lorcan!"

"Huh?"

He knew Orla was lonely in the Daimon Gate. They didn't have many friends here, and after what had happened to them on Earth, they didn't make friends easily. It had been a month, and the only time he'd seen the light back in her eyes was a couple of weeks ago when they'd had visitors. Ciaran LeBlanc and his people had stopped by on their way through the gate on a multiversal secret mission that he wouldn't talk about. Some creature had used dark magic on Ciaran, and

Lorcan and Orla had done what they could to help him find out what it was. Orla had used her sorcery combined with Lorcan's computer skills, and for a little while, she had looked happy again. She'd been intrigued and had felt almost like she'd been back at her job on Earth.

They didn't, however, help Ciaran solely out of the goodness of their hearts. Ciaran made it clear that he knew that Lorcan had died on the 46th floor of the century tower, and that Orla had brought him back with her own dark magic, using it to cheat Lorcan back to life. He had used that as blackmail, and he'd also appealed to their sense of justice. Ciaran was to rule Eudaiz, a universe with hundreds of billion people who relied on him for their safety. Those two things combined had won them both over, and there was nothing else they could do but help him.

The Daimon Gate was a universe full of virtue— governed by virtuous people and operating on virtuous principles. The most serious crime in the universe was cheating any system for personal gain. Lorcan had passed the test that they'd given him and then demanded a deal to get Orla to come with him. The fact that Lorcan had cheated death and come back would be a grave offense, and considered cheating, because he might not be the same person who had initially passed the test. He also hadn't told them Orla's real identity, or the fact that she was a trained sorceress. That was something else that could be considered cheating the system. Lorcan's crimes were grave indeed, but no one knew about them yet. If Ciaran told anyone, then Lorcan would face death by a thousand lightning bolts. That was the vision Orla had just gotten in her delirium.

Ciaran had promised not to reveal their secrets to the Host of the Daimon Gate, and they trusted him. On the other hand, although Ciaran was the king of Eudaiz, if he traveled in the Daimon Gate, he had to play by their rules. If he got caught cheating the Daimon Gate system, he would be killed before he returned to his world. And Ciaran had cheated the system here, right in this castle. He did it to save a senior gatekeeper of the Daimon Gate, Brandon, the prince of the Red Castle. Brandon committed a crime and was supposed to die, but for some reason unbeknown to Lorcan, Ciaran had manipulated the computer system to change the sentence from death to demotion. If Lorcan reported that incident to the authority of the Daimon Gate, the next time Ciaran traveled via the gate, he would be killed.

"Do you think the EYE recorded my use of magic?" Orla asked.

Lorcan shook his head. "I don't think so. The gatekeeper you fought had blocked the signals well enough. But why did he want to expose Ciaran? The only reason I can think of is that someone is opposed to the fact that Ciaran saved the prince and the princess.

But I would imagine there are many other ways to harm Ciaran. Why this way? And why would a gatekeeper of the Daimon Gate want to harm the king of Eudaiz?" he questioned.

Lorcan's wrist unit beeped. Text had come across the screen suggesting the call was made from the Host residence, asking Lorcan to come and meet with the Host of the Daimon Gate. His nerves started to heighten his senses, and he began to sweat. Had the gatekeeper reported Ciaran and Orla already?

Virtue is the core value of the Daimon Gate. As the Host of the Daimon Gate, this man had to be the most virtuous man in the Cosmo, Lorcan thought. Given that, the Host wouldn't tolerate cheating from anyone. Lorcan shook his head, trying not to think about what may lie ahead of them. There were nine thousand gatekeepers at work here—why would this one want to cause them trouble? Without telling Orla what the call was about, Lorcan strode from the bedroom, making a beeline toward the control room.

The Host only dealt with high-level executives within the gate and top-level executives from the participating worlds. No one knew who the Host really was, though rumor had it that he was once human and used to live on Earth. Lorcan was nervous. He answered the call, and almost instantaneously, a hologram appeared. The image was life-sized, and the man looked like a kindly old grandfather in his late sixties. He had a British accent, and it made Lorcan wonder if the two might have been neighbors at one point.

"Lorcan?" Before the Host could speak, Orla poked her head into the room. She saw the hologram in front of her, and her mouth dropped open. Not very many people had the honor of meeting the Host, for security reasons, but now that the two of them were seeing him in the hologram, they were a little starstruck. Lorcan excused himself hurriedly to the Host, rushed over to Orla, and ushered her outside.

"I'll be with you in just a second, okay honey? I don't think the Host would care for you to see him." She nodded and sat in a chair, clutching her stomach. Lorcan returned to the control room. The holocast of the Host stood in a beam of light, waiting. It had taken Lorcan a good two weeks to adjust to this universe's way of communication. A holocast was like a telephone on Earth, but the technology was a lot more advanced. The significant difference was not only the life-sized hologram, but the fact that the person could choose to step out of the light beam and enter the environment of the person he was speaking to.

"Lorcan, how are you and Orla faring? Have you had a chance to settle in properly?" The soft British accent calmed Lorcan's nerves a bit, but he still felt a chill in anticipation of what was coming. The Host wouldn't drop by his place simply for a cup of tea.

"We're doing fine. Sometimes it gets a bit lonely for Orla, but we're managing. I've made some progress with the project. Would you like a report now?"

"Lorcan, I'm going to speak to you off the record now. Whatever you say will be between us only. No record of it will appear anywhere or be recorded." The hologram of the Host took a few steps forward until he was completely out of the beam of light. His fuzzy edges solidified, and his unintelligible details became concrete. Something about him looked familiar, but then again, it could just be that he had one of those kindly old man faces. "Is there anything you want to tell me off the record before I tell you the reason I am here?"

Lorcan contemplated and then shook his head. He didn't think he was breathing, but he must have been. No one could hold their breath for that long. He swore he could hear the sound of a clock ticking, even though time in the Daimon Gate was different compare to Earth, and they didn't use clocks. It must be the countdown of his life he was hearing.

"Let me give you a hint. The EYE reports a glitch coming from your system here a couple of weeks ago, resulting in inconsistencies. Any idea what might have caused the problem?"

Lorcan felt as though the floor under his feet was shifting. He cleared his throat. "I don't know. What sort of problem? I sent out a lot of signals daily while working on your project."

The Host nodded. "That's how I figured out there was an inconsistency. I'm taking a preemptive step here. The computer hasn't reported the issue to the council. But soon, the tech department at central will put a report together, and the issue will be picked up. Are you sure you didn't do anything different?"

Lorcan matched the Host's gaze. "No. Nothing. If the EYE picked up discrepancies, please let me know, and I will formally address it."

The Host smiled. "You're a good man, Lorcan. It wasn't a mistake recruiting you. Thank you for protecting the person who sent out the discrepancies from your system."

Lorcan shoved his hands into his pockets and remained silent.

"The EYE can't record private conversation, Lorcan, you know that."

Lorcan nodded. "It seems you've fixed the discrepancies and know who caused them, so why are you telling me?"

The Host sat. "While I was looking into that particular issue, I came across a nuance, a piece of information from a computer database on Earth that recorded something about you and what happened at Century tower."

Lorcan whirled around. "How is that possible? The EYE can't see into private places."

"I said the information is from an *Earth* database."

"But it was recorded into the LeBlanc security system. It's not possible for an outsider to . . ." Then the truth dawned on him, and Lorcan gasped. "You . . ."

The Host smiled. "You did Ciaran a favor, so I will return the gesture, and I hope you appreciate it. I am Ciaran's father, so of course I have access to the LeBlanc's security system. That information alone is a life and death matter for many people. Although Ciaran didn't expose you and Orla, the information *was* recorded. Sooner or later, it will leak."

"It already has, I'm afraid."

"I beg your pardon?"

"My wife was attacked by a gatekeeper just before your holocast. He forced her to use her magic and threatened to report us if we don't expose Ciaran."

"A gatekeeper?"

Lorcan nodded. "But I don't know who he is or his ulterior motive." Lorcan's hands were clenched into fists.

"How did he attack Orla?"

"He pulled his gatekeeper's walls from dimensional holes."

"He used his resources. There will be a record. I'll find out who he is. But that can't be good for you. When he has to answer to the incident, he will reveal your information."

Lorcan was pacing now, his face clouded over, his eyes stormy. He kicked an empty chair in frustration, sending it through the row of other chairs and creating quite a mess. The Host smiled calmly. "I would never come to you with an unsolvable problem. I appreciate your keeping your promise to Ciaran. So I have a suggested solution."

Lorcan stopped pacing. He shoved his hands into his pockets and stared at the Host, waiting for him to continue.

"There is an artifact, a key that we lost. It is the key to the life force of one of our gatekeepers. A long time ago, an unknown creature from another universe attacked the gatekeeper of Gate 131. The Daimon Gate connects to nine thousand portals, and this particular portal is an Eastern gate. The creature trapped the life force of the gatekeeper inside of a rock with the key of Psuche, locked the gate with the same key, then fled. No one can travel through that gate, and the gatekeeper can neither die naturally nor be saved. As to the creature's whereabouts, or even what it is, we have no further information. If you can obtain the key of the Psuche of Gate 131, it will solve your problem."

"How so?"

"Although I don't understand magic, and I am not a true believer, there is no rule set in stone saying you cannot use unexplainable resources in the Daimon Gate. The problem is that you have to report it and get it approved. The Eastern gate is a perfect example. That gatekeeper used to be a wizard on Earth."

Lorcan cocked an eyebrow.

"Yes, you heard me right. It was long before my time. Because of the gatekeeper's origin, it is deemed appropriate that you would recruit someone with expertise such as Orla's. I can put your case to the council, stating that I was aware of Orla's talent before I recruited you, and that you are now both recruited for the mission."

"You would lie to the council for me? I . . . I thought . . ."

"That I have to be the most virtuous man in the Cosmo? Well, I suppose I am. And I'm not lying. I will simply move the time I received the information about Orla up a little earlier." The Host smiled.

Lorcan ruffled his hair. "Thank you. I'll get you the key."

"It's not going to be a walk in the park. If it were, it could have been done long time ago."

Lorcan nodded. "I see. Thank you very much. I appreciate this."

The Host nodded and turned on the holocast beam. "I should return to my residence for tea." He smiled gently, like a grandfather, and turned on his heel, vanishing into the light beam.

CHAPTER 3

Orla had waited a few minutes to make sure the holocast was gone before she entered the control room and strode toward Lorcan.

"You were eavesdropping?" Lorcan cocked an eyebrow at her.

Orla shrugged, put her arms around him, and snuggled into his chest. Then she rose up on tiptoes to kiss him. She had no idea how they were going to find this unknown creature, but she knew that if anyone could do the impossible, it would be Lorcan. She was going to make sure that she was there with him. They did everything together, and she wasn't going to take a backseat and just watch his next adventure from the sidelines.

When he had regained his footing after the bone-melting kiss, Lorcan combed his fingers through her long black hair and kissed her forehead. "I guess you want to work on this with me?"

"Are you saying I'd never love you without having an ulterior motive?"

He smiled. "No and no. You always love me, the same way I love you. And that's unconditional. And you *always* have an ulterior motive for anything you do, irrespective of whether love is involved."

Orla pressed her body against Lorcan's and pushed him against the wall. "Well, this has no motive whatsoever." She slid her hands underneath his shirt and up his torso. Lorcan grabbed her. He kissed her jaw, trailing his kisses down her neck, rubbing against her smooth milky skin. He turned her around, pressing her against the wall. While his mouth was busy on her lips, his hands fumbled with the buttons of her blouse. She removed his shirt in one swift move, but Lorcan was unable to take hers off, fumbling again and ultimately yanking it open, tearing off all the buttons.

It was unusual of him, Orla thought. He knew every seam of her clothes, every zipper, button, and what-goes-where of a woman's dress. Sometimes Orla wondered how and where he got that knowledge.

Lorcan stopped. He looked at the buttons rolling across the floor. He then pulled her again into his arms and pressed his forehead against the wall. "I'm sorry," he whispered. "I'm out of my depth this time, Orla. I'm going to do my best to save us, but if I can't, I want you to get yourself out of here, do you hear me?" He had her face in his hands now, and they were standing forehead to forehead. She pushed him away.

"I saved your ass twice on Earth, and you think I'm useless now?"

"No. But you heard the Host. If it's doable, why hasn't anyone done it before? I can dig and find any data we need. I can fight. I can even kill. But magic! I don't even know where to start with that."

"Isn't that the very reason you'll need me? And if I'm not mistaken, I'm officially recruited in the mission, too. Do you seriously think I'm going to sit here and let you go on with this alone? And if we don't know anything about this creature, then you're going to need me there to help you find it!" The more she said, the angrier she became, and the higher in pitch her voice rose. Lorcan did his best to catch her fists as she angrily enunciated her little speech with them.

"Orla, I don't want you to get caught up in this. If I don't know what I'm doing, I can't let you go with me. It's dangerous." His voice was calm and neutral, but she knew that he was just letting her blow her steam off. She started crying, and he pulled her in close.

"If it's going to be as dangerous as you let on, then I'm not going to let you do it by yourself. You need me, and I need you. Please don't make me stay behind and worry about you. I want to come with you." When he saw the tears in her eyes, his voice became more soothing.

"All right. If that's what you want, then you can go with me. I don't want to be separated from you, either. But promise me if I fail, you'll go back to Earth and find my family. They will protect you because you are mine."

"I won't let you fail." They stood there in the middle of the control room, holding each other for countless minutes.

It was as dark and creepy as it could be inside the Daimon Gate. Lorcan approached Gate 131 with caution, pushing Orla behind him. He wasn't sure if coming here was a good idea, but they had to start somewhere. The aura of the area made it easy to imagine zombies lurking just around the corner. It wouldn't have surprised him to see bizarre-looking creatures darting at them from seemingly nowhere. This wasn't exactly a gate. Perhaps it hadn't been in operation for a long time. There was no door, no lights, no computer, and no sign of living creatures. The dark Gothic archway peered down at them, imposing and full of secrets. "This is used to be a gate, I think," Lorcan speculated.

Orla rubbed her hand along the wall, finding it damp as if it was perspiring. At the corner of the wall, her hand hit something lumpy. She moved closer to take a look, and the wall opened its eyes and blinked, sending her yelping leaping feet away from the wall. Lorcan darted to her, pushing her behind him. These weren't the wall's eyes—they were the eyes on an ancient man's face which was buried in the wall. Orla missed her weapons, the convenience of the rather violent devices she used to have on Earth. They would come in handy right now, she thought. She wagered Lorcan must have thought the same.

Lacking anything remotely threatening, Lorcan pointed his electronic notebook at the eyes of the man. "Don't move," Lorcan demanded, and then realized that was a stupid command—the man couldn't move. He was immobilized within the wall. Lorcan's eyes then widened as he came to a realization. "You were the gatekeeper!"

"He would smile and nod if he could," Orla commented as she had come to the same conclusion as Lorcan. "It must has been a long time since he's seen anyone. You think he speaks English?"

"Only one way to find out," Lorcan muttered. "Do you speak English? Please blink your eyes if you do."

The eyes blinked.

"We're going to find the key of Psuche to free you. Do you have any idea who took it or where it would be? Please blink for yes."

No blinking this time. Orla sighed. Lorcan paced, contemplating the possibilities. "I'm guessing each gate has its own unique key, am I correct?"

The eyes blinked. Lorcan nodded, a wave of energy rushing through him as he felt they were making progress. "You were a wizard before you became the gatekeeper?"

Blinks.

"Among nine thousand gates and nine thousand unique keys, the creature chose this particular gate and this particular key. Why?" Lorcan mumbled to himself. "The key has something to do with where you came from?"

There was no blinking.

"The key has something to do with you being a wizard?"

There was no blinking. Lorcan raked his hand through his hair. Orla approached. "Someone killed for the key, so it must be very important," Orla commented. The eyes blink rapidly.

Lorcan opened his electronic notebook. His fingers flew on the keyboard. He typed and typed, then paused, shaking his head, and resumed typing. In a short moment, Lorcan looked up and said, "The data suggests that there was a change of the gate key before your time. You were recruited to guard this gate and this key because of your magic. Does the key have anything to do with supernatural forces?"

The eyes blinked rapidly.

"Whoever got the key, can that person control the universes?"

There was no blinking.

"What about one particular universe?" The eyes blinked. Lorcan raised an eyebrow. "Eudaiz?" There was no reaction. "Xiilok?" There was no reaction again as Lorcan went through the list of universes connected to the Daimon Gate. The list was long, and there had been no further reaction from the eyes. Orla was pacing impatiently.

"Earth?" asked Lorcan.

Then eyes blinked rapidly. Sensing it, Orla whirled around. "Earth. Our friendly bloody Earth," she whispered.

Lorcan cleared his throat. "We might need to narrow things down a little bit. The Earth is quite large to look around aimlessly. Now this is the Eastern gate, so I guess I can safely narrow it down to the Eastern countries," he mumbled to himself, searching further on his notebook. Then his eyes sparked. "You're from Japan. Whoever took the key, he's from Japan as well?"

The eyes blinked rapidly. "So he stole the key to control Japan?" Orla deduced.

"Hey, don't roll your eyes. We're trying to help you here," Lorcan scolded.

"They stole the key to control the supernatural forces in Japan?" The eyes rolled again. Orla put her hands on her hips. "The mode of communication is that you blink your eyes to confirm a positive answer. Rolling your eyes is not acceptable. Keep doing that, and we'll leave you here to rot."

Lorcan lowered his voice so that he sounded calm. "So the key is in Japan now?"

The eyes blinked.

"Is that all you know?"

The eyes blinked again then drooped.

Lorcan waved his arms in the air. "Right. Japan it is. Not as bad as searching the entire Earth!"

They heard a *whoosh*. Orla's psychic ability had urged her to move just an instant before the arrow hit, so it only scraped her left arm. Lorcan charged in the general direction of the arrow's origination. Then all Orla heard were the sounds of men grunting and of kicks and punches hitting their target. Soon Lorcan emerged, dragging the man who had attacked her earlier. He was barely conscious. Lorcan continued to pound on the man. Whatever frustration he couldn't vent in the painstaking process of extracting information about the key from the entombed gatekeeper, he took out on this gatekeeper.

Orla pulled Lorcan back. "You'll kill him, Lorcan."

He gave the man a last kick before Orla pulled him out of reach of the man. "Scumbag," Lorcan snarled.

Lying on the ground, then man chuckled. "Yes, indeed I am a scumbag. But I'm alive. If you think you can use the Host against me, you're mistaken. I haven't done anything wrong, but you have. Now he's lied for you—he won't last long, Host or not."

"What the fuck are you talking about?"

"What I asked you to do wouldn't cost you anything. Giving Ciaran up is not going to end your world, but reporting me to the Host and getting him to back you will end both your world and his."

The man pulled himself up onto his knees.

"Who are you?" Orla asked.

The man smirked. "You don't need to know who I am. I gave you options. I asked you to do a very simple thing for me, but you didn't. You chose to go against me, and you helped a stranger like Ciaran LeBlanc. Now, no one is going to help you." Then in front of Lorcan and Orla, he surged up, ran at the buried gatekeeper, aimed his crossbow between the eyes, and shot. The eyes of the buried gatekeeper flared up, glassed over, and then vanished. Lorcan snarled and charged at the man, but he swung open a gatekeeper's dimensional hole, dove in, and disappeared. Lorcan didn't bother giving chase. He pulled out his handkerchief and took care of the cut on Orla's arm.

As soon as they entered the hallway of their castle, they could see the lights from the control room and hear the signals echoing down the corridor. The robots announced that they had visitors and the visitors would like to see both of them. "Sure, so we're guests in our own home now," Orla remarked. Lorcan's jaw clenched, and his striking blue eyes darkened. He knew this was serious.

In the control room, they found the holocast of three members of the Daimon Gate council, one of them the Host. One of the other two was a tall creature with a human shape but an alien face. There was no way for Lorcan and Orla to adjust to the appearance of the person from their earthly aesthetic standards. When the man spoke, streams of text translation in English floated in the air in front of him. The other member was a man in his late sixties who spoke with a New York accent.

"I'm sorry to intrude on your private space again. Since we last spoke, something happened in the council, and we need you to clarify some information," the Host said, his eyes locked with Lorcan's. Lorcan knew that was a warning sign.

He cleared his throat. "Sure. I'll give you as much information as I know. But before we start, I'd like to let you know that the gatekeeper at Gate 131 was killed just now. The information will be ready for you at central when you return."

"Killed? By whom?" the Host asked.

"The gatekeeper who attacked Orla came back and shot at us when we were talking to the gatekeeper at Gate 131. Then he shot him dead and disappeared into a dimensional hole."

The alien-like council member raised his voice, "How do you know the attacker was a gatekeeper?"

"He declared himself as a gatekeeper," Lorcan affirmed.

"Gatekeepers kill one another inside the Daimon Gate?" the man with the New York accent asked, shocked.

"We will make sure this is an isolated case," the Host spoke quietly.

The alien-like member shifted. "That's not why we are here. There were some discrepancies in the between the amount of information you provided us when you joined and the information we received just now. When did you declare Orla as a trained sorceress?"

Lorcan shoved his hands into his pant pockets and shrugged. "As far as I remember, we declared it right at the beginning—but not before I took the test because at that point I wasn't sure whether I had passed." A slight smile came across the Host's face. Lorcan continued, "I was always up front about Orla's talents."

"So you're saying that Orla's skills and talents in using magic were what got you both recruited?"

"Absolutely."

"All information was declared to the recruiter before you joined? Can you confirm that again?"

"Affirmative," Lorcan said, his hands clammy inside his pockets. But he trusted his poker face.

The Host showed signs of relief. The man with the alien face seemed happy with Lorcan's responses. The council member with the New York accent leaned back in his chair, contemplating, and asked, "What proof do we have of this?"

"What would you like to see?" Orla asked.

"Well, if you were recruited because of your talents, and you have had more than a month inside the Daimon Gate to learn the system and prepare, when can we expect you deliver the key to us?"

"As soon as you allow us to leave, we can get ready, investigate and dredge up a bit more information, and then we'll be on our way. As for when we can deliver the key, it depends on our progress at the site," Lorcan responded.

"Where's the site?" the alien-like man asked.

"Japan."

The council nodded in satisfaction. They had obviously never been to the place, Orla thought, as Japan was quite an enormous site to search for a little key.

The New Yorker smiled. "You know that the Host guarantees your information with his credibility, so use his trust wisely."

"Understood," Lorcan said solemnly.

Before he left with the holocast of other council members, the Host nodded slightly and smiled at Lorcan and Orla.

Once all the visitors had gone, tears poured down Orla's face. "You don't have a clue where the key is, do you, except that it might be somewhere in Japan?"

Lorcan shook his head. He pulled Orla into his arms and held her tight. "I'll figure it out," he whispered. "It's not just us now, it's the Host's credibility on the line. I don't want to think about the consequences if they find out we bluffed—and the Host endorsed it."

CHAPTER 4

Orla walked into the control room and found Lorcan still hunched over the computer. He had worked for the equivalent of thirty hours straight. They didn't use the same time reference here, so Orla had to use the computer translator for even the simplest of tasks, such as checking how long it had been since Lorcan had set foot outside that control room.

His fingers worked tirelessly on the keyboard as Orla opened the door to his office. He was so caught up in what he was doing that he didn't hear her approach and ask, "Find anything yet?"

He was startled, but he didn't let on. It was bad that he'd already lost his attention to details around him in this dimension. He'd need all of his old skills back for this assignment, and if he was this rusty, it wasn't a good sign. "I think so. I'm checking a few more things just to be sure, but I'm pretty sure I know where we'll be heading to. Are you ready?"

Orla nodded. She was back in the business mode she'd reserved for her jobs when they lived on Earth.

"The bad news is that we'll be going back to Earth. The good news is that I've found a link between the key of Psuche and a secret Japanese society called the Ryojin. We'll be heading to the Kaihanshin Prefecture. A combination of factual data, historical events, and suggestions from my underground sources led me to this conclusion, so it's not just a wild guess."

"Underground sources!" She winked at him.

He winked back, erased all of his research, and closed his computer. "We have a little time before we leave . . . how about a celebratory romp in the sack?" Orla laughed as he picked her up and carried her to their bedroom.

"Aren't you only supposed to carry me across the threshold if we get married?"

"Marry me then. Otherwise I'll be breaking the rules, and that wouldn't be good, now would it?" They both fell silent as Lorcan's innocent line reminded them that they had indeed broken the rules of this place, and death lingered at their door.

"Let's just forget about all of that right now, okay? I don't want to think about serious things right now." She rubbed her thumbs at the shadows that darted in and out of his striking blue eyes. Then she pulled his head down and kissed him, long and hard. He reciprocated her newfound level of energy and lay her on the bed, taking his shirt off before he climbed on top of her . . .

The trip to Japan was a nonevent. Unlike on Earth, where they had to be physically in transit, travel the distance, and face all the troubles associated with international travel, now they had only to open the portal, and in the blink of an eye, they had reached their destination.

"Welcome to Japan. We're in the second largest city in the country, next to Tokyo of course." Lorcan smiled. Orla's eyes were wide, and her mouth hung open. This was the most beautiful place she'd ever seen. It was a mix between old-world Japan and the modernization of the 21st century. She felt like this would be a wonderful place to live out the rest of her days with Lorcan if the mission should fail. She was getting ready to tell Lorcan that, but he was too busy staring at the ground. She nudged him gently, but he still didn't break his focus.

She cleared her throat to no avail. She nudged him again, a little harder, trying to get his attention. He nearly stumbled and finally looked up at her. "What?"

"I wanted you to take in the beauty of this city, but all you're doing is staring at the dirt. What gives?"

He stared at her blankly for a minute, then laughed. "I'm sorry. I was trying to find someone to help us. The contact you gave me doesn't seem to be here."

"Contact?"

"Well, you told me some messenger called Kitsune would guide us. I sent a message and got a response that the messenger would be here. But I don't see anyone."

Orla laughed at Lorcan's confusion.

"Do you plan to tell me what's going on, or am I just going to learn everything as we go?" There was a definite note of irritability in his voice, and Orla knew that it was in her best interest to explain.

"A kitsune is a sort of intermediary between the world we live in and the Japanese otherworld. They're the gatekeepers that protect us from the dragons and demons that try to break through into our world. They're also damn good at finding people," Orla said solemnly, trying to keep a straight face.

"Oh, so it's not a guide-bug."

She lifted an eyebrow. "A guide-bug?"

"Like a GPS, a very advanced one."

"Oh no." Orla laughed again. "It's a magical animal. You'll know it when you see it."

"Right. But now, because we don't see it, we might have to use my robot. We need to find a woman named Chiyo Maki. She's the last surviving member of the Maki family, and they're the head family in the Ryojin group. Chiyo is a medical doctor, and she didn't seem to have much to do with the family business. But at least, it's a lead. The Ryojin group seems to have disappeared a few decades ago, but they might still have some of the items. If we're lucky, they'll have the key."

"Okay, even if they do have it, how are we going to get it from them? It's not like we packed a substantial amount of money or anything. You should have told me that we were going antique shopping." Orla smiled and winked at Lorcan. "Unless you want me to use the skills that I made a living with on Earth." Lorcan laughed. She loved that he laughed. The shadows still hovered in his eyes, but as long as he eased up a bit, she would feel much better.

Then Orla suddenly squatted down and began talking to nothingness. Lorcan blinked. The shape of a little brown fox was slowly starting to become visible. This was very interesting to him. The little thing twitched its tail and then darted off down the street a few feet, turning around to see if they were coming. "That's our guide. Let's go." Orla smiled brightly. "It won't bite. But if it does, I'll protect you." She pecked Lorcan on the cheek and turned on her heel to follow the magical animal.

Two hours later, Lorcan and Orla were shuffling along on very tired feet when the little fox jumped up on a stoop and began to clean its paw. Orla thanked it, and Lorcan watched in fascination as the little fox became invisible. The only thing he could see was a distortion of the objects behind it. Then it moved, and it was gone. They were standing in front of an old Japanese house, tiered with many roofs. Lorcan pushed the doorbell, and a few minutes later, a young woman in her late twenties with long, straight black hair and deep, soulful brown eyes answered.

"Hello? May I help you?"

Lorcan donned his most charming smile. "Yes, we're looking for Doctor Chiyo Maki." He didn't want to divulge information to the wrong person, so he didn't say anything else.

"That's me. What is this about?" Her English carried a strong accent, but both Lorcan and Orla could understand her.

"We're looking to buy a unique piece from an antique collection your family owned long ago. May we come in?" The woman eyed them for a few minutes longer, then stood back so they could enter. Apparently she didn't want to discuss the delicate nature of the Royjin business in the open. She shut the door behind them and ushered them into the kitchen. The decorations were classic Japanese, but the furniture was modern. The three sat down at the kitchen table.

Something was wrong, Orla thought. It wasn't the house, or the air, but maybe the woman. *What are you up to, stranger?* Orla thought. What bothered her was the typical Japanese-style decoration in the house. Minimalist. Everything was squeaky clean. The floor looked as if you could eat from it. The conservative look on the woman's face and the tasteful decoration in the house didn't gel with the fact that the woman would invite strangers inside so easily.

"You have come to talk to me about the Royjin pieces," the woman said. It was a statement, not a question. Lorcan opened his mouth to answer, but she was already on her cell phone, speaking rapidly in Japanese. She snapped her phone shut with a little more emphasis than was necessary. "The business died with my grandfather in the Kobe earthquake of 1995. I have no involvement with it."

"Were the antiques sold to another family?" Lorcan asked.

Chiyo narrowed her eyes. "Yes."

Chiyo was lying, and Orla knew it. Lorcan didn't need Orla's psychic abilities to tell that Chiyo had lied. He glanced at Orla, and then turned back to Chiyo. "We don't mean any harm."

"Oh, I am sure you don't." The woman smiled again. "But I don't have what you need. Would you like some tea?"

"Can you tell us to which family the antiques were sold?" Lorcan asked.

"As I said, I'm not involved with the family's business. So I don't know. I'm sorry I can't help you."

"If you don't have the antiques, and you don't know where they are, then there is no point for us to bother you further," Lorcan commented.

"All right then. I'll see you to the door."

At the door, Lorcan turned around. "Do you know where we can find the family business records? Although you're not involved with the business, you would know some basic facts and some contacts such as accountants or lawyers, right?"

The woman shook her head.

"You don't know? Or you don't want to tell us?" Orla asked.

From the corner of his eye, Lorcan saw a police uniform. "Orla," he called out, gesturing in the direction of the police. Orla saw looked again at Chiyo. The woman shoved Orla and Lorcan outside the door.

"Now ask these questions to the police, you Yakuz spies!" Chiyo slammed the door closed. Orla and Lorcan glanced at the corner street. If they hurried, they could get out of here before the police arrived. They ran. They had just managed to make it a block over when they heard the sirens.

"Crazy bitch! I say we go back there and beat it out of her!" Orla was angry, and Lorcan could understand why, but he had to calm her down before she got them in trouble.

"It's okay. We'll just find another way to get the answers we need."

She cut him off with a groan. "And where exactly are we going to find these answers? Because it looks like Doctor Barbie in there doesn't want to help." Lorcan refrained from laughing at her joke because it would only encourage her.

"I have my portable laptop in the suitcase, and I can look up a few things before continue." He dug around in his suitcase for a little while, then pulled out his laptop. They were near a café, so the Wi-Fi reached their position. He typed quickly, and Orla felt a sense of pride at how good he was at his job. She stood there silently, keeping an eye out for the police while he did his search. When he snapped his laptop shut with a grin, she knew he had something.

"All right, there's a temple not too far from here, and it looks like Chiyo's grandfather's remains are there. It was a big to-do back then when they started to bury the Earthquake victims, so it wasn't too hard for me to find. Let's go."

"Not too far?"

Lorcan smiled. "About twenty minutes, darling. I can piggyback you, if that's what you'd prefer."

Orla groaned at the fact that they would be walking some more, but there was nothing to be done about it.

CHAPTER 5

Twenty minutes or so later, they'd found the temple. From the outside, there was nothing special about it. It was quiet and peaceful. The curvy roofs decorated with beautiful oriental symbols and painted with red and gold were mesmerizing. The landscape and the garden were designed and maintained meticulously with love and passion. Orla admired the temple so much that she totally forgot the gigantic problem now in front of her—the temple equals dead people, and Lorcan suffered from severe necrophobia, a fear of dead things. He had said nothing yet, but he paused on the path and looked at the temple as if it would eat him alive.

She turned and approached Lorcan, reaching out to touch his shoulders and give him comfort and assurance, but he raised his arms to stop her. "I'll be okay."

"You don't look okay." Sweat trickled down his forehead. Orla knew his hands were clammy and his heart was racing. "Are you sure?" she asked.

Lorcan nodded again. He swallowed hard, looking up at the roofs of the temples, seeing the statues of the deities guarding the gates between Heaven and Hell looking down at him. He shook his head, staring down at the ground for a short moment, and then made his way into the temple.

Inside the temple, rows and rows of remains sat in jars, marked by shiny golden plaques. Orla rolled her eyes. All the words were in Japanese. Normally, Lorcan would have automatically whisked out his device for a translation, but given his current mental status, she thought it best to remind him.

"Lorcan."

"Huh?"

"All the words are in Japanese."

"Right." No reaction from Lorcan as his eyes glazed over the rows and rows of jars containing the ashes of dead people.

"Lorcan."

"Huh?"

"All right, honey, I'll need you to get your device out and read the Japanese for me."

"Oh, that's right." He fumbled with his bag and pulled out his laptop. He used a small device to scan the text. They walked past all the plaques, and the Japanese words appeared on the screen of Lorcan's device in familiar English letters. Once they had the translation under control, it wasn't hard to find the remains of Chiyo's grandfather. The names of the individuals were written on plaques, and Orla busied herself scouting out the names.

Orla approached the jar of Chiyo's grandfather's remains to see if she could glean any information. But before she could move closer, a sea of red hair flowed in front of her. A woman slid in, standing between Orla and the ashes. The woman turned around. Her flaming red hair framed an attractive, fox-like face, long and cut with sharp angles. Orla silently admired the beauty of the woman. The woman arched an eyebrow and didn't seem to want to move.

"Excuse me, I need to see this, please." It was hard for Orla to be polite when she was still felt outrage at Chiyo's treatment of them, but she did her best. The woman gave her a look she couldn't read, but she didn't move. Orla's blood was starting to boil. "Look, I'm on a mission here, lady, and you're in my way. So step back for a minute." The woman didn't say anything to her, nor did she step away. Orla grabbed her shoulder to push her back a little, but the woman's hands came up lightning fast, breaking her grip before she'd been moved an inch. Orla's temper got the better of her, and she reached out to slap the woman. The woman grabbed Orla's hand before it hit her. She looked stunned at what Orla had just done. She rocked back on her feet and struck a fighting position. Orla grinned at her and took her own fighting stance—she was in the mood for a good fight.

"No, no, women, we're in a temple, for God's sake." Lorcan charged over to pull Orla aside. At the same time, Fox Face flew through the air and landed a kick which had been intended for Orla, but hit Lorcan's back instead. He stumbled and turned around. "Look, I don't fight women, okay. But if you keep attacking my wife, I'll make an exception."

"We're not married yet, you can't call me your wife, and I don't need you to protect me." Orla snarled and leaped at Fox Face. Fox Face turned quickly and gave Orla a roundhouse kick, connecting with Orla's middle and sending her reeling backwards, rolling outside of the temple.

Orla stood up, wheezing. Lorcan went after her. Once outdoors, he was back to his alert self. Fox Face was approaching Orla, a knowing smile on her face. Orla wanted to wipe that smile off with her foot. She lunged at the woman, tackling her around the waist and throwing her to the ground. Either Fox Face hadn't been trained in grappling, or she was just stunned to find herself on the floor with Orla on top of her, because she let Orla get a good punch in to her face before she began to protect herself.

"I know you understood what I was saying. Want to tell me why you wouldn't move?" Orla was giving her a chance to talk, but it was really just to gloat over the bruise that was blooming ever so nicely on the woman's pale face. Fox Face didn't respond, and that angered Orla even further. But what Orla didn't see until it was arcing towards her chest was the knife that Fox Face had pulled out of nowhere. Orla let out a squeal and threw her arm down at an angle, forcing the blade and its wielding arm go in an entirely different direction. The woman dropped the knife, and it skittered across the worn cobblestones until it came to rest at Lorcan's feet. He picked it up and pocketed it quickly before anyone could see what had happened.

"No, Orla, don't fight. We've got things to do." Lorcan tried to hold her back, but then the woman tried to run at Orla. "Hey lady, calm down. Let's talk." Lorcan stood in the way to stop her from jumping on Orla. She gave him a hard kick, pushing him to the ground. Lorcan stood. "That's enough! This is stupid." He grabbed the woman from behind while she scuffled with Orla and dragged her away. The woman wriggled but couldn't release herself from Lorcan's grip. She snarled and shouted for release in Japanese. Lorcan didn't need the device to translate—he knew what she was cursing about. He refused to let go, dragging her as far away from Orla as possible. As Lorcan's right arm wrapped around the woman's neck from behind, she tilted her head and bit at his right wrist. As soon as her teeth sank into his flesh, he loosed his grip and staggered back. He leaned against a tree, holding on to it to keep his balance. He felt as if the ground under his feet was moving.

The woman stumbled backward. She kept her stance, wiped her mouth, and locked her gaze on Lorcan. Then her skin began to glow all over in a warm shade of light, and seconds later, a red fox sat in front of an astonished Lorcan and Orla. Before Orla could pulled her jaw closed, the fox darted over and bit Orla, then scampered away. It was making its way to the temple exit when Orla pulled her own knife out of her boot and threw it at the fox. The fox stopped and transformed back into the red-haired woman, throwing a blaze of flame in Orla's direction. Unfortunately, the blast of flame rerouted the knife Orla had thrown, and it ended up striking Lorcan instead. He caught the impact of the knife and the fire at the same time.

The fox woman ran away, and Orla threw herself to the ground next to Lorcan. She didn't have to be a doctor to know that he was injured very badly . . . again. "Hey. Hang in there for me, okay? I'm going to take you somewhere where they can help you. Just hang in there for me."

Lorcan opened his mouth to speak, but he couldn't force any sound past his lips. He hated to see the tears welling in Orla's eyes. He tried, but he wasn't able to move. Yet his mind was crystal clear. There was a surge of something strange running through his body, and he didn't care for it. It was burning hot. It wasn't the wounds that held him down. It was something else, something new. He forced his eyes open.

Orla caressed his face. "Okay Lorcan, you have to try for me. I can't carry you. Come on, baby, sit up for me." Lorcan summoned as much energy as he could, and with her help, he sat up. It felt like being inside a front-loading washing machine.

They stood up, and Orla wrapped his arm around her shoulders. Step by step, the made it along the narrow road back to the village. Chiyo was a medical doctor. Orla had no idea where else to go. She didn't know where a medical center or hospital might be. She didn't speak Japanese and couldn't understand the street signs and storefronts. There wasn't any time for her to regret that she could have been a bit more cultural.

She backtracked as far as she needed to get to Chiyo's house, and she only got lost once. Lorcan stumbled to the ground a couple of times, but he kept up. At the house, she rang the doorbell and waited. Chiyo came to the door.

"You again! I will not have spies in my house! I'm calling the police."

Orla leaned Lorcan up against the side of the house and grabbed the woman by the throat. "Listen here. He's very badly hurt, and you're a doctor. We're not spies or lunatics. I just want you to help him. I'm pretty sure your Hippocratic Oath says that you can do no harm. If you send us back out into the streets, he's going to die, and I'm pretty sure that death counts as harm, so how about you let us in and tend to him?" Before Chiyo could answer, Lorcan's eyes rolled back, and he fell face down onto the ground, half in and half out of the house.

The woman reached up and gently removed Orla's fingers from her throat. "If he stays like that, I can't close the door, either with you in or outside of my house. Bring him in. I'll see what I can do." The two women struggled with Lorcan's dead weight, but they were able to lay him on the living room floor, tucked among the cushions. Chiyo disappeared into the next room and then came bustling in with a black leather doctor's bag. She pointed to the corridor. "The guest room is upstairs on the left."

"What?"

"Close the door on your way out."

"Huh?"

"You want me to treat him or not?"

"Yes, of course. Please. But can I stay?"

Chiyo glared at Orla.

"I guess not," Orla muttered and turned on her heel. She didn't go upstairs to the guest room but waited outside. It seemed like decades. Orla sat on the floor, leaning against the wall, and fell asleep. When she woke and tried to get back into the living room, the door was locked. "Doctor my ass," Orla muttered and sat back down on the floor.

CHAPTER 6

Orla wasn't at all happy with being locked out, but she knew she couldn't be pushy right now because Lorcan's life hung in Chiyo's hands. She waited for what seemed like hours, pacing back and forth in the hallway, thinking that she might actually see the carpet start to fray under her feet. When the door finally opened, Orla ran to it and tried to push through, but Chiyo stood in her way.

"He's asleep right now. You can't go in there. He's lucky to be alive with those injuries." Her voice was hard, and she cast a condescending look at Orla.

"Watch your tone, doc. I would've taken the knife for him if I could have, regardless of whether he was happy about it or not." She got the words out through teeth gritted in anger.

Chiyo just shrugged and walked away.

"Listen here. If it weren't for the fact that you threw us out of your house instead of offering to help us, we wouldn't have had to go there to search for your grandfather's remains." That stopped Chiyo short. She turned around, anger flashing from her eyes, and her cheeks growing red.

"How dare you defile my grandfather's memory by looking for him like common grave robbers! I'm sure I'm not the only one who's ever told you no. I think you need to start taking rejection a little better."

Orla was barely controlling herself, and her hands were clenched into shaking fists at her sides when she threw her next verbal barb. "Grave robbers? Look who's talking. This might be beyond your understanding, but in the place we call home, someone from here—very possibly a member of your extended family—robbed a man of a key and buried him in a wall, leaving him to rot. We're simply try to retrieve the key and return it. So don't you dare stick that robber label on us."

"Robbery and murder? What exactly are you accusing my family of?" Chiyo snarled.

"Look at who is not taking criticism well *now*."

"You're only guests in my house. Remember that I can kick you out again at any time."

Lorcan woke in the living room. Opening his eyes and at the blurry edges of his vision, he saw elegant wallpaper and tastefully arranged furniture. He felt his body comfortably tucked under a thick blanket. He could hear the argument between Orla and Chiyo echoing in from the corridor. He tried to shift, but his limbs seemed to weigh a ton. He closed his eyes, concentrated, and tried to take mental inventory. He had been dragging a woman away from Orla when the woman bit him and then turned into a fox. He remembered it now. All of it. The sensation of her teeth sinking into his flesh. It hadn't hurt, but he remembered the inexplicable feeling of something flooding into him. It was like her bite had flipped a switch and opened a floodgate, except what poured into him wasn't water but something else. Exactly what, he wasn't sure.

He opened his eyes again and found his vision and strength had improved significantly. He shifted, freed his hands, and felt the blanket rub against his skin. He lifted it, looking underneath, and as he predicted, he was half naked. The wound on his abdomen had been dressed carefully. Lorcan shifted and sat up. For a split second, he saw the skin on his arm glow an electric blue. He shook his head and looked again—his skin had gone back to normal.

"What the fuck!" Lorcan mumbled to himself and sat up, leaning against a low coffee table nearby. It was clear to him that the two women hadn't been able to move his dead weight without doing more damage to him, so they had treated him right on the floor in the middle of the living room. He felt as if energy was returning to him in strong waves—it was the same healing feeling he'd had when Orla used the dark magic to heal him in London. It was also the very reason they'd had to take refuge in the Daimon Gate. "Oh, why did you do that again, Orla?" he mumbled to himself. He grabbed his shirt, which was folded neatly on the coffee table nearby, and put it on.

Lorcan found Orla with her hands on her hips at the end of the corridor by the kitchen, snarling at Chiyo, who was responding in a no less aggressive manner. The scene made Lorcan want to chuckle, but he didn't think it wise to risk aggravating the situation.

"How's a man supposed to get any sleep around here with you women practicing your Christmas carols," Lorcan said from the doorway. Orla turned around and blushed a little as she came over to his side, hugging him gently.

"You shouldn't be up. You were hurt very badly, and you can't heal if you don't rest." There was a sternness to Chiyo's voice again, and Orla recognized that she'd turned back into a doctor.

"I think you'll find that I'm doing much better already." He winked at Orla, and she smiled.

Chiyo obviously didn't appreciate her patients talking back to her. "Go lie back down, and I'll look you over." She donned an arrogant tone and stared at Lorcan as sternly as she could. Lorcan nodded and returned to the living room. Orla trailed right behind him, being sure to sneak into the room before Chiyo this time so the other woman couldn't throw her out. Lorcan did as he was told and lay back down on the blanket. Chiyo rummaged through her doctor's bag and took out her stethoscope. She listened to his heart and lungs, claiming they were back to a normal rhythm. She lifted the bandage to have a look at the wound.

"You're doing very well," Chiyo concluded. Her tone was as smooth as still water, but her face betrayed her. Catching the look, Orla narrowed her eyes. She opened her mouth to say something, but in anticipation, Lorcan shook his head, signaling Orla not to say anything. She obliged.

Chiyo cleared her throat. "You wound has healed." Orla arched an eyebrow and said nothing as Chiyo began to remove Lorcan's bandages. His injuries looked like they'd been healing for weeks instead of barely an hour. "How did you do this? If you could do this by yourself, then why did you come to me for help? You're recovering faster than I've ever seen anyone recover. It's a medical mystery. One that I would like to study."

"He's not a lab rat in a drug trial. You're not going to study him." Orla spat her words at the doctor. "And if he's healed, may we have a moment in private?" Orla was surprised by the politeness of her voice.

Lorcan smiled. "I need to talk to her, doc. Would you mind stepping out for a few minutes?"

Chiyo glared at both of them, but kept her voice toned down. "You still need rest. The guest room upstairs on the left is yours. You'll have your privacy there. I'm not leaving my own living room."

Lorcan nodded. "Understood. I appreciate that." He stood and went upstairs with Orla.

Inside the guest room, Orla flipped Lorcan's shirt up and stared at the healing wound. "How did you manage to heal so quickly? The first time it was because I helped you, but this time, I know it wasn't me." Orla kept her voice low because she had the sneaking suspicion that Chiyo was listening at the door.

"I thought I was the one who'd be asking the questions. I thought you'd used the black magic again."

Orla shook her head. "I'm not stupid enough to summon my ancestors while we're in a place where we can't go anywhere without your translator and my guide fox. In that case, we shouldn't bother with the key at all because we'd soon be dead."

"The key is no longer just *our* problem, Orla. The Host is now involved in all this."

"I know, I know."

"So you really didn't use any magic on me this time?"

Orla stared at Lorcan. "Hey, you're healed, but not a hundred percent yet. You don't want to upset me."

Lorcan raised his arms, seeking peace and a truce. Orla smiled, tiptoed, and kissed him. She pulled him into her arms and embraced him, her body shuddering with emotions. "Oh God, you went down like a stone." He held on to her and kissed her forehead. "I know I scared you. I'm sorry."

"It's not your fault. The bitch bit you."

Lorcan nodded. "Not everyone have a chance to be bitten by a fox."

"It's not remotely funny."

Lorcan glanced at the small window which overlooked the roof of the ground level of the house. "What are you not telling me?" Orla asked.

"What?"

"You heard me. You have that I'm-not-telling-her-just-yet face."

"I don't even know what that means."

She jabbed her finger at his chest. "You know what I mean. You're a smart-ass. You always know." She pushed him so that he was off-balance and fell down to the futon.

"Now that we have a room to ourselves, what do you say we really celebrate my ability to heal so quickly?" He wiggled his eyebrows at her, and Orla felt herself laugh for the first time in what seemed like weeks. She wriggled against him, and he groaned into her ear. "You know, if you don't stop that, I'm not going to be accountable for my actions, missy." Orla didn't say a word, just wriggled against him again.

A pale fox-like face stared back at her from the mirror. It had been a long time since she had spared a moment for such vanity. People told her she was beautiful, but what was the use of her beauty? she wondered. She was raised to be the female alpha of her werefox clan, a rare group with an important and sacred mission that had started before her time, but now she just wanted to be an ordinary woman, entitled to live a life with the freedom to love and have a family.

She had bitten a man today. The tradition of the werefoxes was that biting was a mating ritual. Unless forced or acting in self-defense, biting marked a mate for life. When a fox chose a mating partner, it all started with an intentional bite. It was like human consensual sex. She smiled at the thought. She spent way too much time with humans.

The rules didn't apply in her case because she had bitten in self-defense, and he was human. She could bite and kill any other creatures except foxes. She touched her lips. The tingling sensation of his blood on her lips and in her mouth still remained. *What is this man?* she thought. She had bitten humans before, but they had tasted nothing like this. His blood had actually forced her to shift into her fox form right in the middle of a fight.

Lorcan stared up to the ceiling, contemplating the next move for both of them. He sat up abruptly and jumped out of the futon. He heard Orla giggle. Lorcan looked down and darted back to the futon to grab his pants and put them on. He pulled out his laptop, started it, and sat on the floor to work.

"What do you have in mind?" Orla asked.

Lorcan didn't hear her. He typed quickly, mumbled, cursed to himself, then typed again. Orla rolled deeper into the blanket. When Lorcan was engaged in his tech world, the smartest thing for her to do was to treat herself to a nap.

"Whoa, whoa! No! Fuck!" Lorcan's curses drew Orla out of her daydream.

"What's up, Lorcan?"

"Lost the signals. Goddamn it."

Orla narrowed her eyes. "You're not hooking up to your system in the Daimon Gate, are you?"

He nodded. "Just a thought coming across my mind. The gatekeeper who attacked you, he wanted to bring Ciaran down. Exposing a computer manipulation is pretty low. But what if that's all he's got? All he was thinking about? Think about that incident again, Orla. Apart from you and me, who else knows about this within the Daimon Gate? No one except Prince Brandon, right?"

Orla sat up. "But Ciaran risked his life to change the data in the system to save Brandon. Why would Brandon want to harm Ciaran?"

"Well, that's what I was checking into before I lost the signals. Ciaran mentioned that the princess had cheated the system—that's why both the prince and the princess were facing the death penalty. Ciaran also said he owed the prince a favor, so he manipulated the system to reduce the death sentence to a demotion."

"Shouldn't Brandon be grateful for that?"

"Well, I would, if it were me, Orla. But a guy like Brandon, a guy who would attack a woman and kill an unarmed helpless man, wouldn't behave in the same way as a rational person would. What if he considered the demotion to be worse than death? Maybe he would rather die than losing his privilege. In that case, by saving them, Ciaran may have actually taken away the prince's right to die in privilege."

"Who would have thought about that?"

"It's not rational. Definitely not normal. But it can't be as rare as being bitten by a fox!" Lorcan smiled.

"You bet. So you think the gatekeeper who attacked me is Prince Brandon?"

Lorcan nodded. "Pretty sure of it now. The data suggested he was demoted from gatekeeper of the Red Castle to a minor gatekeeper of a creek. It was like a sympathy demotion, a token position. That would have been an insult to him. And also, the data suggests that he had dismissed himself from his position yesterday and vanished."

"Vanished?"

"Outside the Daimon Gate. My prediction is that after attacking us at Gate 131 and killing the defenseless gatekeeper there, he knew he would be facing severe punishment, so he fled."

"Sadistic son of a bitch will seek revenge on us. If he returned Ciaran's favor by vengeance, what would he make of us reporting him to the Host and aggravating his already bad situation?"

Lorcan smiled. "He'll turn into a little ghost and haunt us for the rest of our lives."

Orla sat up, pressing her forehead head to her knees. "I can deal with ghosts."

Lorcan crawled over and hugged her. "You're not doing anything by yourself. We'll do it together. Personally, I prefer animals to ghosts," Lorcan whispered.

She looked up at him, "You're thinking of the werefox?"

Lorcan rubbed his nose into Orla's hair and muffled, "Now *that* animal is definitely weird and mysterious. I'm not sure of my preference anymore. Can I lie down for another minute?"

"Sure you can."

CHAPTER 7

Later that night, Orla was snuggling next to Lorcan, trying to sleep, when she sat bolt upright. She thought she'd heard something downstairs. She tried to look into the darkness around her with her dulled vision, but she could see only shadows and vague shapes. She was ready to lie down again, chalking it up to a figment of her imagination, but then she heard it again. It was a faint tapping sound, almost like in the movies where archaeologists tap away at artifacts with tiny hammers and chisels. She reached her hand out to Lorcan, gently shaking his shoulder. He mumbled in his sleep and rolled away from her.

Sitting in the dark, listening to the noises becoming steadily louder, a sheen of sweat beaded on her forehead. She began searching the dark room for something close at hand she might be able to use as a weapon. If she got up, whoever was breaking in downstairs would hear her and probably run away before they had a chance to question him.

"Lorcan! Wake up! Someone's breaking in downstairs." Her voice quavered a little as she whispered, and she was mildly embarrassed by it. She was not usually easily scared, unless it came to Lorcan getting hurt. She felt like one of those hysterical women in horror movies who always ended up dead because they were stupid. She shook him again, and this time he woke up. He opened his mouth to ask her what was going on, but then he heard it, too. He sat up like Orla, looking around as she had for a weapon.

"Do you really think we'll need weapons? I think the two of us can handle him together. Come on. It's the least we can do for our host." The sarcasm dripping from Orla's voice almost made Lorcan laugh, but he held back.

The two of them slid out of the room, inching along the corridor by trying to step only on areas of the floor that wouldn't creak. They managed to get downstairs, although to Orla it felt like it took an hour. As they crept into the kitchen, they could see the soft moonlight shining down on a figure climbing in through the little window over the sink. They stood in the shadows, one on either side of the doorway, waiting for him to come close enough for the first blow. Orla had to control herself because the intruder was really bungling the situation. He'd gotten part of his shoe stuck in the garbage disposal, and she had to ignore the urge to turn it on. Lorcan must have been fighting an urge to laugh as well because she saw his hand go to his mouth.

The man finally got himself situated, presumably cursing in Japanese. He wore a nice suit, and she thought that a little odd for a late night intrusion. He straightened his suit, then reached behind him, through the window, to pick up a small bouquet of roses. Okay, this had now become the strangest break-in that Orla had ever witnessed. And she'd been a part of quite a few. She stepped forward and dealt the man a quick blow to the nose, sending him reeling back. He threw his arms into the sink to steady himself. The roses went flying, and Lorcan ran to catch them. The man was blabbering in Japanese, which neither Orla nor Lorcan could understand, but at one point he raised his voice and yelled Chiyo's name. Not two seconds later, a loud clattering came down the stairs, and Chiyo raced into the kitchen, turning on the lights. She was dressed to the nines, ready for a night out on the town. She'd managed to get a later shift at the hospital, and she'd been waiting for her date.

"Stop! What are you doing?" Chiyo assessed the situation quickly, then darted between Orla and the man, holding her hands out to halt the next punch. "Leave him alone!"

"I don't know if you noticed, but this piece of trash here just broke in through your window. Do you want to be kidnapped and murdered in the middle of the night? It looks like you dressed the part." Orla's drawl made Chiyo's cheeks turn red, and she didn't look happy at all.

"Why don't you sit down, and we'll explain." Chiyo had one hand up to her head like she was suffering from a very annoying headache. The man in the suit sat down at the kitchen table, put his hands in front of him, and waited quietly. Chiyo sat down, too, motioning for Orla and Lorcan to follow suit. They did so, but both of them now had suspicion in their eyes. "I'll start from the beginning. This man is Goro Kagome. He used to belong to the group Yakuz."

Lorcan interrupted. "You mean he's one of those spies that you accused *us* of being? You threw us out without even listening!" Lorcan was beginning to let anger win out over curiosity, and that usually wasn't a good sign.

"He's not Yakuz anymore. He left them. It was difficult because he belonged to the worst branch of them, but he did it. We've been together for a while now, and the only way that we can see each other is in secret. I should have warned you that I had guests, Goro. I'm sorry." Chiyo turned to look at the pair across the table from her. "And I'm sorry that I didn't warn you that he was coming tonight. It would have saved us all a lot of trouble."

Lorcan threw the roses at her. "Then I guess these are for you."

He didn't know how late it was or what kind of nightlife was still going on at this hour, but he did know that he was tired after three rounds of lovemaking, and right now he wanted nothing more than to fall asleep with Orla in his arms. Orla had hoped for a restful and uneventful rest of the evening, but alas, there was no rest for the wicked. She yawned as she rose from the table, and it told Lorcan that she was thinking along the same lines as he was. He put his arm around her, and the two of them headed back up to bed.

The rays of the rising sun were just beginning to peek through the lace of the curtains when Orla sat up again. There was a distinct clicking noise coming from downstairs that sounded like the heels of a man's very expensive pair of shoes. She rolled over and closed her eyes again. There was no way she was going to lose any more sleep over Chiyo's idiot boyfriend. But it took her only a few minutes to remember that she'd seen Goro's shoes, and they were not the kind that had heels that clicked. Eyes wide, she sat up again and listened. Her movement caused Lorcan to sit up, too, and she held a finger to her mouth to indicate that he should be quiet. He took her hand and listened with her.

"I don't think that's Goro. He has different shoes."

Lorcan raised an eyebrow. "We were fighting someone we thought to be a dangerous intruder, and you paid attention to his *shoes?*"

Orla shrugged. "It was after we figured out he was Chiyo's boyfriend. I thought his shoes would look good on you."

"No, thank you. I can choose my own outfits."

"Should we bother to look downstairs? Or will it only be a waste of time?"

Lorcan was silent for a minute, then shrugged. "I think we should at least take a look at what's going on. If there's a plausible reason for another visitor, then so be it. If not, well, we can let the poor bastard have it."

Orla grinned in the semi-darkness. Once again, the two of them crept out of bed and slid down the stairs in near perfect silence. When they came to the hallway, they saw a massive figure looming in the doorway. It was clear to the both of them that this was definitely not Goro. Orla blinked, shook her head, blinked again, and stared. Lorcan's eyes widened.

The man had no eyes. He held his hands out in front of him, and in the middle of each palm was a large, monstrous-looking eye. The pupils were slitted like those of a cat, and they gave Orla the creeps. There was no way that this . . . thing was supposed to be in Chiyo's house, so she did the one thing that she could think of. Orla curved her fists and sent jets of flame at him, setting him on fire. He stumbled around a little bit, setting a few things around him on fire as well, but Orla did a good job of controlling the flames.

A shadowy figure danced in through the open door, darting in and out of the flames with such speed that Orla and Lorcan knew it wasn't human. When the figure paused in front of them, they recognized the fox from the temple. The fox ran up the stairs like she owned the place.

"You take Palm-Eyes, and I'll take care of the animal," Orla said, and before Lorcan could speak, she ran after the fox. She crested the stairs just in time to see the little red tail disappear into Chiyo's room. Orla swore. Now she'd have to protect that hoity-toity bitch, and she wasn't thrilled about that at all. When she threw the door open, however, the room was empty except for the foxy woman digging through Chiyo's belongings. Orla planted herself in the doorway and cleared her throat.

The fox-faced woman stood up. As she had shifted from her fox form back into human form, she was wearing nothing but a tiny red bikini. Orla blinked. The suit must be designed from a special material designed to protect the woman when she morphed into different forms. On top of an exquisite face, Orla had to admit that the woman had a flawless body. It must come with the fox genes, Orla mused.

"What are you doing here? I didn't like you at the temple, and I don't like you now. What are you looking for?" She hoped that her sheer bluntness would startle an answer out of the woman, but she was wrong. The woman turned back into the little fox and darted out of the room between Orla's legs, scampering down the stairs. She screamed out for Lorcan to grab her at the bottom, but she didn't know if he could hear her over the crackling of the flames.

By the time Orla made it to the foot of the stairs, the foxy woman was back, standing over the body of the man with eyes on his hands. She tilted her head back and opened her mouth in a mournful sound that Orla and Lorcan had never heard before. The woman stared them down, and then she began to scream for Chiyo. Chiyo, of course, didn't answer because she still hadn't come home yet from her date.

"Look, I don't know who or what you are, but listen to me and stop that wailing for a minute!" Orla's angry voice pierced through the woman's screams like a hot knife through butter. In utter shock, she stopped her strange noise and looked at Orla. "Thank you. Chiyo isn't here right now, but I want you to know that she's protected. So back off and leave her alone."

The woman shook her head. "If Chiyo is with that boyfriend of hers, then she's going to be in trouble." The woman turned and tried to leave, but Orla and Lorcan were hot on her trail. Waving her hand in an intricate pattern, Orla removed the flame from the building and swung the door closed. She and Lorcan were now in pursuit of the little fox, but it was very difficult to see her in the early morning light. Neither of them were exactly dressed for a manhunt, but they would have to tough it out. They needed to find out who and what this fox was, and why she was after Chiyo.

CHAPTER 8

Orla and Lorcan followed Fox Face as she darted through the city. It really was a lot easier to follow someone when there weren't hundreds of people in the way. As they trailed this mysterious creature, she led them farther and farther away from the center of the city. After a while, it looked like they were in a part of the city that was crammed full of warehouses for the various businesses in town. Fox Face hauled open a door to one of the larger warehouses.

Orla and Lorcan watched from a distance for a few minutes to see if she would come back out. When she didn't, Lorcan swore and motioned for Orla to follow him. The two of them crept in through still-cracked door, and the scene that met them was a grisly one. Chiyo was tied to a pillar in the back of the empty warehouse, her hands above her head and her feet barely touching the ground. There was a group of mooks threatening the young doctor. Tears were running down her face.

The conversation was in Japanese. Lorcan pulled out his palm device and turned it on. It captured the sound signals, and soon English text flew onto the little screen.

"I don't know what you're talking about. I've never seen a key!" Chiyo cried.

A thin man paced back and forth in front of Chiyo, a malicious smile on his face. "Maybe I can help you remember." He snapped his fingers and four mooks came from nowhere, a platform balanced on their shoulders. They set the platform down, and took the dirty blanket off of the misshapen form wriggling underneath. Orla gasped and had to put her hands over her mouth to stifle it. On the platform was Goro, Chiyo's boyfriend. His hands were tied behind his back, and he had a heavy manacle around his neck with four chains coming down to attach to four iron rings on the platform. He was kneeling, and he had what looked to be a dirty bandana in his mouth as a gag. When he saw Chiyo, he struggled, trying to break free and get to her. Orla felt tears in eyes when she saw that. She shifted and turned back, seeing Lorcan looking at her. He kissed her on the cheek.

"Now, maybe you can tell me a little more about the key of Psuche?" the man's voice slid out like poisoned silk. Chiyo yanked at her restraints, and Lorcan saw blood running down her wrists.

"I don't know anything about it! I'm just a doctor! My grandfather had the antique business, but it died with him in the earthquake! Please, let us go. I swear I don't know anything." She was crying now.

Orla wanted to jump in for a rescue. She hopped up, but Lorcan held her back. "We're seriously outnumbered," he said.

"Poor little Chiyo. It looks like things are going to get worse for you before they get better. Think hard. Is there anything that you remember? Anything at all?" the man grumbled.

Chiyo was silent for a few minutes. "All I can remember is that it was a metal key with a stone on the top of it. I don't remember what kind of stone—or even if it did anything special. I was only a child, and I had nothing to do with the antique business. That's all I know, I swear. Please, just let us go."

The man stared at Chiyo hard, like he was trying to see down into her very soul to determine whether she was telling the truth. "I believe you. I really do. The only problem is, the mooks don't." He spread his arms wide in an 'I don't know' gesture. Chiyo's eyes grew wide with fear, and he swung his head in Goro's direction.

"No, no, please don't do that!" Chiyo cried.

The man pointed at Goro. "What about you? Do you know?"

Chiyo shook her head. "No no, he doesn't know anything."

"We have no use for him then," the man concluded and signaled the mooks. One of them drew a katana from a sheath at his side, walked up soundlessly behind Goro, and slit his throat with one swipe. Chiyo screamed and fainted.

Lorcan had reached his limit. He stepped out into the open space. Orla started to follow, but she was grabbed from behind. Lorcan and Orla turned around, ready for a fight, when they saw Fox Face.

"You're going to need more than just the two of you." The fox woman's voice was low, and she was trying to speak urgently to Orla without anyone overhearing her.

Before Orla and Lorcan had a chance to respond, Fox Face stumbled backward until she was almost even with the pillar Chiyo was tied to. She didn't even know what hit her. The mooks had made them and had attacked from behind.

Fox Face stood up slowly, rubbing her rib cage, wheezing. Men poured out from nowhere, attacking them from left, right, and center. Orla was separated from Lorcan. Three dangerous-looking goons approached her. She stepped back and saw about ten of them pounding on Lorcan. She clenched her jaw. *You forced me to do this*, she thought as she curved her hands into fists and sent fire balls flying at the criminals. She soon cleared out the three who were attacking her. She turned to Lorcan and saw he had knocked down five men, bare-handed, but before she could do anything, a goon standing behind Lorcan pulled out a knife and stabbed him.

Lorcan slumped to the ground.

Orla thought she had stopped breathing. She darted forward, and fireballs flew at the criminal like fireworks. In the haze of confusion, smoke, and the smell of burnt flesh, she didn't realize she had cleared the entire gang out with her fire and Fox Face had just knocked down the last man standing.

Orla knelt down in front of Lorcan, gently stroking his cheek. "Lorcan? Can you hear me? Talk to me, baby."

He groaned and opened his eyes. "I hate it when women are still standing, and I'm the one lying on the ground. You've got to teach me some of that magic of yours."

"Sure thing." Orla helped him sit up.

"I'll heal, as you've already seen."

"All right. But it'll still take a while. Now stand up for me." She slid her arm around his waist. "There you go." He stood up straight, stumbled a few steps, then straightened up again.

"I'm okay. Where's Chiyo? Did you get her out yet?" Orla shook her head. She slowly led Lorcan toward the other end of the warehouse where Fox Face was standing.

Lorcan tried not to lean a lot of his weight on Orla. He couldn't quite figure out how his healing ability had been triggered before. At the moment, he didn't think it was working. The wound on his back was searing, and blood was streaming out. His vision became more blurry by the second. He walked a few more steps with Orla's assistance and then started to stagger. "I . . . I don't think I can . . ." he slurred out and then dropped to the floor in a heap.

"Oh my God!" Orla cried out. She looked up and saw Fox Face approaching. She still didn't trust her, but she really didn't have a choice at the moment. They carried Lorcan to the corner where Chiyo was tied up, and leaned him against a pillar.

"He'll heal. He's like us. But all creatures have different ways of healing. He might have to shut down his system before the healing can start," Fox Face said.

"What? What do you mean by he's 'like' you?" Orla snarled.

"I thought you knew."

"Knew what?"

Fox Face shook her head. "We have other matters to see to now. I'm not yet sure about him, so it's better not to make assumptions."

"The hell I'll let you get away with this. The last time it took hours for him to recover from your knife. Now you're say he's like *you*? Like what? A werefox?"

"I said I'm not sure."

Orla grumbled some profanity and then pulled Lorcan into her, resting his head on her shoulder. She flipped the back of his shirt up and could see his wound was starting to heal. She looked up at Fox Face and saw a faint smirk flash across her face, but she let it go for now. She leaned Lorcan back again on the pillar. Then she went over to Chiyo and started to pick the lock on her manacles. Fox Face admired Orla's skills.

"Wow, you're good."

Orla looked at her, then decided to swallow her snarky response. She lay Chiyo down to the floor and came back to Lorcan. "We have to get out of here soon. I don't know when they'll be back."

"I agree. We can't stay here for long."

Orla gestured at Lorcan and Chiyo. "Can't go anywhere with these two dead-weight bodies here."

"It's dangerous here. I know a place where we can regroup. But we'll have to wait until these two can walk by themselves. At the moment, I hope the Gods here would protect us."

"Here? In this warehouse? Since when that God has changed his style of residence?" Orla asked.

A wave of sadness poured from Fox Face's eyes. "On this very ground used to be an old temple that was abandoned generations ago. The people in the city think it's haunted, so they don't come here, and they've never had the nerve to bulldoze it down." There was a wistfulness to her tone, and it softened Orla's temper just a little.

"Why do people think it's haunted?" she asked gently.

Fox Face looked down at the ground at her feet.

"This temple used to honor us Kitsune, but almost everyone has forgotten us now. There are still those select few that come here to honor us or pray to us for help, but that number dwindles more and more with each passing year."

"You were after Chiyo. Same with the mooks. You're after the key, too. Do these gangsters know you?" Orla did her best to keep her anger at bay, but some of it bled into her voice anyway. Fox Face dropped her gaze. She didn't want to answer, and Orla realized that she really didn't have any way of making her if she didn't want to. She wasn't a bully, per se, unless she had to be one to finish a job.

Lorcan began to stir. Orla went over, and seeing him open his eyes slightly and smile at her, she knew he would heal quickly from this point. She kissed his cheek. Lorcan was beginning to get that twinkle back in his eyes that said he was alert and ready for danger. His injuries seemed to be healing as quickly as they had at Chiyo's house.

Fox Face spoke up again. "I want to apologize for not introducing myself. My name is Mori. I'm a werefox, a creature of folklore. Even though we sometimes walk as humans, we never forget who and what we are. In order to keep ourselves secret from the world, we tend to go underground a lot. That was how I met the Yakuz."

Orla was very sick and tired of hearing that word and not knowing what it meant. "What exactly are these Yakuz?" If she had to fight them again, then she wanted to know what they were up against.

"They are humanoid in form, but they have certain, otherworldly features to them. The man you killed in Chiyo's apartment? He was a tenome, a Yakuz. You could ask her boyfriend for more information if the mooks hadn't killed him. There are myriad creatures and people belonging to that group—even I don't know all of their names. They are very powerful, and the Kitsune stays out of their way." She blushed at this debasement of her breed, but it was the truth, and so she had to reveal it. "The eyes in the man's palms don't see only the mundane as humans do, they see the ghosts of souls past and what they did when they were alive. He was sent to her apartment to find out what she knew about the key of Psuche. I don't know what he saw, but I know that he didn't gather any information from Chiyo, and the fact that the two of you killed him will slow down the Yakuz as well. Take pride in what you've done. Not very many otherworldly creatures could have rid themselves of him if he had come knocking, and here you are, two humans, taking out one of the Yakuz by yourselves." Mori sounded impressed, even though it was obvious that she was trying to hide that fact from them.

Orla narrowed her eyes. "But you seemed sad when the Palm-eye died."

Mori looked at Orla, "Did I?" Then she came back to her usual silent mode and ignored Orla unanswered question.

They heard a clanking sound at the far end of the warehouse.

"Oh hell, they're back already." Orla stood.

"Yep." Mori darted over, standing next to Orla. Lorcan grumbled and tried to stand up. Orla used one hand to squash him back down to the floor. From the far end of the warehouse, a group of twelve menacing men strode in.

CHAPTER 9

"**H**ow many of them can you take?" Orla asked Mori as she gestured toward the coming men. Orla looked around and grabbed a steel bar close by. Lorcan tried to stand up again. She darted over, not squashing him down this time but dragging him behind the pillar. Lorcan's eyes sparked with anger, but he couldn't resist—Orla was much stronger than he was at the moment.

Mori watched the couple with amusement and felt an unusual feeling slash at her heart. It felt like a pain, but she wasn't sure exactly what it was, so she let it go. "I can take five of them in my human form," she told Orla.

Orla glanced at her. The beautiful woman was in bare feet and wore only her swimsuit. "What about in your fox form?"

Mori grinned. "Well, as an animal, I don't count. But I can take all of them."

"Arrogant bitch. Don't be greedy," Orla snarled.

"I'll leave you a couple then." Mori grinned again.

Orla hated to admit it, but she was starting to like this foxy woman. She shrugged. "Well then."

Mori said nothing further, shifting back into a fox effortlessly. She stared at the group of men.

The mooks were charging now, showering their sparks of power all around them, showing off. Orla growled under her breath, and from the corner of her eyes, she saw Lorcan carrying Chiyo, still unconscious, toward the back of the pillar.

The attackers' clothes all had a symbol, and it stood to reason that this was to show that they were members of the Yakuz group.

"The girl! Get the girl!" They mangled the words in English. Orla wanted to throw her hands over her ears because the voice was so gravelly that it almost hurt to listen. "Give us the girl, and we'll let the rest of you leave here in one piece."

"There were three ladies here, actually—one alive, one unconscious, and a female fox. Which one do you want?" Orla asked.

Orla put herself between the group of criminals that now blocked the only way into and out of the temple and the unconscious doctor who had been half hidden under the altar. She could see that Lorcan had moved to where he could protect Chiyo and still fight if it came to that. The little red fox stood somewhere between Orla and Lorcan, glaring at the gang in defiance. One figure at the back of the group stood out. It was taller and dressed more elaborately than the rest. Orla took this to mean that he was the leader. With a wave of his hand, he sent his minions out to fight his battle.

It was a fight between her magic, fireballs and whatever weapons the goons had with them. She used the last reserves of dark magic that she had to blind the ones in front of them, making it so they could only see the horrors of their past. The three that she was fighting turned and ran blindly out of the temple. She didn't have a second to take a breath before another figure loomed in front of her. This one would have to be handled the old-fashioned way, with fists. It got a strong punch in to her face, and her head snapped back. She shook her head to clear it then came at him with all the fury she possessed. It was like Orla had turned into a wild cat, hissing and clawing her way through its protective clothing to the flesh underneath. When she finally had the joy of seeing her opponent run, she turned to look at Mori and Lorcan.

Lorcan had a few cuts and bruises, but with his new unexplained ability to heal himself, she wasn't too worried about him. Mori had a large gash in her tail, but she seemed to be fine, too. Before Orla could say anything, she saw something small whizzing towards Lorcan's chest. She whirled around to try to stop it, but Mori beat her to it. The little red fox threw herself into the air, was knocked backwards as the object hit her, then fell to the cracked and crumbling cobblestones, shaking.

Orla turned to face the now empty doorway, looking for a target to let her anger and aggression out on, but finding none. When she turned to face the wounded fox, the animal was gone, and the woman stood in its place. Lorcan was reaching out to her, but she only stumbled away, trying to run, but only managing to zigzag dangerously.

"What just happened?" Orla was stunned and wasn't quite sure that she believed her own eyes, so she looked to Lorcan for confirmation.

"One of the bastards shot at me. She copped the bullet." Then he darted after Mori.

"Lorcan!" Orla called out. A wounded little fox and an injured man didn't make a good pack. Orla chased after him.

It was dark outside, and the blood trail Mori left was not easy to find. Lorcan ran and ran. Orla was right behind him. *A wounded fox can't run that fast, can she?* Lorcan asked himself. He didn't think much as he followed, but he actually sniffed the air for a scent of Mori. He followed the faint trace of her in the air, which led him straight to a spot on the road where there was a small pool of blood.

Lorcan crouched and sniffed the air again. Then he looked down at his arm and saw his skin glowing blue for a brief second. He jumped back to his feet and cursed. He didn't like this at all. Orla had caught up, out of breath. They walked a little farther and stopped where the blood trail completely disappeared.

From a distance, Mori could see Lorcan and Orla walk away. She had been watching Lorcan—the way he went after her, the way he sniffed the air, trying to detect her scent, and the determination in his eyes. She knew he wasn't an ordinary human, but as to what he actually was, she didn't know. Mori didn't know how to explain her feelings, but what had been developing in her the last few days was disconcerting. She rubbed at the bullet wound which was still bleeding. She didn't know why she had taken the bullet. She wasn't invincible. If she died for this stranger, that meant she would have abandoned her mission and failed her ancestors and her family.

She peeked her head out, and when she saw that Lorcan and Orla had turned the corner, she limped out. She hadn't walked two steps when she heard a low growl that prickled all of her senses. She knew she was in trouble. Behind her were three gigantic wolves from a clan she had chased away a couple of years ago. She knew they held a grudge, but they had never come close to attacking her. Mori staggered back and shifted into her fox form, a tiny red fox against three large menacing wolves.

The wolves charged at her, teeth bared. For a bystander, this would just look like a dog fight. They charged at Mori. Her clan were too far away to call. If she were to go down now, she would put up a good fight. She lowered her front legs, crouched in a fighting stance, and waited. The wolves came in a whirl of dirt and stone and a wall of howling sound. She was bitten everywhere, but she was sure each of the wolves received their fair share of her teeth.

The bullet in her body was damn inconvenient. The pain slowed her down. She staggered, fell, and got bitten more. She was sure she'd be turned into a pile of bloody meat soon. Then a familiar howl came—that was Roy. The relief made her delirious. She could rest now, she might just lie down for a bit. Mori felt her eyes droop and the energy drain out of her. Then everything was a blur.

She woke to find herself in the backseat of a car. She sat up, groggily, feeling a faint pain in her stomach where the bullet used to be. Her body must have pushed it out, and the wound was healing. She glanced up at the rearview mirror at the front seat of the car and saw Roy's intent eyes looking at her. "Thank you," she said.

"You should lie down." Roy said nothing else and focused his eyes on the road ahead. He was her guard. As a human, he owned a construction business in town. As a were-creature, he had mixed fox and wolf blood. Although he considered himself more of a fox than a wolf, because of his mixed blood, he could never be the male Alpha of the group regardless of how dominant he was or the fact that his father had been the previous alpha in the fox clan. Roy didn't complain—he didn't want the responsibility anyway. He hung around the group a lot because of Mori. He protected her and would always be there when she needed him, with the understanding that she could never mate with him.

"I see that you can't help but manage to put yourself in harm's way."

"Why would I intentionally harm myself?"

"If you'd stay where you're supposed to stay, then nothing would happen. And what's with the bullet wound? What if that bullet had been in your head? There would be nothing I could do to save you. I don't think you put the best interests of your clan at the top of your mind. That's fine, I couldn't care less. But if you die, your clan will be left in chaos, and your people will die. Is that what you want? If I stayed out of town a little longer, would I come back and have to attend your funeral?" His voice exploded with anger.

"I didn't plan this. It was the Yakuz."

Roy hit the brakes, and the car swung and stopped at the side of the road. In the mirror, Mori could see the fury in his darkened eyes. Long strands of hair flopped down onto his forehead, making his long, lean face more mysterious and, she had to admit, beautiful.

The Yakuz had killed his parents. Roy didn't want to be involved in the clan's politics and had said he would not seek revenge for his parents' deaths, but the hatred was ingrained in him, and it soared when his mental shield was weakened. Mori knew him. She could read his mind as if it was the palm of her hand. He cared for her, and at the moment, his anger at her injuries had weakened his mind. She was responsible for fueling it. She wanted him to be at peace, and the only way to achieve that was for him to seek revenge. That was her way. She was the female alpha after all, and he was her guard.

"The Yakuz are after the key again. I don't know what triggered them, but I had to stop them before they came right to our doorstep." Mori's voice was soothing.

Roy nodded and shrugged in agreement. He put the hand brake on, raked his hand through his hair, and leaned back in his seat with his eyes closed.

"There are two strangers from out of town. They're after the key as well, but I don't think they mean any harm. I think they could help us."

"How so?"

"Well, if they really are good people, and they can take the key to a safe place far away from here and protect it, it will be an enormous load off our shoulders."

"But how can we be sure they're good people?"

Mori shrugged. "I guess that's the problem. But at the moment, they could use some help. And . . . and . . . there is a thing . . . I think I bit a were-creature."

Roy's eyes flung wide open, making Mori cringe and want to sink into the car seat. "You did what? You bit or you didn't bite? What does that mean by you *think* you bit a creature?"

Mori waved her arms in defense. "I thought he was human. I *still* think he's human, just his blood didn't taste human. The bite wasn't intentional."

Roy cracked up. "You know what, I think the biting ritual is rubbish, okay? So, I don't care if it was intentional or not. It means nothing to me. But the simple truth is, if you open your mouth, use the strength of your jaw muscles, aim, and sink your teeth into someone's flesh until it bleeds, you can't say it was unintentional!"

Mori shrugged. "Just wanted to let you know."

"Why?"

"Nothing."

"Ah. So I guess you bit the from-out-of-towner?"

She nodded.

"Was he severely hurt?"

"Not because of the bite."

Roy cocked an eyebrow.

"I kinda threw a knife at him as well, and his girlfriend helped with a fire ball. But don't worry—he's completely healed from his injuries now. Plus, I copped a bullet for him, so we're even."

"Right."

"Oh, and the Palm-eye spy we placed in the Yakuz, he's dead now. So we've lost that lead. Our only lead. The Yakuz kidnapped Chiyo and killed her boyfriend."

Roy leaned his forehead on the steering wheel. "Do you need more time to write a list of all the unfortunate events that occurred when I was out of town for less than a week?"

"No. That's it."

CHAPTER 10

Lorcan and Orla returned to the warehouse after chasing Mori, and found Chiyo had regained consciousness. They shouldn't have left her alone to chase the werefox, but they did, and it was a relief to see that she was fine. She sat next to the Goro's body. Lorcan helped her to her feet, and she wobbled a little. Her face was cold, and tears still fell from her eyes intermittently, but that was something neither Orla nor Lorcan could help her with. Not many people had to watch a loved one executed right before their eyes—that was a traumatic experience that would never go away.

The young doctor allowed herself to be led home, and she didn't speak until they got there. Even though Orla and Lorcan stumbled a bit, trying to make their way back to her house, she didn't help them. For the first time, Orla felt a kinship to her. She knew what it was like to lose someone she loved. Lorcan had died twice, but she'd been able to bring him back. Chiyo didn't have the power to do that for Goro. Even if she did, now that Goro had been dead for a while, there was no telling what he would come back as.

"I don't understand." They were the first words Chiyo had spoken since she'd come to, and they startled Orla and Lorcan. "How could I have been so vulnerable? I've depended on the two of you for my safety and protection. I'm embarrassed that I couldn't do it for myself. And for Goro." She fell silent as the name passed her lips. Whether she wanted them to be sympathetic to her or not, Lorcan and Orla couldn't tell, and they remained silent instead.

Orla and Lorcan looked around the house to check for signs of intruders. The body of the man with the eye on his hand was gone. Orla had been right. The Yakuz had come straight to Chiyo's house, looking for them. They'd barely gotten away with their lives last time, and they were both still worried about Mori, who'd taken a bullet for Lorcan.

"It's not your fault." The silence had gotten to Orla, and she wanted to break it. "You had no idea what you were dealing with, and even if you had, would you have believed it was happening?" The gentle tone with which Orla addressed Chiyo surprised Lorcan, and he raised an eyebrow. Orla scowled at him and turned back to Chiyo, who was now shaking her head.

"No, I guess I wouldn't have. You're right. But how could I have been so blind?" Chiyo, her head down, was now making her way to the kitchen table, and when she reached it, she sat down and lay her head on her arms. She looked so broken and lonely that Orla wanted to put her arms around the woman in comfort, but she didn't trust her completely. Just because they were protecting her didn't mean she would necessarily play nice in the schoolyard.

Lorcan sat on the other side of the young doctor and put a hand gently on her arm. "I don't know if it's a good idea for you to stay in this house. They obviously know where you live, and they could send more monsters after you when we're not here to protect you. Is there somewhere else you could go for a little while?" Lorcan tried to make the possibility of more trouble seem less likely than it was.

Silence ensued for a few minutes, then Chiyo raised her head. Her eyes were blank and staring, but she said, "I need you to take me to see someone."

When she didn't elaborate after a few minutes, Orla became impatient. "Okay, and who is this person? Someone you can stay with? Someone who can protect you? Can you give us a little more to go on?" Lorcan hid his smile. He'd been worried about her for a little while, but it looked like she was back to her normal self now.

"He's an old man who lives on the edge of the village. He used to be good friends with my grandfather. He might even know something about the Rojin and this key that everyone's trying to get their hands on." Chiyo shrugged innocently.

Orla jumped to her feet. "Why are you just telling us about him now? Why didn't you help us find him when we first came to you?" Anger blazed in her eyes, and as far as Lorcan could tell, she was ready to do battle. He positioned himself on the edge of his chair, just in case he had to dive between the two women.

"I thought you were Yakuz at first. After that, well, there really hasn't been time, has there?" Chiyo's voice was almost dreamlike. Grief did strange things to people, that was something that Lorcan knew about first hand.

"Okay, let's say for argument's sake that we take you to see this old man. Then what?" Orla asked.

Chiyo shrugged again. "He might be able to help you. He claims to be a wizard, and he's the last remaining member of the Rojin group. He might know about that key you were asking me about. It seems like everyone wants the damn thing now." The last part she mumbled more to herself than to her audience, but they heard her just the same.

"Do you know how to find this wizard? I assume he's within a walkable distance?" Despite her best efforts, Orla couldn't keep the sarcasm out of her voice. Chiyo turned to face them again and nodded. She didn't seem at all aware of the growing tension in her new friends. "Then let's go. I want to see if he knows anything, and the sooner the better."

Silently, Chiyo led the group through the winding roads of the city. Now that it was early morning, traffic was picking up, and the streets were considerably more crowded. Orla and Lorcan kept their eyes darting everywhere—they couldn't afford another attack. The walk took them just over two hours, but they arrived at a little hut on the outskirts of the village that looked like it might have grown out of the earth. There was a heavy metallic scent in the air around it, and Orla thought it had to be another breed of magic. Chiyo squared her shoulders and marched right up to the front door, hesitating only slightly before giving the old wood a sound beating. She retreated a few paces, trying to appear less of a threat. As they waited, a chill crept down Orla's spine. She sidestepped, moving a little closer to Lorcan, muttering under her breath, "Something's not right." Lorcan looked around, tense and on edge, but he didn't see anything alarming.

"What do you mean?" The whispered conversation wasn't meant for Chiyo's ears, and since she hadn't turned around, they were safe in assuming that she hadn't heard them.

"I just get his feeling that something's off about Chiyo. I can't put my finger on it, but I feel a wrongness."

Lorcan shrugged. "Her boyfriend's throat was cut right in front of her, I'm surprised she didn't go mad. It's to be expected that she's behaving a little oddly."

"I'm telling you that from a magical standpoint, something is off. I just don't know what." She huffed as she stepped further away from him. Lorcan was going to make a smart remark back to her, but at that moment, the door opened, and a stooped, wizened old man came out.

"Can I help you?" The old man opened the door wide. Chiyo took a step forward and began speaking hurriedly in Japanese. The old man listened politely, and when her river of words dried up, Chiyo fell silent, waiting. The man looked over her shoulders at Orla and Lorcan. Then he looked at her, focused. He had a genuine and calm smile. He said something, and she looked up at him. It felt like the warm reunion of very familiar acquaintances. In Western culture, people would jump up and down, embracing each other in joy and tears. But here, it was expressed in polite nods and bows.

The old man said nothing to Lorcan and Orla, but motioned them to come into his hut as well. Orla wondered if he knew the concept of robbery, or if a stranger had ever pulled a weapon on him. Maybe not, judging by the way he enthusiastically ushered them into his home. The man waited patiently for them to come into his kitchen before he closed and bolted the door behind them. "Please, sit down. We have much to talk about." The trio of visitors stood awkwardly, not sure if they should do as he said, and casting furtive glances at one another. The old man sat down, then spread his arms out to encompass the other seats in another silent invitation to sit down. Chiyo was the first to obey. Orla and Lorcan followed, but they sat stiffly, ready to spring into action at a moment's notice. "You can go ahead and relax. We're safe here as long as my wards and shields are up. I know a little of what you're going through from what Chiyo told me, but I can assure you that nothing can attack you in my house." For some reason that she couldn't explain, Orla believed him, and she sat back in her chair, keeping her hands in her lap.

"Chiyo, you have grown up a lot since the last time I saw you. I am sorry to say that I might not have the answers to all of your questions. I don't know much. But there is something I have to tell you. Are you comfortable for me to speak in front of your new friends?" the wizard asked.

Chiyo's eyes widened, and she nodded slowly. "Your father was a shape shifter." Chiyo's mouth dropped open in astonishment. "He could turn into an eagle, but only that one animal. Your mother knew all about it, of course, because she was part werefox. Her family thought that she was marrying beneath her, and they weren't happy at all with the union between them. Then they had you. You were the deadliner in their family." The old man paused, waiting for his information to sink in. Chiyo was shaking her head.

"No. My parents were normal. They had no special abilities, and they never did anything to get them noticed. I didn't even know that my mother had a family on her side."

When her words subsided, the old man spoke again. "You were to end the magical abilities in their lines. You have no powers and do not have the ability to pass any on, either."

Chiyo finally came back to herself and waved away the explanation as if she wasn't interested. She changed the topic of conversation quickly. "Now about this key. You were in the Rojin, and you were friends with my grandfather. You have to tell me what it is and where I can find it."

The wizard looked sharply into her face then crossed his arms over his chest, contemplating. He leaned back in his seat. "I'm not comfortable talking about that key, and I don't have any information to give you."

Chiyo's face clouded with anger, and she jumped to her feet. "You told me that you would answer the questions that I asked truthfully! How dare you go back on your word!" She shook an accusatory finger in the old man's face. Orla and Lorcan had both shifted a little in their chairs once she'd jumped to her feet, but they'd remained seated.

"I did tell you that I would tell you the truth, and I have about your family. I'd rather not discuss that key. If you have any other questions you need answered, I would be more than happy to tell you what I know." His tone was measured and even, but Orla could see electricity in his eyes. He might seem like a kindly old man, but she knew better than to take anything at face value when there was magic involved. He was giving Chiyo a clear warning that she wasn't heeding. Chiyo begged and pleaded, screamed and cried, but no matter what she did, the wizard wouldn't tell her anything about the key of Psuche. The trio left the wizard's house in disappointment, each with their own reasons.

"That key has to be somewhere close by! If it wasn't, he wouldn't be so secretive. If we start looking, I bet we can find it," Chiyo said and stomped ahead. Lorcan increased his pace to follow, but Orla grabbed him and shook her head.

A misty breeze whirled up from the ground, and an eerie cold wind crept out from the gaps between trees and small shrubs along the road. They were outside the remote village, and Chiyo didn't seem to be heading in the direction of civilization.

If Orla wasn't mistaken, there was a reptilian hiss hovering in the air, and she was praying that it wasn't coming from snakes. She wasn't afraid of them, but she never knew which way they were heading, and that gave her a disadvantage in combat. Lorcan heard the sound, too.

He glanced around uneasily.

CHAPTER 11

Chiyo was now suddenly bound and determined to find the key, and it made Orla uneasy. She'd been swearing up and down that she knew nothing about it and wanted nothing to do with it this whole time, but now she'd made a complete one-eighty. It was as if her personality had changed somehow, like something else was directing her body and mind without her knowledge. Encouraged by the weird aura surrounding them at the moment, Orla decided to try to pry into Chiyo's mind. This was a shady area of magic she hadn't touched since she was a kid. But it was needed now.

Unbeknownst to either of her companions, Orla began to weave her fingers in a complicated pattern, spinning dark magic in her mind for a spell. It would let her touch Chiyo's mind to see what she was really up to. It took her only a few minutes to complete the spell, and then she held her hand up to her face. The small ball of purple lightning that crackled in her palm didn't look like much, but it made Orla smile. She blew it gently in Chiyo's direction and waited. The ball of lightning spun on the air currents towards its intended target. When it reached Chiyo, it drew even with her ear and then lengthened before slowly seeping into her ear like water into a gutter.

Orla gasped and stumbled. Lorcan glanced back at her, but she gestured him to go on ahead. She regained her footing, but she still couldn't wrap her mind around what her magic was telling her was real. Chiyo's mind was empty. The ball of lightning couldn't gather any information from her because there was none to be had. Orla's body was still walking, but she was trapped now in the link between her own mind and that of Chiyo. Orla's body fell to the ground, unconscious; her path back to herself was cut off.

Hearing the sound of Orla's body thumping to the ground, Lorcan turned back. "Holy crap," he called out and darted back to her. "Chiyo," Lorcan called out for the doctor. "Please help." He shook Orla's shoulders, but her body seemed completely shut down. Lorcan was panicking. "Come on, honey. Open your eyes for me. Tell me what's going on. Chiyo!"

Silence. No response from Chiyo. Lorcan looked up.

Chiyo began to laugh, a loud, guttural sound that sounded inhuman. Chiyo's hair began to shrink upwards, like her scalp was reabsorbing it. She grew taller, and her smooth skin began to break out in bumps and ridges like that of a lizard. He watched as the creature reared back on its hind legs, returning to where Orla lay on the ground.

Lorcan sprang into action, trading blows and insults with the Godzilla wannabe in front of him. He made sure to keep himself between this creature and Orla. The more that Lorcan began to think his moves out in advance, the faster he became. His agility increased after every few moves until he was darting around like a little fox toying with a much larger predator. The lizard whipped her tail and dealt him more than just a glancing blow to his midsection. Lorcan let out a howl that didn't even register in his own mind.

Lorcan swore as he reminded himself of what Orla had whispered to him in front of the wizard's hut. She'd said something about Chiyo not being normal. That something was amiss with her now in a magical sense that hadn't been wrong before. Lorcan had thought nothing of it. He promised himself to take whatever she said about magic more seriously from now on—*if* they had a chance to move on after this. The thing in front of him was awfully big, and he didn't have a weapon. But he'd be damned, though, if he'd let this overgrown iguana harm Orla.

The lizard stomped toward Lorcan. He lunged at it with all he had. At the moment, he realized that his only weapons were his will and his fists. Punching the lizard felt like punching rusty metal panels. His knuckles tore and bled, and he swore it wasn't his imagination that the lizard grinned at him. It swung a gigantic tail at Lorcan, and he was knocked four feet, rolling and scraping against the dirt road.

The lizard then turned toward Orla. Lorcan charged at it again, and copped another blow from its tail. He reeled up, his nose bleeding, his face scratched. This wasn't smart, fighting bare-handed with the creature, he thought. But what choice did he have? The lizard was approaching Orla, and he couldn't figure out how to stop it. Fury increased inside him, boiling his blood. He grabbed a tree branch and swung at the creature. It broke the branch with its tail, and Lorcan took another hit. There was only so much his human body could take. The thought raised a wave of strange energy in him.

He needed something heavier. He saw a large rock on the ground. When he reached to pick it up, his hands—or what used to be his hands—were now paws at the end of hairy electric blue animal legs. He turned to look at the lizard, and his vision was strange, rounded with blurry edges, and his viewpoint seemed to be very low to the ground. He was totally confused. He wanted to move forward but found himself tangled in his clothing. He shrugged off his jeans and shirt and lunged at the lizard. He wanted to grunt, but the sound erupting from his mouth was not a grunt, it was a howl.

The lizard turned around, paying him some attention now. It waved its tail and thumped it on the ground, sounding almost like the rumble of a small earthquake. Lorcan walked around, circling the lizard. He realized he was walking on all fours now, and admittedly, he felt comfortable and very agile. He wanted to say something, but the words wouldn't come out of his mouth. He jumped at the lizard, climbed up its back from its tail and over the top of its head, biting down on its soft weak spot, the eye.

The lizard roared. Lorcan wagered if it were a dragon, it would have let out a stream of fire. But unfortunately for the reptile, it was merely an ugly lizard. It swung its head, hurling Lorcan to the ground. He howled in pain and then saw the lizard's foot about to crush him. Springing to his feet to get away, he felt the lizard step on his tail. Tail? Lorcan turned to see that he had a large, furry tail. He tried to drag it out from under the lizard's foot, but it didn't seem to move. He saw another foot coming down. This might be the end . . .

Suddenly, a blast of icy blue energy sizzled over Lorcan's head and hit the lizard square in the chest. He whipped around as the lizard began to scream in agony and saw the old wizard coming to the rescue, using his staff as a wand of some sort and shooting out blasts of energy from the tip. A final blast threw the overgrown lizard back about ten yards before it collapsed and lay still.

The wizard turned, looked at Lorcan, and gave him a warm smile. "It's a shape shifter. Just like you. But it's gone now, you needn't worry."

Lorcan was still standing protectively in front of Orla's immobile form, but he couldn't lift her up with his paws. The wizard crouched down next to him, "If this is your first time, it must be hard for you."

Lorcan felt lightheaded. He staggered away, stumbling as his limbs stretched out unexpectedly. He lay down on the ground, gripping the earth for balance as his world seemed to spin out of its orbit. He looked down to see his human hands grabbing the dirt, and then he blacked out for a brief moment. When he awakened, Lorcan sprang to his feet, shivering in the cold. He looked down and saw he was completely naked. He dashed to the pile of clothes he'd shed earlier and put them on.

The wizard smiled and waited patiently. He then knelt at Orla's side. He murmured some words and ran his hands the length of her body, pushing a green energy into her. Orla's eyes snapped open, and she gasped. Sitting up hurriedly, her chest heaved in fear. Lorcan gathered her up into his arms. He crooned to her, calming her down until she stopped trembling.

"If you could learn to control your dark magic, child, you could be very powerful indeed," the wizard said.

Orla stared at him, not knowing how he'd gotten here or what he was talking about. "What do you mean?" she asked groggily.

He smiled at her like a kindly old grandfather. "I'm familiar with your branch of sorcery, dear, and if you could refine the use of your powers, you could be quite formidable. If you'd like, I can try to teach you." Orla looked from him to Lorcan and back again. The old man nodded, understanding that she make her decision later. "As for you, son, what happened was powerful. Use it to your advantage. You need to practice and see what works best for you."

Lorcan said nothing in response.

The wizard nodded. "I'm sure both of you need some time to adjust, make sense of what just happened, and discover your natural talent. Come to me if you need help. Remember, things like this happen for a reason. Don't take it for granted."

The wizard smiled, stood, and walked quickly away in the direction from which he'd come.

"What was he talking about?" Orla asked.

"You passed out, and Chiyo turned into a gigantic lizard that I had to fight off."

"What?" Orla sat up and saw the dead creature. She got up to her feet and inched toward it. "That's why its head was empty."

"What?" Lorcan asked.

"I was attempting to get into Chiyo's—I mean, the lizard's—head. I think it must have figured it out."

"Are you saying you used your magic without telling me?"

"There wasn't time to tell you. How did you fight this huge animal with your bare hands?"

"Well, it wasn't me who killed it. It was the old man with his magic."

"What was he talking about? Your talent? I know you're a good fighter, but it sounded like he was referring to something else completely."

"Well, I turned myself into a dragon, flew fifty feet into the air, threw jets of fire at the lizard, and killed it in one go. How does that sound?"

She smiled. "Not funny."

Lorcan pulled her into his arms. "I know it's not, but please laugh anyway." When she pasted an awkward grin on her face, he shook his head. "That look could scare little children." He embraced her tightly and kissed her forehead, his body shuddering with emotion. He knew she could feel it. The moment he'd seen his paws and felt that he couldn't protect her, couldn't speak, couldn't call out for her—the helplessness of that moment came back to him now in a blast of emotions.

Looking up at Lorcan, Orla stared into his eyes and felt like she could lose herself in them for the rest of eternity. "Thank you," she said.

"I didn't exactly . . ." She stopped his words with her kiss.

They stood in the chill air for a while, then reality came flooding back. "Lorcan, I don't think the Chiyo-lizard that attacked us was the real Chiyo. I know you won't believe me, but I feel like there was something different about her. My magic picked up on it when she was knocking on the old man's door. Something different about her presence."

"Then we should ask the wizard for his opinion. Also, I think you should take him up on his offer."

"What offer?"

"To teach you how to control your dark magic."

Orla raised her arms. "You think I can't control my magic?" Lorcan grabbed her arms. "No, please. I can't handle two episodes from you in a day."

CHAPTER 12

The pack gathered at their secret meeting place at a small temple on top of the hill. Mori walked in, Roy flanking her right side. There were twenty other werefoxes around, now in human form. Mori sensed a strange aura in the air, but said nothing. As usual, she walked to the middle of the room as the leader of the group. Five senior members of the clan sat on chairs on a raised platform in a corner of the temple.

Roy glanced at Mori to be sure she was okay. She limped a bit but seemed to be moving fine. Mori looked up and caught his deep brown eyes—her fierce gaze always made any other fox flinch, but not him. He smiled at her instead.

An old man standing at a corner grumbled, "Why was this meeting so urgent? I need to work for a living. If you can't bring in the money to support us, at least give us some room to maneuver. You can't expect us to drop everything to be here on a whim."

"This is urgent." Mori gave him a stern stare. "Don't speak before I do. And don't speculate on whether or not it's important. The clan's matters come first and are of utmost priority. If you can't make a living doing what you're doing, the clan will support you financially, but you have to earn your way first."

Everybody turned to look at the old man. He stared back at them, shoving his hands into his pockets and casting a condescending look on Mori. She ignored him and spoke slowly and clearly, "The Yakuz were looking for the key again." She waited for few seconds, letting the information sink in while she gauged the reactions of the senior members. The five sitting on chairs looked at one another.

"What proof do you have of that?" one of them asked.

"I know someone in town who might have information about the key and its location. This person was attacked, kidnapped, and tortured for the information. Our spy in the Yakuz was killed during the process," she answered.

"The Yakuz!" There were rumblings among the people in the temple. They looked at one another. Amid the confusion, Mori knew, there was fear. It wasn't the Yakuz, but the fear that worked to destroy the morality of her clan. It was her worst nightmare.

She projected her voice to the far end of the room. "And before you ask, I don't know what triggered the attack. I don't know why they want the key . . . or why now. But it's our mission to protect it and the secrets that come with it, so we must delegate more members to the location—just in case they find out where it is and decide to hunt for it."

The old man who spoke before raised his voice. "Are you saying you want to send our people to that place? Are they supposed to remain there for the rest of their lives? I, for one, am not volunteering for this."

"And I'm not asking for volunteers." Mori stared at him, demanding his silence. "As I said before, I don't know what triggered the Yakuz attack. But war is coming our way, and we have to live up to our sacred mission."

"We've sacrificed enough for the mission," said one of the senior members.

"What do you mean?" Mori asked him.

"You are too young to know. I have seen deaths. I've seen the battle, and I think we've given enough," the old man muttered.

"What are you talking about?" asked a young member on the floor.

The crowd fired up with questions, and Mori didn't know which one to answer first.

Sai, a man in his mid-twenties, stepped out to the middle of the room. He had inherited his family's fortune and was willing to throw money at anything that money could buy. The only thing he didn't have to go along with his wealth was the alpha bloodline. "The Yakuz are deadly. You ask us to protect the key, but what do you do to protect us, Mori?" he asked, broaching a sensitive topic. Everyone quieted, allowing Mori to answer.

"I'll handle this. I'll negotiate with the Mahito family. They've been supporting us for generations," Mori responded.

"You are too young and inexperienced to handle this," said a senior member. "I can help with the negotiation. I've established good rapport with the Mahitos," said another senior member.

Mori smiled, but Sai jumped in and cut her smile short. "She's the alpha—she should be negotiating. The Mahitos are outsiders. They don't understand fox business. If you need money, you have only to ask me," he grinned. "But money isn't going to buy back our long lost power in the werefox world, will not buy back the lives we have lost protecting the key."

Mori narrowed her eyes. "What are you proposing?"

"I want to protect this clan. I want everyone to be safe. And I can do it for real. Not just talk. We don't work for nothing. Guarding the stupid key is equal to working for nothing, and I don't like that." Sai paced, circling Mori, looking her up and down. He moved a step closer but then felt Roy's hand on his shoulder, gripping him like a pair of iron pliers. Sai glanced up and gauged Roy's eyes, eyes that looked as if they could shoot fire at Sai. He knew he'd be at a disadvantage against Roy, so he withdrew.

"No, we don't want to do this. Whatever it was, the mission began before our time. Now we have families to take care of," a middle-aged man added from the far end of the room.

His comment triggered a round of similar protests.

"We won't honor this mission."

"We've done our fair share."

"If I can't protect my family, what the hell am I doing protecting a mysterious key?"

Mori raised her voice over them. "But you know what will happen to the city if the key lands in the wrong hands. We'll all die. You family's survival is a moot point in a dead city."

Silence. Just when the crowd seemed to be on the verge of agreeing with Mori, Sai spoke again. "Yes, the key protects the city and keeps it safe. But it's been our responsibility for such a long time. We've given more than enough. It should be someone else's turn now. If the Yakuz want the key, let them have it. They won't destroy the city in which they live. They'll protect the key and stop attacking us. It's a win-win solution."

"You want to give the key to the Yakuz?" Mori stared hard at Sai. She smiled as the pieces started to come together for her. "What's in it for you, Sai?"

"As I said, I act only on the best interests of our clan."

"So you think it's best if I give up the location of the key to the Yakuz? That way, we don't have to fight?"

Sai nodded enthusiastically.

"Do you want to be the leader of the clan, Sai?"

He shrugged and said nothing.

Mori smiled. "I was wondering how the Yakuz found out about the family who knows the secret of the key. How they'd known my whereabouts that night and where I sent our spy. I also wondered how the gray wolf clan knew when I was alone and injured so they could attack me."

As Mori advanced, Sai staggered backward. "Don't you accuse me of anything! I challenge your leadership!" Sai growled.

"Challenge my leadership?"

"Yes, I'll fight for it. The old-fashioned way. If I win, I lead."

"And if you lose?"

"I'll spend the rest of my pitiful life guarding the stupid key."

There were rumbles in the room.

"No, this is not a good time for it."

"I'm supporting Mori. She's been a good leader. I don't want a fight."

"If you don't want to fight, go elsewhere."

"An alpha has to be able to defend her position in battle."

"Battle my ass, it was ancient."

A wave of arguments. People talking over one another.

Mori and Sai circled threateningly, looking into each other's eyes, about to fight.

A senior member raised his hands. "Stop this. Stop. Do not fight."

"This is tradition. If she insists we follow tradition and protect the key, then she should defend her leadership," Sai snarled, shifting into a formidable fox.

Roy darted over, grabbing Mori's hand before she shifted. "You don't have to do this. Please don't, Mori."

"I don't want to fight. But this is a leadership challenge, not a threat. You can't protect me from this, Roy." And then she shifted.

The crowd got excited now. "Fight! Fight! Fight!" they cheered.

Mori and Sai charged at each other. Mori's supporters argued with Sai's. The observers began to shift and fight amongst each other. The inside of the temple was a blur of dust, flying objects, and the sounds of wounded dog howls.

"Stop!" Roy yelled but nobody was listening. "Stop this!" he yelled again, but it made no difference. He pulled a gun and fired into the air. Silence ensued, but Sai and Mori were still snarling at each other. Both were badly injured. Blood was everywhere. Roy said nothing further, but walked to the middle of the room, snatched fox-Mori up, and swung her over his shoulders. She passed out.

Sai growled, and Roy pointed the gun at him. "Between your teeth and my gun, my money's on the gun. To all of you—I've had enough of this nonsense. You want to shift, then shift. You want to bark, fight, and kill one another, that's your problem. I'm taking Mori out of here." Roy turned on his heel and exited the temple with Mori on his shoulders.

Halfway down the hill, Mori opened her eyes, finding that she had shifted back to her human form and was dangling from Roy's shoulders. "Let me down, let me down!" Roy didn't stop. "Let me down, Roy."

"I just saved you."

"Saved my ass."

"Yes, and that, too." Roy kept walking, ignoring Mori's wriggling and verbal abuse.

Orla and Lorcan went back to the warehouse to look for a sign of the real Chiyo and found nothing. Not only they could they not find Chiyo, but Goro's body had disappeared as well. The building was empty, save for the eerie chilled air that filled the place. They decided to go back to the wizard for more information. The old man greeted them at the door with a warm smile as if not surprised that they had come back to find him.

He made them tea, then brought the steaming cups over to the table as he settled in for a long tale. Lorcan began their story with finding the kitsune that had brought them to Chiyo's front door. From there, Orla related how Chiyo had kicked them out and they had found the temple holding her grandfather's remains. The old wizard's eyes grew sad as they spoke about his old friend, but he didn't interrupt. They next explained what had just happened and how they'd ended up at his door. When Lorcan fell silent, they waited to hear what the old man had to say. He shook his head as he thought, silently coming up with ideas and dismissing them just as quickly. When he finally settled on one that he thought might work, he smiled and looked up at the young couple in front of him.

"When she accompanied you to my door, I sensed it might not be the Chiyo I knew, but I hadn't seen her for such a long time. I wasn't sure. I don't think she's with the Yakuz, but I think it's more likely that we'll receive bad news than good. If they'd gotten the information out of her, they wouldn't have sent in the lizard shapeshifter. Don't blame yourselves—you couldn't have known."

"The shapeshifter speculated you would have information about the key. You killed the lizard—will its group know that? Will they go after you?" Lorcan asked.

The old man looked at Lorcan and smiled. "You are both looking for the key as well."

"Yes, but we were forced to do it for reasons important only to us. We're not interested in any benefits the key would give the holder. We're not gold diggers," Orla jumped in.

"I can tell that much." The wizard gave her a fatherly smile. "But as you can see, trouble follows whomever possesses the key—or even those with a whiff of information about it. What you don't know won't hurt you."

"What does it do, really?" Lorcan asked.

"Power. The key can open the source of God's power."

"What sort of power? Energy? Magic? Knowledge?" Lorcan pressed on.

"Curiosity killed the cat, young man."

Lorcan smiled. "When we put our lives on the line for this key, we're half dead already. If we can't find the key, not only will *we* be dead, but we'll put at risk the lives of other people who depend on it."

"That's the very reason I have to do whatever it takes to keep the information to myself. The key is safe now. You need not worry. But you cannot take it with you."

"We came all this way. If you want us to go away empty handed, then can you at least give us an inkling of what this key is all about? If we—and many others—are going to die because we can't have it, can you at least let us know that our cause is nothing compared to the disaster you're protecting humankind from?" Irritation overflowed in Lorcan's voice.

The old man took a few minutes, contemplating. Then he spoke slowly. "One of the power sources that the key can control or release is the water element. That was why the sea dragon wanted it. The sea dragon wanted to flood and drown the entire city. It needs the water element to do so."

Orla's eyes widened. "Sea dragon's territory expands with the water. Of course, it would want water everywhere."

The wizard nodded. Lorcan buried his head in his hands for a while, trying to gain control over his sneer. He smiled. "Sea dragons exist in children's fairy tales. There are explanations for this. At a very basic level, tides are the rise and fall of sea levels caused by the combined effects of the gravitational forces exerted by the moon, the sun, and the rotation of the Earth. Let's say someone could somehow affect the celestial rotation and ultimately impact the orbits of the related planets. That person would create tides that would drown whole city. But I can't see why someone would want to do that . . ."

"The sea dragon. The sea dragon would want that, Lorcan," Orla explained.

"Orla!" Lorcan exclaimed.

"Had I mentioned that information comes hand in hand with trouble? It's here already."

They old wizard bolted to the door with lightning speed. Lorcan and Orla were amazed to see him move so fast. They followed him, rushing out the door.

CHAPTER 13

The wizard rushed toward a shadow along the dark road. It slithered away quickly, similar to the movement of a gigantic python. Within only a few steps, the wizard had lost sight of the spying animal. Orla and Lorcan caught up with him.

"We've lost it. What was it?" Orla asked.

"A python," the wizard answered.

"Lizard, python . . . what'll be next?" Lorcan muttered. The wizard shook his head and turned back toward the house. Lorcan stopped him on his way. "Come on, we have to do better than this. We can help you. Tell us what you need. If we leave here and the Yakuz attack you, what are you going to do?"

The old man stared at Lorcan. "I'll take the secrets to my grave."

"That won't save people's lives. I can guarantee you that we can take the key to a very safe place. No one on Earth will ever have access to it. Isn't that a better solution? Think about it. You might be able to keep certain information secret, but what if they found the key in some other way? What would you be able to do about it?" Lorcan was losing his patience when the wizard suddenly turned back.

"What is the place that you're talking about? How can you be so sure it's perfectly safe?"

Lorcan pulled out his wrist unit, put it on, and pressed a series of keys. A light beamed down from the sky, and the portal to the Daimon Gate opened. The wizard could see a glimpse of the goings-on at the entrance. Then Lorcan shut the portal and put the unit away. The wizard gasped, looking at Lorcan with a newfound respect.

"You never mentioned that you could wield magic, young man." His tone was borderline accusatory, but Lorcan just grinned at him and shrugged.

"I wouldn't call it magic, exactly. I'd just call it using my resources to get what I need. That is the place where I will keep the key safe. It's not on Earth—it's another universe. There are many worlds just like the world you live in now. The place I showed you doesn't give access to evil men from Earth. The Yakuz and the sea dragon could never get the key. Do you understand?"

The wizard hesitated.

"I'm trusting you with our lives now, and it's not the first time. Can't you trust us just a little bit? I can build a data portfolio for you about all of Japan's natural disasters. I can locate places you think the sea dragon might be. I can dig up information on the Yakuz for you. I have access to a system off-planet that can do that and more. Everything, that is, *except* magic."

The wizard looked at him for a long time, then seemed to silently consent, sinking in to himself a bit. To Orla, it looked like the old man struggled with a load too heavy for his frail shoulders to bear. He nodded, but before he could say anything further, a group of shapeshifters swooped down from the sky as hawks, attacking them with their sharp talons. Orla had the presence of mind to duck, but the old man and Lorcan had been caught unaware. Lorcan's face was gouged, and the old man was knocked over. Orla decided it was time for her to vent her anger from the close call she'd experienced at the hands of the lizard, and as these punks were obviously working for the same side as the reptile, they were fair game.

She began to chant under her breath, and purple lightning formed at her fingertips. Her eyes were open, following one bird, and then another. Once her gaze settled on one, lightning bolts flowed from her fingers, and the bird was zapped badly enough that it fell out of the sky and thought twice about trying to attack the group again. She was losing time trying to focus on one of the hawks at a time, but she was the only one who could fight them off. Lorcan had no way of getting to them, and the wizard was dazed, though valiantly trying to get back to his feet.

"You won't have to handle them alone. I'm adding my magic to yours." He let her know he was with her, and that somehow helped Orla gather her strength and courage for a major attack. She had her back to the wizard, and so she didn't see that five of the hawks were flying in carrying a net with a large boulder in it. The old man was busy chanting with his eyes closed, and Lorcan was ducking to avoid an onslaught of vicious talons. The hawks let loose, and the boulder fell . . . right onto the old man. It crushed his chest, and that drew Lorcan over to him to try to protect him as best he could while Orla killed the rest.

She was stunned by the sight she saw when she turned around, but it only served to anger her more. The bolts of lightning were now thicker and seemed to have minds of their own. She no longer had to aim for individual birds—the lightning was doing it for her.

She fell to her knees near the old man, apologizing for being watchful and asking if there was anything she could do to save him. He patted her hand. "No, child. You can't help me, but you can help by taking the key to a safe place. I have a map that will lead you to the temple. Please do it as soon as you can . . ." His body tensed, his eyes closed, and he took his last breath.

Orla took the map from the man and unfolded it. They were, indeed, very close to the temple. But before they could determine anything further from the map, Lorcan sniffed the air. "Mori," he whispered.

"What?" Orla was astonished, not because he had spoken Mori's name but because he had sniffed the air and known it was her. He obviously didn't even realize what he was doing. "Mori," Lorcan repeated. He stood and glanced around. All of a sudden, a car raced out from a hill coming from a small road in the bush. Mori appeared to be tied up in the back seat of the car. She was kicking and shouting at the driver. The car swerved onto the main road and headed into town.

Lorcan chased the car. "Lorcan!" Orla called out. "You can't chase them on foot!" Lorcan kept sprinting. "Lorcan!" Orla called again. Lorcan stopped.

"He got Mori. Someone got her."

"I can see that, but we can't chase them on foot."

"What do you suggest?"

Orla ran to a side street. She saw a scooter parked in an empty front yard. She made a run for it, ducked down by the scooter's side, and picked the lock. It took her only a few seconds. "Sorry," she mumbled to the absent owner as she pushed the scooter away toward the corner where Lorcan waited.

"We'll return it, of course," she said when she saw the look on Lorcan's face.

"Do you know how to drive one of these?" he asked.

"Can't be more difficult than riding a horse."

"It is. A horse has four legs and can stand by itself."

She shrugged. "You want to get Mori, here's your chance."

Lorcan looked at the vehicle, considered his options, and then hopped on.

"Are you sure?" Orla asked.

"There's no other way. It can't be more difficult than riding a horse, as you said."

Orla grinned and hopped on.

When they were on the road heading into town, Orla noticed Lorcan sniffing the air repeatedly for Mori's scent.

"Do you realize that you're sniffing the air?" Orla asked.

"What?"

"Obviously not. Never mind."

In town—Orla called it a town, but it was actually much smaller than a village in England—they stopped in front of a small traditional Japanese house. Wrapped in manicured gardens, it was quiet and peaceful, as was the street. Orla and Lorcan surveyed the area from a hidden position around the corner.

"How do you know she'll be here?"

Lorcan shrugged, "I just know."

Shortly, the car they had seen at the village approached and parked in front of the house. From inside, a man exited, a grocery bag in one hand. Lorcan charged at him from across the street. Without speaking a single word, Lorcan landed a punch on the man's face. The groceries fell to the ground. The two men pummeled each other.

Orla helped Mori from the backseat and realized she wasn't tied up. She moved stiffly, though. "Are you okay?" Orla asked. "Don't worry, we're here . . ." she said, but stopped when she saw the worried look on Mori's face when she saw the men fighting.

"Stop fighting! Stop that! Stop!" Mori cried out.

The men ignored her and continued fighting. Orla grabbed a load of bread lying on the ground and whacked at the two men. "Stop fighting!" Orla yelled. They stopped, but they were still snarling and swearing at each other.

"You get off her," Lorcan growled.

"What the fuck!" The man ran at Lorcan again, but Orla jumped in front of him.

"Hold on. Hold on. She's all right," Orla said to Lorcan.

Lorcan turned to Mori. "Are you okay, Mori?"

Mori gingerly pressed her palm into the injuries she'd sustained in the fight with Sai. "I'm all right. It's not his fault. I'm not hurt . . . much. He was just trying to help me, Lorcan. That's Roy."

"Yes, finally, thank you!" Roy punctuated every word like a curse. "I was just trying to help." Roy paced back and forth, looking as if he needed something to punch.

Mori couldn't move quickly—she leaned against the car. "I'm sorry, Roy. Don't get mad at me." A tear dropped down onto her cheek.

Roy was astonished, and his fury evaporated into thin air like smoke. He'd never seen Mori's tears before. A woman like this didn't cry easily, and when she did, she could deflate a man's gigantic ego, Orla thought.

Roy darted over to Mori, taking her arm. "Please don't cry. Let me take you inside."

"Would you like to come in?" Mori asked Lorcan and Orla.

Lorcan was about to refuse, but Orla chimed in with an agreement before he could utter a word.

That night, Orla and Lorcan stayed in the guest room of Roy's house. Snuggling on the futon, Orla toyed with a strand of hair on Lorcan's face and looked into his striking blue eyes. He smiled at her. "We haven't had a proper wedding yet. I'm sorry." He smoothed her hair and pulled her into his arms.

"The wedding is just a formality. You haven't proposed properly."

He hopped up on his elbows. "I did, in London." She lay down on her arm. "Really? I can't seem to recall."

"That's all right. I'll do it all over again." He inched closer to her, and his hands began to get very busy on her body. Some nibbling here, some kisses there, gentle touches in other places. Her man knew how to please a woman, Orla thought. Soon, their bodies tangled in the sheet as they drove each other to the peak of satisfaction.

Orla's biological clock had adjusted to the time difference. She woke naturally in the morning, but not Lorcan. He was a sleepyhead regardless of the planet he was on. She snuggled into his chest for some of his familiar warmth, thinking of another round of activity to lift the morning mood. Then she gasped and bolted out from under the blanket and off the futon, landing on her backside and dragging herself backward on the floor.

Lorcan sat up. He intended to ask if she was okay, but what came out of his mouth was a woof.

Backed against the wall, Orla calmed down instantly as she registered what had happened. "Shhhh, it's okay, Lorcan." She smiled as graciously as possible. "You see, it's okay. I'm okay," she repeated herself. In front of her was a magnificent electric blue fox. She recognized his eyes, and she could tell he was in a panic. It was not the time for her to freak out. She smiled again.

She could tell he was totally confused. He whirled around, walking back and forth, making a pitiful little moaning sound. She inched toward him. He sat down on the futon. She reached out her hand and touched the soft fur on his head. He shook her hand off his head. As he turned around, he saw his bushy blue tail. He sprang up to all fours, jumped off the futon, and landed on the floor in front of the mirror. There, he saw it. In the mirror was a large blue fox. He snarled at himself.

"No, no, Lorcan, it's okay. We'll figure out how to handle this." Orla reached over to him, but he bolted out the door and outside to the garden.

"Lorcan!" she cried out and ran after him. He was too fast. He disappeared into the bush. Tears streamed down her face. Orla ran back into the house. Her scream woke Mori and Roy. She stuttered so much they couldn't understand what she was saying. Eventually, she summoned all of her strength and put the words together.

"Lorcan turned into a blue fox. He was totally confused, and he just ran off into the bush." And that was all she could say. She cried.

"He didn't know?" Mori asked. Orla shook her head. The thought of losing him forever tore at her heart. Roy said nothing. He shifted into a large black fox and ran out the door. Mori sat Orla down and fetched her some water.

CHAPTER 14

It had turned dark before Roy made it home. He walked into the house, gloriously naked with fox-Lorcan on his shoulders. He walked straight into the guest room and threw fox-Lorcan down on the futon. His blue fur was soaked with wet patches of blood, his left eyelid was torn, his right ear bled, and he was apparently not conscious.

"Oh my God, what happened to him?" Orla asked in panic.

"I beat him up. Stubborn son of a bitch. He'll heal fast. You don't need to worry," Roy said. Mori came in with a medical kit. She gave it to Orla, and then took a few bandages out and fussed over Roy's injuries. It looked as if Lorcan had put up a good fight. Mori took Roy back to his room.

Orla cleaned up all the mud and blood on Lorcan, literally from head to tail. She smoothed his magnificent blue fur. She had never seen such a beautiful animal. The thing was, he was all hers. A little later, Orla found Roy and Mori sitting in the living room. Mori poured Orla a cup of hot tea.

Sitting on the sofa, her hands still shaky, Orla couldn't make sense of the whole thing.

"He's different. I think he's a mix." Roy broke the silence.

"Like you? Fox-wolf?" Mori asked.

Roy shook his head. "I don't know. You're right, Mori, his blood tastes very strange."

Orla followed every single word in Roy and Mori's conversation, wanting to gather as much information as possible about were creatures so she could understand Lorcan better.

"How come he didn't know? Were blood is genetic. Unless he's a dead-liner who could live his whole life not knowing. But it's obvious he can shift. He can't be a dead-liner. In that case, he had to have been shifting since he was a kid. How could he live his whole life not knowing?" Roy asked.

"The other day, after Mori bit him, I think things started to change. I don't think he knew. I don't know his family, but I really don't think he knew about this ability."

"It doesn't look like he's taking it well," Mori commented.

"But were blood is, well, blood. You have it, or you don't. It's not a thing you can trigger," Roy said. The conversation continued, Mori and Roy discussing what they would do if they weren't werefoxes.

People always wanted things they couldn't have, Orla thought. She finished the tea, excused herself to go back to the guest room with Lorcan. Before she left, she asked, "When do you think he'll be able to shift back to his human form?"

"We can't speak for Lorcan, but we shift whenever we want," Mori said. "The only time I was forced was when I bit him." Orla nodded and left to be with Lorcan.

During the night, she snuggled next to Lorcan, stroking his fur and whispering into his ears that she loved him. She knew he heard her. Then she fell asleep. She felt his warm rough tongue on her cheek as she slept. She smiled at the feeling, but it might have been just a dream.

When she woke the next morning, Lorcan was still in fox form. He opened his eyes and looked at her. He stared right through her, then he closed his eyes again.

She lay down next to him, stroking his fur, but he turned his head away from her. "All right, if you just want to lie here, I'll lie with you." She lay down again next to him. Then she started talking about different things, about the time they were in London and the time when she left home and he didn't find her until three years later, and what she did in between.

Hours passed, and she kept talking. She cried, she got tired, she fell asleep, she woke, and she kept talking. Still, Lorcan just lay there in his fox form. In the evening, Mori came in. "Orla, you've got to come out and eat something. You look worse than he does."

"If he wants to do this, I'll do it with him," Orla said as a tear rolled down her face.

"I'll give you tonight. But by tomorrow morning, if you guys aren't up, I'm throwing you out. You're not going to die and rot in my house," Roy said from the doorway.

When Roy and Mori had left the room, Orla reached over, pulled fox-Lorcan into her arms, and cuddled. "Well, one more night, and then we'll have to die on the street. If that's what you want." Still no sign of a response from Lorcan. She lay there for a little longer, and then she got up.

Orla went to Lorcan's computer bag and pulled out the pouch in which he kept his lucky little love stone.

The yellow stone stared back at her, both encouraging and daring her.

She palmed the stone and went back to Lorcan at the futon. "I know you can hear me right now, so I'm going say this once and for all. You thought I was six and didn't have a clue what you meant when you took this stone. You were wrong. I understood, and I secretly wished you had kept your promise. I was raised a sorceress—I'm not allowed to wish, to have hope, or to love. So I thought if I wished for your love and kept it a secret to myself, then my sorcery demon wouldn't know. So I kept it a secret. Through all those years when you hadn't yet found me, that was the only thing I hoped for. When you showed me the stone in London last month, I thought my secret hope had finally paid off. But I was wrong after all . . ."

Tears streamed down her face now.

"I had been so wrong my whole life! You said you'd love me regardless of what I am. How noble of you. You don't think I can love you in the same way? Maybe the next thing you're going to say is that I want you for your money. But if you want to say so, you might have to shi—"

His mouth was on hers.

He pushed her to the futon, his hands caressing every curve of her body while his mouth ravished her. He was starved for her. He'd shifted back to his human form in lightning speed. All six-foot-one of him wrapped around her long, lean body. He kissed, he fondled, he soothed, he wiped away the tears and the worries that dulled her eyes.

The next day, Lorcan went for a run with Roy in their fox form. Roy taught Lorcan essential survival tips for controlling his shifting activities and how to utilize his were-abilities. After all, Lorcan was very new to the *were*-business. When the two foxes came back, Orla observed the magnificent sight of them. While Roy was large and quite bulky in the chest, he had short and shiny fur. His golden irises glowed. It seemed to her that he must have had some leopard in him—half-wolf, half-fox didn't quite explain his eyes. Lorcan looked more like a wolf than a fox with his long, glowing blue fur, especially around the face. His eyes were the same, striking blue. Both of them, Lorcan and Roy, were long, lean, and muscular, with the strength of predators. Seeing them, Orla made a mental note to never confuse were-creatures with ordinary pets—she could lose body parts that she desired to keep.

When the men came to the living room, fully dressed, Orla said, "I guess it's time for us to leave. Thanks for your hospitality."

Mori nodded. "I guess we part here. It was a pleasure meeting you."

Roy went to the kitchen to get himself a cup of tea. He sat down on the couch and said nothing.

"Very well then. Thank you again." Orla stood with Lorcan, about to leave.

"We can work together," Roy said and sipped his tea.

"Roy!" Mori sent Roy a disapproving look.

Roy shrugged. "That's what you told me. You said they could help by taking the key to somewhere safe."

"That was before what happened in the temple. Before . . . before . . ."

"Before Sai tried to rip your throat out . . . after he failed to kill you by tipping his wolves that you had been wounded by a bullet?"

Lorcan's eyes darkened. "You mean the bullet intended for me? I haven't had a chance to thank her for that yet. And you're saying someone was trying to kill her because she took that bullet?"

Roy leaned back in his chair. "There's nothing personal about her taking that bullet for you. She bit you without knowing you had were-blood. Your blood mixed, and you were both naturally bonded for a short period of time. The issue is that a dickhead in her clan, possibly a traitor, took the opportunity to send three wolves after her when she was injured."

"We don't have proof of that, Roy," said Mori.

"You speculated that yourself at the temple. Think about that, Mori. I know you think troubles follow you, but the truth is, we're stronger together. You can't go back to your clan."

"Why not?" Tears started to form in Mori's eyes.

Roy couldn't handle Mori's tears, and Orla knew they needed Roy to stay cool. Before he could utter insensitive words in response to Mori's tearful reaction, Orla jumped in. "But *we* need you, Mori. Really. We need your help. We need the key, or people will die, including us. We will protect the key because it's . . . it's our lives we're talking about . . ."

Lorcan sat down next to Orla and was about to say something, but Orla cut him off. "Roy, how do you think we could help? Come on, we need this."

Roy looked at Mori, waiting for a signal, then he said, "Sai was bought off by the Yakuz, Mori, and I'm afraid that the majority of senior members in your clan were, too." His voice was as cold as steel. Tears rolled down Mori's face now.

"At the temple, Sai gave you two options. He challenged you. If he won, he'd lead the clan and be in a position to access the key. If he lost, what did he promise you? It seemed to be fair at the time, right? If he lost, he'd spend the rest of his life guarding the key, meaning he'd know exactly where it is. Either way, it leads him directly to the key."

Mori sobbed, but Roy pressed on. "You were in the middle of it, so of course you couldn't see. But the other members of the clan were pushing you toward one of Sai's options. Think about it, Mori. I know it hurts. You love your clan, and you worked for it your whole life. You believe in it. But the Yakuz is the force of evil. You can't fight against it. I don't want to lose you, Mori."

Mori looked at Roy and nodded. Roy smiled, but it didn't last long. They suddenly heard the loud squawking of birds. Looking out the window, they saw a sky full of black hawks streaming at the house. There were similar to those that had attacked and killed the wizard—and they knew the old wizard had given Orla the map.

Orla darted toward her handbag which rested in a corner close to the door, but it was too late. The front line of the birds threw their bodies at the glass entrance as if on a suicide mission. The door shattered, and a cloud of black birds invaded the house. Roy pulled the cover from the sofa and wrapped Mori up, tightening his grip so she couldn't wriggle out. He drew his gun and shot at the birds with his free hand.

"Through the back door!" Roy yelled, dragging Mori out the back door with him. Lorcan grabbed his bag with one hand, and tried to protect Orla with the other. There wasn't much Orla could do from inside the house. They ran to the back yard, and once out in the open, Orla began to throw her fireballs. This time, the fire was lethal to the birds.

They ran toward Roy's car. He opened the front door and shoved the squirming Mori inside. He darted to the driver's seat while Lorcan and Orla jumped into the backseat. A few remaining birds hurled themselves at the car, but figuring they had no chance against metal, they flew away.

Roy drove away quickly.

"Where are we going?" Lorcan asked.

"To the key," Roy said briskly and focused his eyes on the road. Mori finally broke free from the sofa cover. She looked at Roy, and her voice was shaky. "You're scratched. Oh my God, you're scratched."

Roy shook his head. "It's okay."

But Orla knew it wasn't okay—she could see where the shoulder of his shirt was torn, the scratch marks had turned black. She swung her eyes to Lorcan and saw that the scratch marks on his arms and shoulders were bleeding, and the blood was red. "Are you okay, Lorcan?" she asked. Lorcan nodded, but he could see Roy's trouble as well.

"What is that, Mori?" Lorcan asked. Mori looked back at him, her eyes filled with tears already. "It's the Yakuz's poison. It's designed for were-creatures."

"Why didn't it affect me?"

Mori shook her head and said nothing more.

CHAPTER 15

Roy drove the car straight to the wooden dock. The wheels spun as he braked hard, and the car did a three-sixty and stopped with one wheel dangling over the edge. He pushed at the door, bolted out, and slumped to the ground. Roy was on his knees, breathing heavily. His eyes were dazed, and a stream of black blood trickled from of his mouth. Mori wrapped her arms around him, but he shrugged her off. He tried to yank at his shirt to pull it off, but Mori wouldn't loosen her grip.

"No," she said firmly. "You're not going to shift now. You're not going to die. You have to stay with me." He struggled again but couldn't loose himself from Mori's hold. "Get the boat, please," Mori directed Orla and Lorcan.

"Shouldn't we take him to the hospital?" Lorcan asked.

Mori shook her head. "It wouldn't help him. We have to get him to the temple, where the key is. It's a sacred place, it will heal him." Lorcan stared at her in disbelief, but as Orla rushed toward at the boat, he followed her.

"Do you really think that's best for him?" Lorcan asked.

"Mori knows best. We should take her word." She gestured at the boat. "It looks like you'll have to drive this beast. Ever driven a motorboat, smarty pants?"

"I'll look for the 'on' button," Lorcan said, letting Orla go to help Mori bring Roy to the boat.

Mori sat at the back of the boat, Roy in her arms. He was weakening by the second. In no time, they were sailing across the sea, Lorcan having figured out how to operate the boat. Roy shivered with the cold breeze. Mori gathered whatever she could find to keep him warm, but it didn't seem to help. His face had turned pale as a sheet, and his lips had blackened. She just gathered him into her arms and rocked, saying things in Japanese.

Orla didn't need Lorcan's translator to know Mori told him she loved him and he had to stay alive for her. It was all too familiar for Orla, the things a desperate and woman in love would say. But Orla wasn't sure Roy could hear any of it. Orla didn't realize, but tears were streaming down on her face. She felt the warmth of Lorcan's body when he wrapped his free arm around her shoulder, his other hand manning the steering wheel.

Roy opened his eyes and muttered something. Mori called out for Lorcan and Orla. Lorcan slowed the boat and rushed toward the back.

"Where you come from, is it a safe place?" Roy asked.

Many responses flashed through Lorcan's mind, but he simply nodded.

"Can you take Mori with you?"

Mori said something in Japanese—Orla knew she was begging Roy to stop saying things that sounded like his last words. But perhaps they were. Lorcan nodded again.

There was a loud bang on the side of the boat.

Lorcan thrust Orla behind him and moved toward the origin of the noise. At the front of the boat, he saw the whirlpool. In the center of the swirling water, an electric blue shape was surfacing. It had a long snout with fringe hanging from the bottom jaw, and it looked almost exactly like one of the ancient Japanese dragons he'd seen depicted in fairy tales. It had a serpentine build, and its head was large enough to swallow the boat whole. It stared at them, opening its enormous jaws wide, and shot a jet of water which hit the hull of the little boat with such force that it punched a hole in the bottom. That meant they'd soon be swimming. A second jet tore through the old wood. The third jet wasn't water, but looked like a pure bolt of lightning.

"We have to jump!" Lorcan said. They darted toward the back of the boat. Lorcan threw Roy overboard and jumped in after him. Mori and Orla followed. Roy sank like a stone, and he was too heavy for Mori to pull to the surface. Lorcan swam to her and grabbed Roy, floating to the surface with his unconscious body. The boat had not sunk yet, and it blocked their view of the monster. The group quietly tread water, moving silently toward something that looked like land in the distance.

When they looked back, they saw more lightning strike the boat, causing it to catch fire and explode. They swam for what seemed like hours to them, but finally came to a small island where they could drag their tired bodies from the water and flop in the sand. The sky in the direction from which they'd come looked inky black, illuminated here and there with lightning bolts.

Mori said nothing, but hurried to Roy and performed CPR with tears streaming down her face. A short time later, Roy spat out some water and took a deep breath.

He was breathing, but barely. Lorcan looked at both Mori and Roy. Orla knew he was furious at how hopeless their situation was. Then he pulled out his wrist unit.

"Oh my God, don't tell me it's damaged. It's our only way back to the Daimon Gate, Lorcan."

"It's fine. I'm going to call the Host for help. We don't have any other option, and we don't have time to explain to Mori. The last thing we want is . . ." Orla raised her hand it stop Lorcan. She turned and ran toward Mori, pointing behind her.

"Look out!" Orla shouted. As soon as Mori turned to look, Orla landed a punch on the side of Mori's face, knocking her out cold. She turned back to Lorcan. "Does that help?" He nodded and punched commands into his wrist unit while Orla dragged Mori toward a large stone, away from the wind.

After Lorcan had called, a beam of holocast appeared. Inside the beam was the hologram of the Host of the Daimon Gate, and he didn't look happy. "You're on a mission. It's inappropriate to directly contact me like this."

"I know, I'm sorry. But this is urgent, and we need your help. We're so close to getting the key. But the man lying there, he's been poisoned by those who stole it from you. He's the only one who has access to the key. We need to save him."

From the distance, in the dark, Orla raised an eyebrow as Lorcan lied right to the Host's face—without his usual obvious squirming. Most of the time, lying was her job.

"Lorcan, I'm not the right person to call on this matter for several reasons. I cannot help you regardless of how much I want to. The right person to contact is Ciaran."

"Ciaran! But how can I contact him? He's in another universe. Not only . . ."

"That's the only plausible way I know. I'm sorry. I have to go." The Host and the light beam of the holocast vanished.

"Wait," Lorcan said helplessly, although he knew the Host could no longer hear him. Then he saw a small object lying on the sand. Lorcan picked it up and grinned at Orla. "Wicked old man," he muttered.

"Hush. What if he can hear you?"

Lorcan grinned again. In his hand was a wrist unit. It must be the communicator that connected directly to Ciaran. Lorcan entered the commands, and a holocast arrived, casting a circle of light in the sand. Inside it stood Ciaran LeBlanc, with a face that God had created when he was in a very good mood and the body of a warrior. Ciaran looked to be in a hurry, his hair tousled and his shirt unbuttoned. Ciaran was astonished to see Lorcan at the other end of the holocast.

"Lorcan?!"

Lorcan nodded.

"Do you realize you just hit the panic button of my private contact?"

"By private contact, do you mean your father?" Ciaran's eyes darkened, and Lorcan's requested more time to explain before Ciaran leaped out of the light beam and slit his throat. "The Host gave me the unit because I'm on a very important mission for him, and I need your help. He trusts me with the information about your relationship. You know the Host is not supposed to interfere with anything outside the Daimon Gate. He risked his life giving me this unit to contact you because he knows what I'm doing is important."

Ciaran stopped pacing. He nodded. "After the prank I pulled on my father, I deserve this."

Lorcan remembered vividly how Ciaran had tricked his father to get some information past the Daimon Gate's scanner. It was a big deal, and Ciaran felt remorse about it. The worst part was that Lorcan had helped Ciaran to carry it out. "Don't be too harsh on yourself. It wasn't exactly a prank. You needed the disc—it was important," Lorcan said. "Same with this now, Ciaran."

"All right. What do you need?"

"If you come a bit closer, you'll see a man lying in the sand. He's been poisoned." Lorcan walked toward Roy so Ciaran could follow him. The light beam circling on the sand around Ciaran shed enough light for him to see Roy.

"My father asked you to call me. Does that mean this guy couldn't be saved by any earthly means?"

"We're stranded on an island. He might not last long—even if I *could* get medical help here."

Ciaran nodded. "All right. I'll get my medical doctor. But he's never been to Earth before, and I can't risk him stepping outside the holocast. I'll have to bring your guy inside."

Lorcan nodded. "One more thing . . . Roy is a werefox. I think your doctor should be aware of that."

"I beg your pardon?"

"A werefox is . . ."

"I know what a werefox is . . . by superstition only. I can't believe you're using the term as if they exist in the real world . . ."

"Why would you say that?" Mori darted out from the dark toward Ciaran, followed by Orla, who was trying hold her back without success. "Please try to save Roy. We're werefoxes, yes, but we're not bad people."

"I didn't say that you were."

Mori shifted into her fox form, and then shifted back. "If you didn't believe, now you've seen it. Now you should believe. Please help him. Please."

Ciaran could see the devastation in Mori's eyes. He nodded and entered a command into his wrist unit. A tall young man in his thirties with blonde hair and an angelic face arrived. "Please step back," Ciaran said and then expanded the light circle. The two men approached Roy. The circle gradually grew wider until Roy was lying inside it under the bright light.

From the distance, Mori gasped. "They look so human. Beautiful."

Orla smiled. "I don't know about the doctor, but Ciaran *is* human. He's from London."

Inside the light circle, the doctor examined Roy, shook his head, and discussed something privately with Ciaran. The conversation seemed intense. Ciaran paced back and forth a bit, then came to the edge of the light and signaled Lorcan to come close to the light wall.

"I can't talk to the woman, Lorcan. Please ask her to stay over there." Lorcan turned around and saw Mori trying to move closer and Orla struggling to keep her away. Lorcan gestured for them to stay.

Lorcan put his hands into his pockets and spoke to Ciaran. "If you can't save him, just say it."

"It's up to you. I need your decision."

"Why me? Why not his woman?"

"She's too emotional. She'd agree to everything. You called me here. You're responsible for this, so you have to make the decision. Can you honestly tell me Roy is trustworthy?"

Lorcan realized he hadn't a clue. Their encounter had been too short for him to tell. Lorcan shook his head. "I don't know. We just met him. But he protects Mori—he loves his woman. And he took me into his home the day before yesterday, without even knowing me. I was in bad shape, and he kicked my ass just to shake me up. After an earlier attack, the poison was eating him up, but he still drove us to the dock. He knew he was going to die, but all he worried about was keeping Mori safe."

Ciaran nodded. "That's good enough for me. The doctor can't cleanse the poison already in his bloodstream, but the corrupted blood can be replaced with a clean substance."

"Substance?"

"Yes . . . kind of like a special type of blood. It has several good attributes, but the down side is that once we use it, we can't simply take it out and replace it with normal human blood. He'll be partially Eudaizian."

"It'll turn him into an alien?"

"Whatever you want to call it—it's just terminology. You live in the Daimon Gate, so technically you and Orla are aliens as well." Ciaran cocked an eyebrow.

Lorcan nodded and raked his hand though his hair. "Right, right. Sorry, I'm awfully confused right now. I guess the blood isn't the biggest issue here?"

Ciaran nodded. "Right. What I have to put into him is a secret substance only used for important people in

Eudaiz. I'm in charge of more than six hundred billion citizens in Eudaiz, so I can't afford to risk anything when it comes to security. If Roy turns against us, if he gives a sample of this substance to our adversaries, I will have to kill him. Do you understand that? Can you relay that to his woman after this?"

Lorcan nodded.

"The substance is only sustainable in the Eudaiz environment, so he'll have to be our citizen. And as you know, we don't adopt people easily. If his woman isn't qualified, we might be able to take him only."

Lorcan shook his head and felt a pang of pain in his chest. This was all too familiar to him. It was the exact scenario he and Orla had faced when they were torn apart because of her family sorcery, and that was the reason he had entered the Daimon Gate. Lorcan knew he'd been lucky to cheat their way in, and now they were paying for that cheat. But what if Roy couldn't pull it off? That meant the decision made now would set them apart forever, should Roy survive.

"This should be Mori's decision." Lorcan shook his head.

"No, this should be Roy's decision, but he can't speak for himself right now. You called me here. I'm willing to risk our substance to save him. But the next part you will have to decide for him—and take complete responsibility if things go awry."

"Why does it have to come to this?" Lorcan raked his hair again.

"Welcome to my world. He hasn't much time. What do you say?"

Lorcan turned and looked at Mori. Then he turned back to Ciaran. "Do it."

Ciaran nodded at the doctor. The doctor pulled out a small box containing several pieces of compact medical equipment and crouched next to Roy. Ciaran was right next to him for assistance. Ciaran knew the exact procedure. After the doctor injected something into Roy's arm, Ciaran held his body down when he tensed up and convulsed. He tilted Roy's head to the side so that he wouldn't choke when he vomited. Ciaran took his shirt off, wiped the black blood from Roy's mouth, and cushioned his head.

From a distance, Mori's eyes widened. "Is Ciaran a doctor?"

Orla shook her head. "Not really. But he has a wealth of knowledge, and he cares a lot for a great many people. He's a good man." Orla was thinking that she was glad she and Lorcan had decided not to betray Ciaran. She glanced at Lorcan, and when she saw him looking at her, she knew he was thinking the same thing.

Roy seemed to settle. Ciaran snapped a wrist unit on his right wrist and then came to the edge of the light. "What he has now is temporary," he said to Lorcan. "We will fully charge him in Eudaiz. The wrist unit must stay on him at all times, or he will die."

"How temporary?"

"I'd give it a week. As for you, never use that button again. Return the unit to my father. If you ever need to contact me, this one is yours." Ciaran put another wrist unit on the sand. He turned to signal the doctor it was time to leave.

"Wait," Lorcan said. "Brandon attacked us in the Daimon gate and wanted us to expose your activity to the council. We didn't. Your father knows about it now. I thought I'd let you know."

"Brandon? Prince of the Red castle?"

Lorcan nodded. Ciaran rolled his eyes and shook his head. "All right, I'll handle that. Thanks." Then Ciaran, the doctor, and the light beam vanished.

CHAPTER 16

When the sun came up at the horizon of the magnificent sea, Roy stirred and awoke. Mori gathered him into her arms and burst into tears. "A magical man came and saved you."

"Well, it wasn't exactly magic. The work Ciaran and the doctor did was completely scientific. How do you feel, Roy?" Lorcan asked

"I feel like I could move a mountain." Roy stood. He was six feet tall, but at the moment, he seemed to grow two inches taller, and he was glowing with energy and virility.

"You look well," Orla said.

"I should ask Ciaran for some of the substance for myself!" Lorcan muttered. Then he whispered into Orla's ear about Roy's one-week lifespan. Orla squealed and walked away, waving her arms in frustration.

Lorcan looked at Roy and Mori. "She didn't like my joke," he hastily explained as he scurried after Orla.

When Lorcan caught up with her, Orla lowered her voice so Roy and Mori wouldn't hear. "One week? How are you going to explain that to him? How are you going to tell Mori?"

"I didn't have a choice. Plus, he won't exactly die within a week—but he does have to go to Eudaiz. As long as he's alive, we can sort things out, right? Let's try to look at this in a positive light, shall we?" Orla contemplated and then nodded.

They returned to Roy and Mori at the beach. Lorcan spent some time discussing the wrist unit with Roy, letting him know how important it was to keep it on at all time. He gave Roy a sketchy description about what had been done to save him, but he withheld the information about one-week life span on Earth. Roy seemed to be open enough to accept whatever information Lorcan offered.

Once Roy's briefing was finished, Orla moved on impatiently. "Now that the stupid birds have the map, we've got to hurry to get to the key before they do. We need your help on that. How long is it going to take to find the key?"

"It's not far away—just over there." Mori pointed to a strip of land floating close to the horizon.

Lorcan squinted as he looked to where she pointed. "Right, let me just call in a chopper," he said sarcastically.

"Really?" Roy asked.

"No, not really. I don't have access to resources like that." Lorcan rolled his eyes.

"Then how are we going to get there?" Orla asked.

"We'll have to swim," Roy responded.

Mori dove head first into the cold water. She swam like a fish. Roy followed. Lorcan rumbled and dove in at Orla's push. Not much later, they'd reached the stretch of land Mori had showed them. It had looked farther than it actually was. As they gathered on the dry sandy beach, Mori glanced around, and her eyes clouded. "They're here. The Yakuz are here already."

"Where is the key, exactly?" Orla asked.

"In a temple on top of the hill. I have guard foxes permanently placed there, but I'm not sure how many men or creatures the Yakuz have brought with them, or what kind of weapons they have."

"We were chased out of the house. We've got nothing to fight with. Even Roy doesn't have his gun now," Lorcan said.

Orla and Lorcan looked toward the interior of the island. In front of them was a gigantic hill of sand. The coastline curved away, and they couldn't see the other end unless they went around the hill. Bleached white sand carpeted the entire area, black rocks hopping up here and there. Sand as far as the eye could see.

"What are the Yakuz anyway? Mysterious creatures? Criminals? We've run into all forms on them since we came, and everyone has referred to them with fear, and with one word—Yakuz," Lorcan muttered.

"They majority of them are human outlaws. But they have a lot of money, so they hire creatures with magical talents and abilities, including were-creatures, witches, wizards, sorcerers, you name it. If any magical forces have reached the high ranks of the Yakuz, I don't know about it. And whether any other groups have enough power to hire the Yakuz to do their bidding, I have no clue," Roy said.

The four of them walked slowly around the sand dune. Mori signaled everyone to hide in the shadow of a large rock. Via a gap, they could see large groups of furry black wolves pacing.

"Werewolves?" Lorcan asked.

"Too far away to tell, and too many of them to go ahead on," Roy said.

"Werewolves or not, let's see how they do against hard shells." Orla rushed back to the water, Lorcan at her heel. A slow smile curved her luscious lips as she dipped her hands into the water.

"What's your plan, Orla? I don't like surprises."

"They have their minions, and we should have ours." She stretched her hand out into the water. Small jolts of purple lightning danced from her fingertips out into the waves. Small granules of sand began to swirl around her fingers.

She was forming crabs out of sand. They began to scuttle around on the bottom of the sea. She made their color more substantial, bright red, and then sent small bolts of lightning into them, forcing them away from the island to grow rapidly to roughly the size of a man before coming back.

Mori and Roy approached, and Orla grinned as she gestured toward the sea. The red claws of an army of crabs slowly crept out of the water and headed up the hill to where the wolves kept watch. It was show time. From behind the rock, they soon heard the howls of wounded wolves echoing out from the other end of the sand hills. Peeking through the gap again, they saw the bodies of wolves scattering the sand field and the red-claw army retreating back to the sea.

"The entrance of the temple is right on top of the hill, facing east. Once inside, I can show you where the key is. My foxes should be guarding all the way up to the entrance of the temple," Mori said.

"It's more than a hundred yards from here to the bottom of the hill. And then we have to fight our way up. Do you have any idea how many there are on the other side of the hill?" Lorcan asked.

"I'll go and take a look," Roy said.

"No, Roy. You're not going in by yourself."

There was a low growl behind them, and they slowly turned around. Six wolves approached the, teeth bared. Roy, Mori, and Lorcan immediately shifted into their fox forms. The trio was magnificent in blue, black, and red. The fight broke out and soon became a flurry of flying sand. Lorcan took on as many as he could to keep wolves from attacking Orla.

In this world of were-animals, Orla felt a bit out of place. She looked over to the rock, strategizing a way to approach the temple gate. The trio had knocked down the attack wolves with ease, but the noise they'd made may have alerted the Yakuz at the top of the hill. There was no way they could make it to the sand hill and then fight their way up. Orla tried to recall all the lessons and practice she had received during her short training in Ireland.

She closed her eyes and willed herself to summon the dark force. She knew Lorcan wouldn't approve of this, but she had no other option. She crouched and braced her hands on the cold sand. Power, she needed the dark power. She started chanting. Gradually, she could feel it rising inside her. Waves of fire energy stormed into her like a tsunami. She felt as if she could move mountains, drain oceans, and draw up wild storms.

Orla stood, her eyes blank, her body and hands glowing with magical light. The foxes had won their battle and shifted back to human form. Lorcan saw Orla, and it instantly registered what she had done. He ran to her, and she stared right through him. She raised her arms, sending lightning bolts streaking across the blackened sky and smashing into the entrance of the temple. Thousands of bolts struck all the way down the hill. The trees on the hillside caught fire, and Yakuz bodies and body parts flew into the air.

Orla heard Lorcan call out to her from somewhere amid the noise and destruction, but she couldn't stop. Nature's attack kept crashing into the hillside until not a sign or sound of live creatures echoed their way. Orla's eyes were completely blank, and her long black hair trailed in the wind, the air whirling into eddies of freezing air when she lifted her arms.

"Shall we go!" she whispered into the wind and raised her arms, palms up, singing a strange chant. The ground underneath their feet rolled in waves, curved up and surged into a gigantic sand wave, carrying the four of them right to the shattered entrance of the temple.

Once on the ground again, Orla's arms flopped down to her sides as if the power was exiting her body. Her eyes came back to normal. Lorcan knew too well what would happen next, and he dashed toward her to catch her before she fell head first onto the stone floor.

"Orla, Orla, honey, come back to me, please." He had seen her use magic, he had seen her sending people—including himself—to Hell and back, but he had never seen her work with such magnitude. He wasn't sure she could come back from this at all. If he lost her here and now, the whole ordeal wouldn't mean a damn thing to him. But shortly, she stirred and opened her eyes. Lorcan squeezed her into his arms. "Oh God. Please don't do that to me, ever again. Promise me? Please?"

She smiled groggily and nodded.

Roy and Mori came back after a quick search around the outside of the temple. "They killed all of my guard foxes." Tears swam in Mori eyes, and Roy hugged her tightly.

"You couldn't have known. If anything, I bet this is Sai's doing," he said.

Lorcan helped Orla up. "Can you walk?" She nodded.

They cautiously pushed what was left of the temple door open. The last piece of wood crumbed as Roy touched it. The temple was eerily quiet.

"The key is at the far end." Mori entered through the doorway, intending to lead the group, but Roy pushed her behind him. They had only gone a few yards when a string of men cut off the corridor. Lorcan swore under his breath and stood in front of Orla.

She rolled her eyes. "I can fight, Lorcan. At least this is men on men. We're a level playing field now."

Lorcan glanced at Roy, who was ready for a fight. "You take the back row, I'll take the front row, and we'll meet in the middle when we're done." Lorcan's voice was casual, and he didn't seem worried at all.

Roy gave him a curt nod, then began walking toward his appointed gaggle of goons, trying to draw them out one at a time. Orla turned and sauntered toward the other end of the corridor where she found a few men lurking. She kept one hand behind her back as she walked toward them, carefully and stealthily building a ball of purple lightning in her palm. She paused in front of the middle person and smiled. Six feet still separated them, but she was close enough.

"I'm going to go out on a limb here and say that there's no way that we can work this out civilly?" she asked sweetly.

Silence met her question, and she could feel herself getting more irritated. Finally, in answer, the line of warriors took on a fighting pose, ready to attack. She refused to be intimidated. Sneaking her other hand behind her back to make a second ball of energy, she watched and waited.

The first attack came from the far left. There were five of them, but the one on the end leapt into action, spinning a katana above his head as he began a complicated dance to move closer to her. Orla threw a ball of energy at him, and he was engulfed and lifted into the air until he hung about fifty feet above the ground.

Even as the panic showed in his face, he didn't make a sound. The bubble disappeared, dropping him back to the hard-packed earth of the floor. Orla waited with baited breath, but he didn't move again.

The second ball of energy easily dispatched the next attacker in the same manner as the first, and she turned to the three that were left. All three of them were advancing on her, weapons out. That put her at a distinct disadvantage. The first guy lunged at her with a katana, and she managed to squeak by without harm. The second one had nun chucks, and he was moving quickly toward her, swinging them in an impressive pattern. Orla reached her hand out, lightning fast, trying to grab one of them to wrest it away from him, but she only succeeded in getting a wallop on her hand that made her think she'd gotten a broken bone in return.

"Okay, Little Miss Nice Girl is gone." Her snarl came out of nowhere, and it was enough to make the third one hesitate a bit. He had a crude bow and arrow that she thought wasn't going to do him any good fighting in such close quarters. She sent a bolt of energy at it and watched as the weapon disintegrated in his hands. He looked up at her incredulously, and she pretended to blow smoke off her fingers like she'd just fired a gun. They stared at each other for a while, but then the enemy turned and ran.

CHAPTER 17

Orla came back to the main entrance and saw that everyone had gathered there. Lorcan glared at her and said nothing. She knew he was mad because she'd sneaked behind his back and went in for a fight. But it was done now. She merely smiled in response to his scowl.

Seeing the tension between them, Mori smiled. "Glad to see you came back to join the party."

Orla sneered. "Not much of a party for the goons."

Roy chuckled and pushed at Lorcan's elbow. "Come on, we have a key to fetch. Cheer up!" Lorcan mumbled something and shuffled along the corridor.

"Lorcan, do you know where you're going?" Mori asked.

He shook his head, then stopped and waited for the group to catch up with him. "I'm sorry about your foxes," Lorcan said to Mori.

"Don't worry. It couldn't be helped. If we can just get the key and put it in a safe place, perhaps that will give these foxes peace—and justice."

"Then who will give *you* justice, Mori?" Sai's voice exploded from the right corridor. They turned and looked down the hall but found no sign of him. Lorcan had thought the voice and the echo were a bit odd, so instead of looking toward the right, he looked to the left, thinking the sound had perhaps bounced from the left in the opposite direction. He was right. From the left corridor, Sai charged out with a gun in his hand, aiming straight at Mori. Lorcan had enough time to push her aside, but he took the bullet in his shoulder.

Without losing a second, Roy charged at Sai, grabbing a metal candleholder on his way. Before Sai could register Roy's movement, Roy had whacked the gun out of his hand. Roy pounded on Sai, who was at a great disadvantage in size, strength, intelligence, and willpower. After a good pummeling to his attacker, Roy let Sai flop to the floor, but as soon as Roy turned his back, Sai surged up, knife in hand. Mori yelped. Quick as lightning, Roy turned back, landed a final blow on

Sai's face, grabbed his hand, and turned his own knife on him. In a flash, the knife sank up to the hilt into Sai's chest.

Lorcan was on his knees now, and Orla was holding him. The pain was bad, but he said nothing and willed himself not to pass out. He grabbed at the floor for purchase and breathed heavily. Roy crouched. "You have to let go. You have to pass out or your body won't start healing. I told you, Lorcan. Our healing processes are all different. That's how your body works. Just lie down, right here. We'll guard you."

Lorcan's eyes were blurry. He flopped to the floor, but pushed up again. "There's no time for it. We're in the middle of this. I can't lie down. We don't know what else might be coming." He stood. And then they heard a muffled cry for help. The sound was very familiar.

"Chiyo," Orla said. They searched the area and found Chiyo tied up and blindfolded in a dark room at the end of the corridor. When they entered the room, Chiyo withdrew, "Who are you? Don't touch me. Please don't beat me. I don't know anything."

"It's us. We'll get you out of here." Orla took the blindfold off. As soon as Chiyo saw Lorcan and Orla, tears streamed down her face. Orla untied Chiyo. She wore the same clothes she had worn when they captured her at the warehouse. Her wrists were marked with bruises and dried blood. Her hair was tousled. Lorcan helped her up and let her cling onto him, although he could barely stand by himself.

"We should go get the key and find a safe place to stay tonight," Roy said.

Mori nodded in agreement and led the way. They wound their way along another long corridor that ended at a double door leading to the main part of the temple. As Mori opened it, a beautiful woman stood in front of them, smiling. Mori moved back and hissed. Roy muttered loud enough for everyone to hear, "Hina, the virgin princess of the Yakuz."

The woman was nearly naked, wearing only the sheerest of long, gossamer robes. She looked more like a sex symbol than a virgin, Orla thought.

"Welcome to my temple," she said. "You must be Roy, the mixed-blood hero. And you two are the travelers from a faraway land." She nodded at Lorcan and Orla. Her voice was as clear as a bell.

"This is not your temple," Mori growled.

The woman smiled. "You must be Mori."

Hina had advanced slightly toward Mori when Roy snarled, "One more step, and I will cut your throat out."

Hina stopped and withdrew. "You need not fear me . . ." But before she had finished the sentence, her right arm shot out like a snake, flew over the thirty feet of distance between her and Mori, and grabbed Mori's neck, pulling her over like a rag doll. She pulled Mori close against her body, her fingers at Mori's neck now morphed into five sharp steel blades.

"I'm going to have to borrow her for a bit. Please excuse us." She pulled Mori out the door and into another corridor. The group followed but Hina didn't stop them.

"She needs Mori to pull the key. She's the chosen one," Roy growled as he followed Hina and Mori. He picked up a knife lying on the floor next to a dead body.

Hina's eyes glowed with insanity the closer they got to the key. They entered the main chamber. At the far end of the room was a raised platform which looked like some kind of monument. There was a golden padlock on it, and a gigantic golden key fixed inside. Hina dragged Mori toward the platform. She pushed her face at the key.

"Draw the key out and give it to me."

Her fingers cut into Mori's neck, and streams of blood flowed out, but Mori stood still.

"Pull the key!" the princess roared.

At her back, Orla's hands curved into fists as she began to form fireballs. But reading her thoughts, Lorcan grabbed at her hands and shook his head.

"Give me the key." Hina tightened her grip. More rivulets of blood ran down Mori's neck.

"Give it to her, Mori, please," Roy begged.

Mori nodded slightly and raised her right hand slowly, and as soon as she touched the key, it glowed in recognition. She turned the key three times until it clicked and pulled the key out of the lock. As soon as she had removed it, she used her left hand to grab Hina's right wrist so she couldn't swing and slice through her throat with her blade fingers. Still holding the key in her right hand, she shoved it into Hina's eyes. Hina roared, staggered back, and loosened her grip on Mori's neck. Seizing the opportunity, Mori freed herself.

Seeing Mori was out of the danger zone, Roy charged at Hina. Before he could reach her, Orla had sent a fireball right at her. She fell but managed to throw her snake arm out, slashing at Roy. He fell to the floor. Mori was furious. She picked up Roy's knife, threw the key toward Lorcan, and flew at Hina. Dazed by the strike from Orla's fire, Hina didn't react quickly enough to avoid Mori's knife. It pierced the woman's heart, and she dropped dead before she could speak another word.

Mori rushed over to Roy. "Roy, talk to me." Roy moaned and got up. "I'll heal." Mori wrapped her arms around his waist to help him up. Orla checked on Hina to ensure that she really was dead. They heard Lorcan grunt, and he rolled back into the room, lying on the floor with a fresh gash on his arm. Outside the door, Chiyo stood with the key in her hand. She punched a button at the door, and the steel bar doors fell down, blocking ways out to all corridors.

"Why, Chiyo?" Lorcan asked.

The woman smiled. "Chiyo was sacrificed for my God a long time ago. I have lived in her skin and have been waiting for this for a long time. I'd almost lost hope before you two came along." She looked at Lorcan and Orla. "I haven't thanked you yet for that. If you hadn't stirred this up, I wouldn't have gotten this far, and the Yakuz would have gotten the key by now. We deserve the key much more than the Yakuz."

"*We?* Who are *we?*" Mori was furious. She grabbed the barred door and shook it fiercely, but it wouldn't budge.

"I'm sorry but your Fire Fox clan is doomed and gone," the woman said and turned on her heel, disappearing down the end of the hallway.

The entire building shuddered. "It's going down. The temple is going down," Roy said. Everyone searched for a way out, but all exits had been barred. The temple shook, and dust from the ceiling and loose objects started falling to the ground. Lorcan and Roy ran to a storm drain at the corner of the room and lifted the lid. Roy climbed down first. Hopping back up, he said, "It's okay. Come down." He helped Mori and Orla down, and Lorcan slid down the hole just before a stone column collapsed right on the spot.

They followed the drainage system until it opened up into a tunnel. They ran in the dark as fast as they could. For a while, they'd seen a glimpse of light at the end of the tunnel. Finally reaching it, they bolted out the other side of the sand hill. They looked up to the top of the hill, watching as the temple crumbled, caved in, and collapsed. Dust and smoke formed enormous balls which hovered in the air, their shadows looming over the sand island.

At the far end of the curved sandy beach, they saw the woman they knew as Chiyo removing her clothes in a ceremonial manner and walking toward the sea with the key in her hand. On the horizon, the dragon creature that had attacked their boat surfaced and raised its head high above the water. The sky around it darkened and storm clouds gathered.

Mori and Roy sprinted toward the woman. Orla ran after them. Lorcan was staggering, his wounds bleeding badly. He slumped to the sand, shaking his head and trying to stay alert. Orla returned to Lorcan, but he waved her away.

"They need you. Help them." As Orla ran toward Roy and Mori, Lorcan reeled toward the bodies of guard werewolves they had killed before.

The woman had entered the water and was walking out to the open sea. The water was at knee level, and soon she would be swimming toward the dragon. Mori bit her hand and tried to yank the key out. Roy sprung up from the water to land on the woman's shoulder, intending to bite her throat. The dragon slung a water jet at Roy, deflecting him before he could get to the woman. Roy dropped into the water. The woman screamed and cried at the same time, she tried to shrug Mori off so she could swim toward the dragon. It appeared as if the dragon couldn't strike Mori as he would have to hit the woman as well.

Orla curved a fireball in her hand and threw it at the woman. It had just left the tips of her fingers when the dragon shot a hard spray of water at her. Orla fell onto the sand, skidding away several feet. Her fireball flopped to the water and fizzled.

The woman had disentangled herself from Mori, and Mori dropped to the water. She could see the dragon aiming in her general direction. As the woman turned again toward the open sea, Lorcan darted out from the sand hill will a knife he had found on one of the guard wolves. He threw it at the woman. The knife spun in the air and then stabbed into her from the behind, plunging into her heart. She turned toward Lorcan, and he could see the life draining from her eyes. Lorcan looked at his hand in disbelief—he had never thrown a knife in his life.

Mori pulled the key from the woman's hand as she fell into the water and paddled safely back to land. Roy also returned. In the distance, the dragon's strident roar seemed enough to crack the ozone layer of the Earth. It turned to glare at the four on the beach.

One look at the dragon, and Orla knew disaster was imminent. She yelled out to Mori and Roy. "Come inland! Quickly!"

CHAPTER 18

Under the blackened sky, the dragon had raised up fifty feet in the air. Its eyes glowed with a blood red fury. Orla knew it was conjuring a tidal wave. Mori and Roy had reached her, and Lorcan approached from behind. Orla turned toward them, yelling, "Get back, get back, give me some space!" She looked at the dragon, concentrated, raised her arms, and her eyes once again went blank.

Mountains of water rushed in toward the shore, enough to swallow the entire island. Orla chanted her spells. In opposition to the dragon's rough seas, she was as calm as still water. She didn't rush, didn't panic.

Lorcan stood right behind her, flanked by Mori and Roy. If they were to die on this island, they'd die together, fighting as one. As Orla chanted, the sand moved. They could feel the ground grumbling. The island shook. Orla raised her arms again, uttering a command that was completely foreign to Lorcan.

The tidal wave came close to the shore. It was so enormous that it blocked their view of the dragon. Similarly, the dragon couldn't see them. The sand surged up in the air like a row of skyscrapers or an army of gigantic sand soldiers. In a flash, before any of them could register anything, the sand met the water. The giant wave broke and shattered, and sank back into the ocean. The dragon roared his protest and vanished.

Lorcan ran to Orla, thinking she would collapse. But she turned around and looked at him gently, saying, "I'm okay. It wasn't the dark magic that I used. I'll thank the late wizard later. But now, we need a shelter. The dragon will return soon, and I'm running out of resources."

They hid behind a large rock on the beach. "We can't risk swimming back to the mainland. Water gives us nothing but a disadvantage at the moment," Roy said.

"It'll swallow the island on the second attack," Orla said, flopping into the sand. Lorcan sat, leaning against the rock, his eyes rolling back and his vision blurry.

"You have to let your wounds heal, Lorcan," Mori said.

Orla reached over to pull him into her arms. "Come on, lie down here."

Lorcan raised his arm to stop her. "I can't. We have to get out of here." He pulled out his wrist unit and started to program it. His hands shook, and his vision got worse by the second.

In the distance, they heard the low growling sound of the dragon coming back.

"Roy and Mori, we came from the Daimon Gate, a universe far from here. Orla and I can go back via our portal, but I'm not sure how it works with you. The Daimon Gate doesn't accept uninvited guests. If we violate any rule there, you'll die . . ." Lorcan had to stop speaking to take a breath. "So I'm programming it so that we only get to the transitional zone. Then I'll go into the Daimon Gate and seek permission to take you in."

"It sounds like a reasonable plan," Roy said.

Lorcan shook his head, more to stay alert than in response to Roy. "The transitional zone is nobody's land. No one is in charge, and no one governs it. You could be attacked by any number of creatures while waiting for me. That's the risk, if you're willing to take it."

"How likely is it that we'd be attacked?" Mori asked.

"I don't know. I've never been."

"I'll risk it. I'll go with you. How about you, Roy?" Mori asked.

"I don't have a better alternative. Any place is better than in the stomach of that thing." Roy pointed.

Lorcan cursed under his breath and turned back to the unit to finish the program. Soon, a ring of light appeared inland, and their portal opened. It was two hundred yards away, and they had to run across an open sand field. Lorcan lay back on the sand, on the verge of passing out.

"You go," he mumbled, closing his eyes.

"No, no! Look at me, Lorcan." Orla shook his shoulders, but he wouldn't open his eyes.

Mori dragged Orla away from Lorcan. Roy kicked a pile of sand right into Lorcan's face. Lorcan grabbed at his face and grumbled.

"That'll wake you. You wouldn't let yourself pass out when I asked you to . . . but now is *not* the time," Roy growled, hooking Lorcan's arm over his shoulders and hoisting him to his feet.

The group raced toward the open portal. The dragon saw them go and hurled as much wind and water as it could toward the group.

They jumped into the ring of light, and the light withdrew and vanished. From above, they got a last glimpse of the island as it was swallowed by the dragon's tidal wave.

The transitional zone was as dark as the tunnel in the island had been. "I don't know where we are. It's not supposed to be a tunnel," Lorcan said. They kept running, searching for some light. Lorcan pulled out the unit Ciaran had given him and punched the alarm button. The group kept moving forward. Freezing wind blew through the tunnel, drawing them toward the far end. At the side of the tunnel, a beam of light flashed on, and the door of a spaceship opened.

"Thank you, Ciaran," Lorcan said and ran to the door. They all jumped in, the door closed, and the ship lifted off, hovering and then zooming away smoothly. Lorcan slumped to the floor of the spaceship and finally passed out.

A while later, Lorcan opened his eyes, finding Orla smiling at him. He was snuggled comfortably in her arms. "How are you?" she asked and kissed him.

"Perfect." He smiled up at her. "How did you beat that dragon without dark magic?"

"The late wizard told me to utilize my talents, remember? My talents don't lie in dark magic. I have an extended family, and some of my relatives are white witches. They taught me all sort of things. I can conjure up astrological elements to serve whatever purpose I want. The water element is what the dragon used, and earth is the element that destroys water."

Lorcan chuckled. "Indeed."

"I missed your blue fur. Can I rub it, just once?"

He stopped smiling.

"Too soon?" Orla pouted.

Lorcan rolled his eyes. Then Orla saw her blue fox looking at her with puppy eyes. She grinned, burying her face into his long fur, but then got his mouth instead. He had shifted back.

"That's cheating," Orla said but continued to kiss him. Afterward, Lorcan rolled to his side and saw Mori and Roy seated stiffly on the floor across the spaceship. Lorcan chuckled.

"Can you tell us where we're going?" Roy asked.

Alarm bells rang in Lorcan's head, and he realized it was time to tell Roy about his new blood and the deal with Ciaran. Lorcan sat up.

"This is Ciaran's spaceship, so I'm guessing we're going straight to Eudaiz. I've never been there, so I can't tell you much, but from what I've heard, it's a heaven, a universe of beautiful and happy people. It's a universe of true happiness."

"A universe?" Mori raised an eyebrow.

"Well, just like our Earth, our world, there are many universes that exist that we haven't visited," Lorcan responded.

"Alien?"

Lorcan shook his head. "As long as you're not talking about the green aliens you often see on TV, I can live with the term. It's a very long story. But you'll see it for yourself."

"So I'll have a chance to thank Ciaran for saving me. It's good to hear there's a place where true happiness exists," Roy said.

Orla rolled her eyes. "Try a universe of virtue," she muttered, thinking of the Daimon Gate.

"I'm sorry?" Roy asked.

"Don't worry about it. The less you know, the happier you'll be," Orla said.

"Humm." Lorcan ruffled his hair.

"What? Why don't you just spit it out? I can take it." Roy raised his voice.

Lorcan cleared his throat. "Right. Here's the thing. Ciaran couldn't cleanse the poison from your system, so he had to replace part of your blood by a substance only available in Eudaiz. It's no big deal, really. You can become a Eudaiz citizen and receive the supply for the rest of your life. Ciaran owed us a favor, and he's willing to take you in because of that. He's a very fair man. But he doesn't necessarily have to take Mori."

"And what the fuck does that mean?" Roy growled.

"Ciaran doesn't know you. He's responsible for a lot of people, and it's difficult to take in random strangers. Having said that, once he gets to know you, I don't think it will be a problem. But you have to be patient. We can't expect to go there and have them lay out the red carpet for us immediately." Lorcan kept his voice as low and calm as possible.

"What would the worst scenario be?" Mori asked.

"That would be going back to Earth to be eaten by that dragon monster," Orla answered.

The spaceship seemed to have come to a stop and was now hovering. Lorcan stood, hauling Orla up with him. "We're here!" Lorcan exclaimed.

As the door slid open, a robotic voice spoke, "Welcome to Xiilok. You have arrived at the residence of Prince Brandon."

"What the fuck?" Lorcan yelled, "Wait!" to stop Roy and Mori from reaching the door.

"Close the door, close the door!" Orla shouted.

Roy pushed the door closed. The spaceship shuddered, and the lights were cut off.

The group stood in darkness.

CHAPTER 19

They struggled in the cabin of the spaceship for what seemed like decades. Except for the sound of the machinery clicking and humming, there was no other sound in the dark that was recognizable. Lorcan knew that in a few seconds, their enemies—whoever or whatever they were— would break in, and that might be the end of them. He concentrated. *Where did he go wrong?* They were on Earth, they were being attacked, he had opened the portal so that they could travel to the transitional zone in between the universes. Lorcan braced his hands against the control panel in the dark and probed for the buttons. The lights had been cut off as well as the energy. The air would be the next thing to run out. Lorcan raked his hands through his hair, retracing every step again from the beginning, from when they first escaped the Dragon's attack to when they ended up wherever they were at the moment. He couldn't figure out what he had done wrong.

The spaceship was hovering now, and the creatures out there could roll it over any moment. The sounds of footsteps, claws, and hard objects hitting the outside of the spaceship echoed inside, making every nerve in his head throb. *They were not going to die here,* Lorcan thought. He wouldn't let anything happen to Orla, or his friends.

Whatever was out there was shaking the spaceship now, it had to be very big and strong, and there would be many more of them around. Hand-to-hand combat was not a wise solution at the moment. They had to stay put inside the cabin.

But the air was getting thinner by the second. Every breath they drew could be the last one.

Nobody said anything, which made things worse as the creatures' roars and squeaks outside became more prominent and haunting.

Lorcan's hand hit a square button. All the other buttons were round, but this one was square. He bit his lips, pressed the button, and prayed that it was not the one that opened the door automatically.

It was not.

Instead, a dim light lit up in the corner of the spaceship's cabin. Lorcan turned around. He could see now. Mori and Orla held the doors together to keep the creatures outside. Roy helped from the middle, pushing the handles of the two doors tightly together. All three were pale and exhausted, and they looked ready to give up any second.

The spaceship was shaken again, tilting left and right, up and down.

"I'm going to get this thing moving," Lorcan said.

"Hurry, Lorcan!" Orla exclaimed.

"If memory serves me right, this is my very first time operating a spaceship. It's most likely a lot more difficult than you think," Lorcan said in frustration as he typed a series of commands into the control panel. The spaceship jerked, lifted, swung a bit, and then moved backward. The movements were so jerky that everyone thrown to the floor. "Great, we're going backwards, but at least we're moving."

They were moving backward at an incredible speed.

"Do you know where we're going?" Roy asked.

"The place where the spaceship was taking us was obviously wrong. I'm trying to un-go, if it's at all possible," Lorcan mumbled. "Maybe we could . . ." But before Lorcan could finish his sentence, the spaceship hit a hard object from the behind, the wall caved in, and the spaceship started to dive. Lorcan grabbed at the control handle, and pulled. In response, the spaceship stopped diving. Lorcan entered a landing command, and prayed that it worked. It did, and they landed. Before they could say anything, the electrical wires sparked into fire. "Get out!" Lorcan yelled.

Everyone dove from the spaceship, just a split second before it exploded. They crawled on the ground, trying to get back on their feet. When they stood, they could just make out a small army of creatures in the distance, approaching them and brandishing weapons, claws, and foreign objects that weren't recognizable to them.

"Holy shit," Roy said.

There was no way that they could fight, especially when they didn't have any weapons. Just then, from behind them, they heard a male voice say, "Get down."

They dropped to the ground, without question or hesitation. A small spaceship came to a stop behind them, and from inside it, black laser beams sliced through the air, slaughtering the space creatures and obliterating the army. The group stood and turned around to see who had saved them. From the small spaceship, Ciaran LeBlanc stepped out, a formidable presence with the aura of a dark angel. He holstered two laser guns and approached the group.

"Does the king of Eudaiz normally engage in combat alone?" Lorcan asked.

"No, I have soldiers and armies of people working for me when it comes to engaging in real combat, both on Earth and in Eudaiz. But I consider saving idiots to be my personal problem, and for that I spared my people the chase. You hit the panic button to call for my help, but you had left the position before my people arrived. Do you know how dangerous it is for me to send my soldiers to the transitional zone? If I hadn't jumped on my personal spaceship and followed my instincts, you'd probably be tucked cozily in those creatures' stomachs by now," Ciaran fumed.

"We ran into a tunnel, and then that was the only spaceship we saw, so we jumped on. Then it went in the wrong direction. We didn't have a choice," Roy said.

"Whose spaceship was that?" Orla asked.

"I thought it were one of yours," Lorcan explained.

Ciaran looked at the spaceship, at the moment no more than a pile of scrap metal, with disdain. "I don't know, it's not qualified to be called a spaceship, and it's certainly isn't mine," he said.

"The spaceship sent us to Xiilok and Brandon's residence. It seems Brandon has taken residence in Xiilok, and he's out of the control of the Daimon Gate," Lorcan said.

Ciaran shook his head. "Brandon would rather be an outlaw of all the universes than be a minor gatekeeper in the Daimon Gate. It takes all kinds."

Roy staggered a bit and walked toward the corner, leaning against the wall. Mori asked, "Are you okay?"

Roy tried to respond to her question, but his body had a mind of its own, and his eyes rolled up before he slumped to the ground.

Mori grabbed him. "What's happening to him?" she asked.

Ciaran quickly checked the wrist unit on Roy's right wrist, and he said, "He's out of energy. I gave him seven days' worth of energy, but because you took him traveling across multiple dimensions and across the transitional zone, his energy level has been depleted."

"Can you give him more?" Orla asked.

"Yes, but it's only temporary. I have to get him to Eudaiz ASAP."

Ciaran took a small square black patch from his belt and snapped it into the wrist unit that Roy was wearing. The glowing green light of the level indicator on the wrist unit lit up.

"This is very temporary. And again, because we have to cross dimensions of time and space, I don't know how long it'll last. He has to go with me now. Whatever you need to do with the Daimon Gate, you will have to do it without him," Ciaran said.

"All right then," Lorcan confirmed.

Roy opened his eyes and sat up. He had heard the last thing Ciaran said. "What about Mori?" Roy asked.

"She'll have to go with Lorcan. I can't take her to Eudaiz now. I haven't discussed it with my council," Ciaran said.

Roy stood and walked away. "I can't leave Mori."

"I gave you the energy, but I can take it back at any time. It's your choice." Ciaran's patience had run out.

"Look, Roy, this is temporary. Go with Ciaran now to get yourself fixed up, then we can reunite later. I'll get a guest pass for Mori at the Daimon Gate. You're both going to be fine," Lorcan said.

"If we hang around here any longer, and the creatures come back, we'll all be dead. It's not just about you," Orla snarled.

At the back, another small spaceship arrived and parked. A couple of uniformed officers stepped out and approached Ciaran. He nodded in acknowledgement.

"My officers will take you to the entrance of the Daimon Gate. Roy, what's your decision? If you go with them, you'll die in a few minutes," Ciaran said.

"Roy, please go with Ciaran. We'll meet again soon," Mori said.

Roy nodded reluctantly. Mori, Lorcan, and Orla entered the newly-arrived spaceship. Ciaran waited until it had departed safely before he took Roy into his ship.

Once inside, Ciaran verified himself using his left palm and activated the machine.

It hovered smoothly and then swiftly darted into the holo-space. "Destination, Eudaiz, Sciphil Zone, Tower Three."

Ciaran gave a verbal command. After the computer acknowledged the destination, he turned, about to ask Roy something, but his wrist unit flashed a signal. Ciaran glanced at the information on the small screen, then looked at Roy.

"What did you try to do for the Host of the Daimon Gate?"

"We tried to get the key of Psuche to the Daimon Gate for safekeeping."

Ciaran nodded. "And that required a fight with some sort of creature at sea?"

Roy nodded.

"You killed it?"

"We barely escaped with our lives."

Ciaran cocked an eyebrow.

"It's a dragon, as big as a mountain. How would you expect us to kill it?" Roy asked in frustration.

Ciaran shook his head and gave a verbal command to the machine. "Change destination, entrance of the Daimon Gate. Engage holocast communication with the Host of the Daimon Gate immediately."

A CHAPTER OF VOLUME 2 – UNCURSED IS ON THE NEXT PAGE

CHAPTER 1

Heat. That was all he could feel. A wave of fire that carried incinerating heat was flying toward him. Lorcan stared at it as if it was a movie clip shown in slow motion. Once that fire brushed over him, Lorcan knew all that would be left of him was a pile of ashes. He was stuck beneath a collapsed brick dome, half of his body was buried, and his legs were crushed. He didn't think there were any bones left intact, so even if the bricks and stones didn't crumble down upon him, he wouldn't be able to move out of the way of the fire anyway.

As death loomed close, he thought of Orla. He hadn't had a chance to marry her properly. He thought of his family in Ireland, too, and regretted taking their love for granted. If there were a God—and somehow that God was compassionate enough to grant him another chance—he would take Orla to Ireland to meet his family and marry her. On top of that, he would go to church every week.

Brandon's laughter still echoed in the air—the sound of evil. How could a gatekeeper in a virtuous place such as the Daimon Gate turn dark so quickly? Lorcan wondered. As he closed his eyes, awaiting the coming fire, he heard the sound of a spaceship moving closer. Turning toward the noise, he saw it had parked close to where he lay. From inside the spaceship, Ciaran jumped out and rushed over to Lorcan.

"Go away! There won't be enough time, Ciaran!" Lorcan yelled. That man must have nerves of steel, Lorcan thought. Without a word, Ciaran blasted his weapon at the loose bricks around Lorcan and then used his daggers as levers to lift the large stone from on top of Lorcan. Ignoring Lorcan's verbal abuse, Ciaran hauled Lorcan up and half-carried, half-dragged Lorcan into his spaceship.

The door closed and sealed immediately after their embarkation.

"Heat defense mechanism on!" Ciaran shouted. The spaceship shuddered, and they heard a click.

"Affirmative and ready," a robotic voice said.

Then the storm of fire hit them.

The spaceship tilted slightly when hit, but regained its balance soon after. As the counterbalance mechanism kicked in to compensate for the heat outside, the air inside the spaceship dropped to freezing. The storm continued to attack the spaceship from the outside. They heard the sound of hard objects hitting metal, and the force of the air blew through gaps in the outer body of the ship, creating a hellish howling noise.

Then it quieted down, the fire went past, and the spaceship seemed to settle.

Lying on the floor, Lorcan's vision became blurry. He knew he needed to pass out so that his body could begin the healing process, but he had to tell Ciaran about his healing ability first or he would think that his system was collapsing. "Damn it," Lorcan thought. He couldn't force a word past his lips. And as he'd predicted, Ciaran was trying to prevent him from passing out because in the same situation, a normal person would pass out and go into cardiac arrest due to the shock of the injuries and the extreme changes of environmental conditions they had just experienced.

"Lorcan, come on. Open your eyes for me. You're not going to die on me. Come on." Ciaran shook Lorcan's shoulders so hard that there was no way he would be able to pass out and start any healing process. Lorcan wanted to scream, but again, he couldn't get any words out. Ciaran ran to a small compartment and pulled out an emergency medical kit. Lorcan opened his eyes and saw Ciaran preparing a syringe. It had to be adrenaline, Lorcan thought, which normally he wouldn't mind, but if that kick-ass chemical was injected into his system now, he'd be forced to remain conscious and deal with this excruciating pain.

Lorcan summoned all the strength he had left and said, "No."

Ciaran cocked an eyebrow. "No? It's only adrenaline. I know what I'm doing."

"No," Lorcan repeated, but Ciaran approached him, still ignoring his weak protest. Ciaran crouched next to Lorcan, but before he could inject the adrenaline, something hit the spaceship so hard that it almost tipped the craft over. Ciaran fell, dropping the syringe on the floor, and it rolled away to a far corner. He hurried toward a control window to look outside, mumbling some profanity as he went.

On the floor, Lorcan took his opportunity and slipped into his needed unconsciousness.

After a while, Lorcan opened his eyes to find himself alone, lying on the floor of the spaceship. His body had healed. Getting up, he went to the window to see what was going on outside. A short distance away, Ciaran and a group of soldiers had barricaded themselves behind the ruins of a gothic dome and were firing at a small army of space creatures. To protect Lorcan, Ciaran shot and killed any creatures veering toward the space vessel.

Lorcan immediately recognized the ambush attempt that had caught him off guard before. He searched the spaceship for the weapon compartment. He grabbed two long laser beam guns. He'd never used them before, but in looking them over, it didn't take him long to figure out where the triggers were. Unfortunately, as soon as he touched the handles of the guns, a line of text flashed on a small screen located above the trigger: Unauthorized User. Lorcan swore and ran to the control panel. He slammed his palm on the verification screen and, ignoring the machine's protest, hacked into the system. It didn't take him long to prompt the system to give him a pass for weapon usage. Lorcan scanned the receiver of the gun over the verification screen dashboard and the recognition mechanism on the gun flashed a green light.

Outside, Ciaran had nearly wiped out the small army, still keeping an eye on the spaceship to be sure no stray creatures wandered near it. He felt a sudden blast of heat and dust pressure coming from behind, an area that, oddly, backed up to a dead end wall of rock and stone. Ciaran was sure that nothing could penetrate the wall to come out at him from that corner. But it then dawned on him that he was fighting at a transitional zone in between universes. The dead end could be merely an illusion, and a dimensional hole could open before he had a chance to react. He whirled around to face the general direction from which the blast had come, but it seemed to be too late. He shouted to his soldiers to take cover and dove behind a rock.

The pressure came like an explosion. He and all of his soldiers were thrown feet away, tossed around like rag dolls. Dazed, Ciaran tried to sit up and see through the dust storm. He saw nothing but the shape of a man walking toward him. He groped for his weapons on the ground nearby but found nothing but dust. He could feel the warmth of his blood streaming out from a gash on his left shoulder. Ciaran tried to spring to his feet, but his body wouldn't obey. Looking up, he saw Brandon standing right in front of him, a cold smirk on his face.

"Never thought you would face death like this, did you, Ciaran?"

"Why? I saved your life."

"Well, you should have asked me if I wanted that. You think you know it all, Ciaran? You, the Host, and those stupid humans are trying to obtain what doesn't belong to you."

"The key of Psuche? What does it have to do with you?"

"I could take the time explain to you why you must die today, but I'm not feeling compassionate at the moment. So goodbye, Ciaran LeBlanc, king of Eudaiz. You will die on the battlefield like a common soldier."

Brandon raised his crossbow, aiming at Ciaran's head, but Ciaran swung his leg and kicked the weapon away. His second kick landed on Brandon's abdomen, sending him staggering back and falling to the ground.

Still groggy, Ciaran struggled to his feet and was then assaulted by Brandon's two-leg kick. He skidded backwards and fell back to the ground. As Brandon stood up and ran to recover his weapon, two streams of laser beams blasted at his chest. His clothes became engulfed in flame, but he pulled a lever and the fire died out instantly. Brandon released a black smokeball and fled the scene.

Lorcan hurried into the dome of dust and black smoke to drag Ciaran out.

"I've got this! Let go!" Ciaran shrugged off Lorcan's support and walked out of the dust on his own. He inhaled some clean air and coughed out the dust that coated this throat and lungs, recovering swiftly. Then Ciaran turned around, looking at Lorcan. "Are you okay?"

"Yes." Lorcan grinned.

"Did you know the best way to kill a creature in space is to aim at the head? You're using two laser beamers, and all you did was set Brandon's clothes on fire!" Ciaran exclaimed.

"I've never used these before, so that's good enough, isn't it? I didn't miss totally!"

"Brandon ran away—again," Ciaran mumbled, clutching his bleeding shoulder. He glanced around, taking stock of the situation. "And he killed seven of my best soldiers."

"Shouldn't you be relieved he didn't kill you, too?"

Ciaran said nothing and headed back to his spaceship. Lorcan followed, and Ciaran asked, "How can you walk like that now? A short while ago, you were dying."

"I knew that would be the first thing you'd ask when you saw me! I wasn't dying. I have the ability to heal myself, heal my injuries very quickly, but I have to shut my system down first."

They were inside the spaceship now. "You can heal yourself?"

Lorcan nodded. "Yes, as long as I haven't died, I can heal myself from injuries. To what extent, I don't know. It's all new to me, too."

"Right." Ciaran rolled his eyes.

"Ciaran, I know it's hard for you to accept anything you can't explain scientifically. It was hard for me, too. But when your life partner, the person you've spent your entire life with, tells you she's a sorceress, you kinda learn to accept things that seem a little beyond reality."

Ciaran nodded. "Are there any more special abilities you and your group have that I should know about?"

"Apart from what you already know—Roy and Mori are werefoxes, and Orla is a sorceress—nothing else. Anyway, why are you here? I thought you were taking Roy to Eudaiz."

Ciaran shook his head. "I got a message on way to Eudaiz with Roy. I came back for you, and the girls said you'd gone. What happened?"

"I was on my way to the Daimon Gate to get the guest pass for Mori. Brandon ambushed me exactly the way he did you just now. He thought I had the key with me, and when he couldn't find it, he left me buried in the ruins and went after Orla. We have to get to her."

Ciaran shook his head. "I've sent for her. They'll be here soon." He glanced at his wrist unit. "My officers just confirmed. They're safe and sound."

The sound of an incoming holocast interrupted, and a beam of light flashed inside the spaceship, inside of which stood the life-sized hologram image of the Host of the Daimon Gate.

"You're injured, Ciaran?" the Host asked.

Lorcan nodded, acknowledging the Host. The Host responded in turn.

Ciaran winced and walked toward the medical compartment. He pulled out a square medical patch and cleaned his wound. "I don't have the ability to heal myself quickly, but this will help clean things up. It should look better by the time my wife sees it." Ciaran flashed Lorcan a brief smile and then addressed the Host. "I called for you because one of the missions you sent people to complete on Earth might have caused collateral effects that I don't think you'll be happy about. I placed our intelligence system on Earth to keep an eye on things, and the system has just reported that a sea creature is gathering a massive amount of energy under the seabeds of all continents on Earth. That amount of energy could create a series of tsunamis."

Ciaran looked straight into the Host's eyes. "It's going to drown the entire human population. This creature has something to do with the Daimon Gate. What can you tell us about the key and the mission you ordered?"

The Host arched an eyebrow and stared at Ciaran. Ciaran shrugged. "I can certainly find out myself, but it will take precious time that we might need in order to save the humans on Earth. I still have interests on Earth, so I'd like to protect the people there," Ciaran explained.

The Host nodded. "There was a myth before my time that the key of Psuche can give the holder the ability to control the water level of any universe, given the correct lineup of all astronomical elements. For me, it's simply a key to secure one of our Eastern gates."

Ciaran nodded. "For creatures that live in an aquatic environment, water dictates their territories and is a prime motivation for invasion."

"I killed the woman who was supposed to give the key to the creature. It looked quite pissed. I'm not sure if it was because of the woman's death or because it couldn't get the key. But whatever the reason, if we go back to Earth to kill that reptile, do you think it would solve the tsunami threat?" Lorcan asked.

Ciaran nodded. "It's speculation, but it's better than doing nothing."

Lorcan pulled out a little pouch and put it on the floor. "Here is the key. I'll leave it with you, and we'll return to Earth for the creature." He looked at the Host.

Ciaran arched an eyebrow. "I thought you said you didn't have it with you?"

"I'd hidden it before Brandon attacked me. Just got it back now."

"Brandon?" the Host asked.

Ciaran nodded. "He was trying to kill me, too. He's taken residence in Xiilok, outside your jurisdiction. And now he—or the person who took him in—wants the key, too. Maybe the myth has some truth to it—perhaps the key of Psuche does have magical powers," Ciaran mumbled sarcastically. The Host stepped forward, moving the light beam up to encircle the pouch on the ground. He then bent down to pick it up.

"Oh, no." The Host shook his head.

Lorcan and Ciaran watched the Host as he pulled out the key and pointed to its top. "The stone is missing. There's an Indigo Stone that's supposed to be mounted right here."

"So the key won't work without the stone?" Lorcan asked.

The Host shook his head. "The stone carries the power, and the key unlocks the power. They won't work separately. This is now simply a metal key, and the stone an expensive decoration."

"But we took the key out of the patch lock at the temple. My guess is that it had to have the stone attached to it at the time— the Fire Fox clan wouldn't have spent generations and sacrificed many lives to guard a useless key with no power. And the woman grabbed the key from me and ran to the beach. It wasn't long before we caught up with her, and we killed her before she could give the key to the dragon. So what happened to the stone in between?" Lorcan exclaimed.

"Time is relative," Ciaran contemplated.

"How does that explain any of this?" Lorcan raked his hands through his hair and paced in agitation.

"Did anything strange happen between the time the woman took the key and when you killed her?" Ciaran asked.

"Not really. She locked us in the temple and triggered a mechanism so the temple collapsed, and we were buried. We escaped via the drainage system beneath the temple. The only thing that was strange to me was the drainage. It was like a tunnel—long, dark, and confusing . . ." Lorcan trailed of as a thought came across his mind. "Dimensional hole . . . do you think that's what it was, Ciaran?"

Ciaran smiled and nodded. "The woman was obviously going to give the dragon the key without the stone. There must be more to that woman than meets the eye."

Lorcan rolled his eyes. "Yeah, she stripped naked on the beach."

"I beg your pardon?" the Host asked.

Ciaran laughed. "Never mind," Lorcan rumbled and continued, "So I guess we leave the key with you here and go back to Earth for the stone and the dragon?"

Ciaran nodded. "You might be able to kill two birds with one mission. Take these." Ciaran removed handguns from the weapon compartment and programmed them.

"These are specially designed for the transitional zone, so I think they'll work on Earth. They'll definitely be superior compared to the current technology there and won't be detected by any detecting device." Ciaran gave Lorcan the guns. While Lorcan assessed the weight and the feel of them, the Host shook his head.

Ciaran merely smiled at the Host and muttered, "I'm sorry your peace-keeping mission isn't working out. But my friends are still on Earth. I'm not going to let them die because of this stupid reptile."

SPECTRUM DUOLOGY
VOLUME 2

UNCURSED

http://www.narrativeland.com/spectrum

D.N. LEO'S LATEST NOVEL LIST
http://www.narrativeland.com/dnleo-novels

A SHADE OF MIND SERIES
Main characters: **Ciaran and Madeline**
Supporting characters: **Tadgh, Jo, Jennifer**
Characters from related series: **Lorcan, Orla, Zach**
Book 1: Random Psychic
Book 2: Forever Mortal
Book 3: Elusive Beings
Book 4: Imperfect Divine

Thank you for reading.

If you enjoyed reading **Cursed**, I would appreciate it if you would help others enjoy this book, too.

<u>**Recommend it.**</u> Please help other readers find this book by recommending it to friends, readers' groups and discussion boards.

<u>**Review it.**</u> Please tell other readers why you liked this book by reviewing it at Amazon or Goodreads. A few sentences will make a significant difference to me. If you do write a review, please send me an email at info@dnleo.com so I can thank you with a personal email.

Connect with me online:
Web: narrativeland.com; Twitter: @dnleostory

To join my mailing list, please click here

Facebook page of the Outlanders of the Multiverse series
https://www.facebook.com/Outlandersofthemultiverse

COPYRIGHT

CURSED
Spectrum Duology - Volume 1

By D.N. Leo